Charles Dickens's
David Copperfield

Charles Dickens's *David Copperfield* (1849–50) is one of the most fascinating and enduringly popular works of the nineteenth century.

Taking the form of a sourcebook, this guide to Dickens's classic novel offers:

- extensive introductory comment on the contexts and many interpretations of the text, from publication to the present
- annotated extracts from key contextual documents, reviews, critical works and the text itself
- cross-references between documents and sections of the guide, in order to suggest links between texts, contexts and criticism
- suggestions for further reading.

Part of the *Routledge Guides to Literature* series, this volume is essential reading for all those beginning detailed study of *David Copperfield* and seeking not only a guide to the novel, but a way through the wealth of contextual and critical material that surrounds Dickens's text.

Richard J. Dunn is Professor and Chair of the Department of English at the University of Washington. He has published numerous studies of Dickens and other Victorians.

Routledge Guides to Literature*

Editorial Advisory Board: Richard Bradford (University of Ulster at Coleraine), Jan Jedrzejewski (University of Ulster at Coleraine), Duncan Wu (St. Catherine's College, University of Oxford)

Routledge Guides to Literature offer clear introductions to the most widely studied authors and literary texts.

Each book engages with texts, contexts and criticism, highlighting the range of critical views and contextual factors that need to be taken into consideration in advanced studies of literary works. The series encourages informed but independent readings of texts by ranging as widely as possible across the contextual and critical issues relevant to the works examined and highlighting areas of debate as well as those of critical consensus. Alongside general guides to texts and authors, the series includes "sourcebooks", which allow access to reprinted contextual and critical materials as well as annotated extracts of primary text.

Available in this series:

Geoffrey Chaucer by Gillian Rudd
Ben Jonson by James Loxley
William Shakespeare's The Merchant of Venice: A Sourcebook edited by S. P. Cerasano
William Shakespeare's King Lear: A Sourcebook edited by Grace Ioppolo
William Shakespeare's Othello: A Sourcebook edited by Andrew Hadfield
John Milton by Richard Bradford
Alexander Pope by Paul Baines
Mary Wollstonecraft's A Vindication of the Rights of Woman: A Sourcebook edited by Adriana Craciun
Jane Austen's Emma: A Sourcebook edited by Paula Byrne
Mary Shelley's Frankenstein: A Sourcebook edited by Timothy Morton
The Poems of John Keats: A Sourcebook edited by John Strachan
Charles Dickens's David Copperfield: A Sourcebook edited by Richard J. Dunn
Charles Dickens's Bleak House: A Sourcebook edited by Janice M. Allan
Herman Melville's Moby-Dick: A Sourcebook edited by Michael J. Davey
Harriet Beecher Stowe's Uncle Tom's Cabin: A Sourcebook edited by Debra J. Rosenthal
Walt Whitman's A Song of Myself: A Sourcebook and Critical Edition edited by Ezra Greenspan
Robert Browning by Stefan Hawlin
Henrik Ibsen's Hedda Gabler: A Sourcebook edited by Christopher Innes
Thomas Hardy by Geoffrey Harvey

* Some books in this series were originally published in the Routledge Literary Sourcebooks series, edited by Duncan Wu, or the Complete Critical Guide to English Literature series, edited by Richard Bradford and Jan Jedrzejewski.

Charlotte Perkins Gilman's The Yellow Wall-Paper: A Sourcebook and Critical Edition edited by Catherine J. Golden

Kate Chopin's The Awakening: A Sourcebook edited by Janet Beer and Elizabeth Nolan

D.H. Lawrence by Fiona Becket

The Poems of W. B. Yeats: A Sourcebook edited by Michael O'Neill

E. M. Forster's A Passage to India: A Sourcebook edited by Peter Childs

Samuel Beckett by David Pattie

Charles Dickens's
David Copperfield
A Sourcebook

Edited by Richard J. Dunn

Routledge
Taylor & Francis Group

LONDON AND NEW YORK

First published 2004 by Routledge
11 New Fetter Lane, London EC4P 4EE

Simultaneously published in the USA and Canada
by Routledge
29 West 35th Street, New York, NY 10001

Routledge is an imprint of the Taylor & Francis Group

This volume first published as *A Routledge Literary Sourcebook on Charles Dickens's David Copperfield*

Typeset in Sabon and Gill Sans by RefineCatch Limited, Bungay, Suffolk
Printed and bound in Great Britain by TJ International Ltd, Padstow, Cornwall

British Library Cataloguing in Publication Data
A catalogue record for this book is available from the British Library

Library of Congress Cataloging in Publication Data
A Routledge literary sourcebook on Charles Dickens's *David Copperfield* /
edited by Richard J. Dunn.
     p. cm.—(Routledge literary sourcebooks)
Includes bibliographical references and index.
1. Dickens, Charles, 1812–1870. David Copperfield. I. Dunn, Richard J.,
1938– II. Series.
PR4558.R68 2003
823'.8—dc21   2003009715

ISBN 0–415–27541–5 (hbk)
ISBN 0–415–27542–3 (pbk)

Contents

4: Further Reading

Illustrations

Annotation and Footnotes

Annotation is a key feature of this series. Both the original notes from reprinted texts and new annotations by the editor appear at the bottom of the relevant page. The reprinted notes are prefaced by the author's name in square brackets, e.g. [Robinson's note].

Acknowledgements

When I first discussed a *David Copperfield* sourcebook with series editor Duncan Wu, I found the project a challenging opportunity. After years of teaching and writing about the novel, I had to decide what to extract from the voluminous text, various contexts and hundreds of commentaries. Thanks to Wu and to Routledge editorial staff, especially Liz Thompson, and consultants, my prospectus and draft manuscript received close scrutiny from which they benefited greatly.

Students and colleagues have knowingly or unknowingly helped me. Cara Lane, Suzanne Pitre, Swan Sheridan and Karen Stewart-Perry as graduates and undergraduates interested in the text and context of *Copperfield* have shown me the importance of this novel's visuality – illustrations, films – and their independent studies are ones upon which my own are more dependent than they may realize. Thanks to Dr Leon Litvack and to his students at Queen's University Belfast, I had opportunity to discuss *David Copperfield* and think about numerous contextual connections and varied theoretical and critical views. For extensive help with special library collections of materials, I thank Sandra Kroupa of the University of Washington Libraries and Andrew Xavier, Curator, and the staff and volunteers of the Dickens House Museum.

The following publishers, institutions and individuals have kindly given permission to reprint materials.

AMS Press Inc. for James R. Kincaid, 'Viewing and Blurring in Dickens: The Misrepresentation of Representation' from *Dickens Studies Annual*, Vol. 16 (1987).

Andrews, Malcolm for *Dickens and the Grown Up Child* (Basingstoke: Macmillan, 1994), reproduced with permission of Palgrave Macmillan.

Dickens House Museum for providing copies of the monthly parts cover and five of the original *David Copperfield* illustrations.

Giddings, Robert for 'Oliver Twist dramatised by Alan Bleasdale ITV 1999' and 'David Copperfield dramatised by Adrian Hodges BBC 1 Christmas Day and Boxing Day 1999' from *The Dickensian 96*, 2000.

Reprinted by permission of the publisher from *From Copyright to Copperfield: The Identity of Dickens* by Alexander Welsh, pp. 115–19, 128–35 (Cambridge, Mass.: Harvard University Press), copyright © 1987 by the President and Fellows of Harvard College.

Mann, Glenn for 'Cukor's and Selznick's David Copperfield: Dickens and Hollywood' from *Reading David Copperfield*, 1990.

Oxford University Press for James R. Kincaid, *Dickens and the Rhetoric of Laughter* (1971); Juliet John, *Dickens's Villains: Melodrama, Character, Popular Culture* (2001); and Philip Collins, *Charles Dickens: The Public Readings* (1975).

Palgrave Macmillan for William J. Palmer, *Dickens and New Historicism*, © William J. Palmer, 1997.

Extract from *Dickens the Novelist* (1970) by F. R. Leavis and Q. D. Leavis published by Chatto & Windus. Used by permission of The Random House Group Limited.

University of Chicago Press for Mary Poovey, *Uneven Developments: The Ideological Work of Gender in Mid-Victorian England*, 1988.

Every effort has been made to trace and contact copyright holders. The publishers would be pleased to hear from any copyright holders not acknowledged here so that this acknowledgements page may be amended at the earliest opportunity.

Introduction

David Copperfield, published in monthly parts in 1849–50, is one of the greatest works by Charles Dickens (1812–70), England's best-known novelist. Because the fictional autobiographer, David, is himself a novelist, the story is simultaneously his personal memoir and self-conscious act of remembering and interpreting his life story. Few works of literature recapture so well the child's viewpoint, for, as the older David recognizes, he had been a child with exceptional powers of observation, 'an innocent romantic boy, making his imaginative world out of [. . .] such strange experiences and sordid things' (Chapter 11). At times revealing and at other times concealing agonies of Dickens's own childhood employment and of his first love, *David Copperfield* also stresses his growing determination to succeed as a writer, a goal towards which he applies confidently the Victorian faith in the value of hard work. The novel is a *Bildungsroman*, a story of growth and development. As early as *Oliver Twist* (1837–38) Dickens had written of the struggles of an orphan, and more recently in *A Christmas Carol* (1843) he had demonstrated the power of childhood recollection to bring about moral regeneration, with Scrooge becoming able finally to 'live in the past, present, and future' (Stave V). David, like Oliver, finds himself cast out and abused but supported by loving friends and relations. David, as had Scrooge, discovers the value of his past life through recollecting it, for, like Scrooge, he has loved and lost.

In its monthly serial form the novel bore the cumbersome title, *The Personal History, Adventures, Experience, and Observation of David Copperfield the Younger, of Blunderstone Rookery: (Which He Never Meant to be Published on Any Account)*. The first hard-cover and all subsequent editions appearing during Dickens's life shortened the title to *The Personal History of David Copperfield*, and, as the book has remained in print ever since, the most frequent title has been simply *David Copperfield*.

The story begins with the curious circumstances of David's birth, moves quickly through first childhood impressions, establishing a recurring pattern in which each new phase of his life puts him in touch with some people who abuse or dupe him and others who nurture him. At the outset, he is beaten by his fierce stepfather, Mr Murdstone, and consoled by his beloved nursemaid, Clara

Peggotty. One of David's most formative experiences comes when he visits Peggotty's family at Yarmouth and meets the bewitching orphan, Little Em'ly, who becomes an important woman-child sister-figure in David's story.

Returning home, David finds his mother married to Murdstone, who sends him to Salem House Academy, run by a self-proclaimed 'Tartar', Mr Creakle, who gleefully abuses his charges. At Salem House, David finds a patron of sorts in the head boy, the dashingly confident and wilful James Steerforth, who becomes the first clear hero of David's life and whose subsequent story deeply affects David and the Peggottys. After the death of David's mother, Murdstone withdraws him from school and relegates him to humiliating employment in London, where he lodges with the novel's most memorable comic character, the irrepressible and improvident Mr Micawber. When Micawber is arrested for debt, David flees to Dover to escape the servitude of his employment and to seek refuge with his eccentric aunt, Betsey Trotwood. Betsey, following the practical advice of Mr Dick, her mad lodger, defies Mr Murdstone's attempt to reclaim David, unofficially adopts him, and sends him to school in Canterbury. David thrives with good schooling and comfortable residence at the home of Mr Wickfield, Betsey's business agent. His daughter Agnes, one of those young Dickens women assuming adult responsibility in the place of a dead parent, soon becomes the second sister-figure in David's life. But just as Murdstone had darkened the Blunderstone of David's childhood, so does the Canterbury Wickfield house and business have its resident demon in the writhing form of Uriah Heep, a falsely humble and always unctuous manipulator of the Wickfields and, increasingly, of David.

Finishing his Canterbury schooling successfully, David becomes articled to a solicitor in London. He soon falls under the spell of Dora Spenlow, the daughter of his employer. Pursuing his daily work, he also learns shorthand, becomes a reporter and, later, a novelist. Reacquainted in London with Steerforth, David and his old friend visit Yarmouth, where the patronizing Steerforth delights the Peggottys. Disaster soon follows when Little Em'ly, engaged to her faithful cousin, runs off to the Continent with Steerforth and David realizes that, because he had introduced Steerforth to her, he was largely responsible for the damage to Em'ly and her family. David marries his beloved Dora but soon finds himself deeply troubled by the childish charm he had adored during courtship. She is unable ever to be, or was not made to be, more than his child-wife. Meanwhile in Canterbury, David's old friend Mr Micawber turns up again as assistant to Uriah Heep, who has illegally gained control of Mr Wickfield's affairs. Heep shocks David by expressing his desire for Agnes. Just as David's friend Steerforth betrays him by seducing Em'ly, so his nemesis Heep threatens the innocent Agnes.

In the last third of the novel a more sobered and uncertain David recalls the devastating results of his mistaken trust in Steerforth and of his impetuous marriage. Dora dies after a lingering illness and Steerforth perishes in a storm at sea off the Yarmouth coast. Em'ly returns to England, is reunited with her uncle, and soon the Peggottys, along with the Micawbers, set sail for a new life in Australia. This part of the story also brings comic resolution to the Wickfield–Heep story, with Mr Micawber relishing his moment of rhetorical glory by exposing and denouncing Heep's infamy.

Devastated and with no clear path before him, David leaves England to travel in Europe. When he returns, he takes Betsey Trotwood's advice to visit Agnes, with whom he had corresponded during his travels, and finds, to his surprise, that she has quietly loved him all her life and that the dying Dora had told Agnes that only she could occupy the vacant place in David's heart.

The three main sections of this sourcebook – Contexts, Interpretations and Key Passages – interconnect essential issues in and around the novel, the personal history of Dickens in relation to that of David, the values and issues of mid-Victorian England, and the principal interests of *Copperfield* critics and readers over the past century and a half. Introductions to each of these sections, shorter headnotes to many of the reprinted materials, and annotations and cross references help the reader to understand the relationship between these Sourcebook parts. Rather, however, than pigeonhole *Copperfield* as literary type (fictional autobiography) or period piece (Victorian novel), or impose a particular critical or theoretical approach (biographical, psychoanalytic, socio-political, feminist), this Sourcebook can help readers to explore the richness of the novel text and the cultural and critical texts which surround it.

1

Contexts

Contextual Overview

The primary *David Copperfield* context is biographical, for the novel is a personal history, with much of Dickens's own life recast as fictional autobiography in the story of David Copperfield. The more we know of Dickens's public presence as the leading novelist of his time, as journalist and editor, prominent public speaker and philanthropic supporter of many causes, and as theatrical public reader of his own works, the better we can recognize *David Copperfield* in relation to Dickens, the man engaged in public events and issues, moral values and concerns of mid-nineteenth-century England.

Like all of Charles Dickens's novels, *David Copperfield* (1849–50) was published in serial parts, with each part completed only shortly before appearing in print. While at work on the novel Dickens kept number plans outlining his ideas < both about the evolving whole and about points to carry forward from one serial part to the next. Five brief lines from the plan for the fourth serial part (Chapters 10, 11, 12) well establish this novel's strong biographical context and also clearly distinguish between Dickens's own experience and that of his title character.

---

what I know so well

I become neglected and am provided for
I begin life on my ⟨account⟩ own account
I go on with life, rather uncomfortably
   on my own account and don't like it
I make a resolution[1]

Dickens set apart the first of these lines, which records his personal connection with the subject matter, from the following lines which are drafts of the serial part's chapter titles. The 'what' Dickens well knows is his secret story at that time

---

1 Dickens's working plans are often appended to modern paperback editions and are discussed in full by John Butt, '*David Copperfield* Month by Month', in John Butt and Kathleen Tillotson's *Dickens at Work* (London: Methuen, 1957), pp. 114–76.

existing only in an unpublished autobiographical fragment dealing primarily with his childhood employment in a shoe-blacking factory (see **pp. 20–2**). The 'I' of this first line obviously is Charles Dickens; the 'I' of the remaining lines is the fictional David. Only after Dickens's death would his readers begin to understand the impact of Dickens's childhood drudgery on his life and the extent to which it was hidden, especially in the fourth serial part of *Copperfield* (see **pp. 107–9**). While at work on this part of the novel, Dickens informed John Forster, the only person then aware of the autobiographical fragment: 'I really think I have done it [used the autobiography] ingeniously, and with a very complicated interweaving of truth and fiction.'[2] So spoke Dickens privately to his most trusted friend, and there is no question that, more than for any of Dickens's other books, the principal context for the whole of this novel is biographical, the story of his early life and of what, at its mid-point, he was making of a career which had already brought him international recognition as writer and also as social commentator, journalist and public speaker. In all these roles, Dickens projected personal experience to address larger social issues and values, some of which are implicit in the working notes cited above. For example, David's 'I become neglected, and am provided for', reflects Dickens's own childhood experiences and also more generally points to the general matter of abused and neglected children's claims for care and attention. Harsh though Dickens may have found working conditions in the months he served in Warren's blacking factory, his was far less hopeless than the situation of thousands of Victorian children doomed to severe, often life-threatening labour as chimney sweeps, mine and factory workers. Parliamentary Factory Acts of 1833, 1844 and 1848 began to address the working conditions of women and children, and in 1850, the year Dickens completed *Copperfield*, came the Factory Act of 1850, known as the 'Ten Hours Act', because it limited women and children to no more than ten hours of work six days a week. Child labour is but one of *David Copperfield*'s social concerns, as it portrays abused and neglected widows and orphans, cast-out women, eccentric and mentally impaired people, victims of literal (death at sea) and figurative (bankruptcy and fraud) shipwreck.

It is childhood most vividly rendered, however, that has attracted and held readers both of *David Copperfield* and of much more of Dickens's writing. David remembers himself as 'a child of close observation' (Chapter 2), and observant child characters were prominent in Dickens's earlier writings. In *Oliver Twist* (1837–38) he idealized the outcast child, showing 'the principle of Good surviving through every adverse circumstance, and triumphing at last'.[3] In *Nicholas Nickleby* (1838–39) he addressed the plight of unwanted children in remote boarding schools. *The Old Curiosity Shop* (1840) introduced the first of Dickens's 'little women', females denied girlhood and thrust into adult, sometimes

2   *The Letters of Charles Dickens*, ed. Graham Storey and K. J. Fielding (Oxford: Clarendon Press, 1981), vol. V, p. 569.
3   For the 1841 edition of *Oliver Twist*, Dickens wrote a preface that stressed the realism with which he had depicted the London underworld and the frankness with which he characterized the prostitute, but the same preface makes this point about ideal, invulnerable, goodness.

parental, roles. This novel's Little Nell supports an addicted gambler who is her grandfather. She, in a situation like that of the ultimately more fortunate Agnes Wickfield in *David Copperfield*, finds relief only in an early death, rendered with the fullest chords of Dickens's sentimentality. In *A Christmas Carol* (1843) Dickens employs the supernatural to effect recollection of childhood as a pathway towards adult moral regeneration. Scrooge's miraculous transformation begins with rediscovery of childhood joys and loves, and ends with his dedicated and gleeful promise to serve the needs of present children, epitomized in the frail, but cheerful, Tiny Tim. In these earlier portrayals of children and childhood Dickens often captured the world of childhood, but not until *David Copperfield* did he ever so fully combine immediacy of childhood impression with adult retrospection. The older David thus sees and pities the 'innocent romantic boy, making his imaginative world one of such strange experiences and sordid things' (Chapter 11).

Dickens's secret story, embedded in the fictional David, was one of rags-to-riches, a chronicle of earnest effort and ever-expanding opportunity. The fictional autobiographer, David, declares that he has dropped the curtain on the stage of his earlier life (Chapter 12), and so had Dickens abandoned and then fictionally veiled past the actual past. In that personal past resided the motive force for Dickens's moral and social views: his life-long sympathy for children, his denunciations of abusive parents and teachers and employers. In that past lie also the roots of Dickens's strong will. As he remembers in the autobiographical fragment, even as blacking-factory drudge, 'I kept my own counsel, and I did my work. I knew from the first that, if I could not do my work as well as any of the rest, I could not hold myself above slight and contempt' (**p. 21**).

By the time *David Copperfield* appeared, Dickens was a famous advocate for the oppressed and was the scourge of the oppressors. As he was composing the novel from month to month, he began a new weekly magazine, *Household Words*, and on more than a half-dozen occasions, while writing monthly *Copperfield* parts, he made speeches on behalf of charities for aged actors, newsvendors and law clerks. Supporting metropolitan sanitary reform, a popular cause after the cholera epidemic of 1847–8, Dickens lauded the suffering poor: 'No one who had any experience of the poor could fail to be affected by their patience, by their sympathy with one another, and by the beautiful alacrity with which they helped each other in toil, in the day of suffering, and at the hour of death.'[4] So put, Dickens stated a popular but controversial idea of the deserving poor as a class to be admired and assisted, but for whom, categorically, there seemed to be little chance of material betterment. The charitable activity with which Dickens was most fully involved while writing *Copperfield* was a home for fallen women, funded by the heiress Angela Burdett Coutts. Dickens took an active part in the management of the home, and the 'appeal' he wrote to prospective residents (**pp. 22–3**) expresses his belief in their capacity to benefit from a disciplined education and to find better lives, probably as emigrants. Prostitution was rampant

---

4   K. J. Fielding, ed., *The Speeches of Charles Dickens* (Oxford: Clarendon Press, 1960), p. 108.

in nineteenth-century London; the journalist Henry Mayhew reported that 'In 1857, according to the best authorities, there were 8,600 prostitutes known to the police, but this is far from being even an approximate return of the number of loose women in the metropolis.'[5] The image of the fallen woman, particularly in the novel's characterization of Little Em'ly, directly derives from Dickens's work with Coutts.[6] Dickens's public pronouncements about the moral strength of the honest poor and his statements and actions on behalf of fallen women provide a context for the novel's emphasis upon the Peggotty family's support of Em'ly, who loses her honour in becoming the mistress of David's friend Steerforth. The Peggottys, and Em'ly in particular, exemplify Dickens's general confidence in human goodness.

Concern about the fallen woman is but part of the novel's attention to the situation of Victorian girls and women, and Dickens provides both conventional and unique versions of the Victorian 'angel in the house'.[7] In a society which sharply differentiated men's education, vocations and avocations from women's into what were largely separate spheres, the ideal woman was the icon of morality and the custodian of home and hearth. Amazingly, this ideal persisted despite the reality of thousands of working-class women, doomed to hard factory and mine labour, or to obscure lives as servants. Among the novel's good women, Dickens comically individualizes David's nursemaid, Clara Peggotty; his eccentric aunt, Betsey Trotwood; and his good friend, the ever-faithful Emma Micawber. He renders more seriously several harsh women: the steely Miss Murdstone, cringing Mrs Heep, and haughty Mrs Steerforth and her embittered companion, Rosa Dartle.

But it is through compelling and sometimes ambiguous characterizations of David's mother Clara, of his childhood friend Little Em'ly, and, particularly, of his first wife Dora, that Dickens shows the ineffectual reality of the angel in the house. Were it not for the number and variety of women characters in this novel, the pair of Dora and Agnes, David's first and second wives, would stand as a greatly oversimplified and sentimentally idealized image of good girls becoming good women. Both characters have prototypes in Dickens's first love, wife and sister. As a young reporter Dickens was infatuated by a banker's daughter, Maria Beadnell, who spurned Dickens because her family considered him beneath them socially. As Dickens, in a letter to her twenty-five years later, let her know, in *Copperfield* she could have found 'a faithful reflection of the passion I had for you, [. . .] and may have seen in little bits of "Dora" touches of your old self sometimes'.[8] Because she is characterized as so petulant, silly and unable to cope

5   *London Labour and the London Poor* (New York: Dover, 1968), Vol. IV, p. 213.
6   *Letters*, Vol. VI. In December 1849 Dickens let Coutts know that he was finding the subject difficult to present in *Household Words*, intended 'for readers of all ages', but that he was working it into *David Copperfield*.
7   Generally readers understand 'angel in the house' as simply the idealized and domestically enshrined Victorian wife and mother, but recently A. N. Wilson sees the concept more broadly as 'domestic Love which exists between men and women'. *The Victorians* (New York: W. W. Norton, 2003), p. 305.
8   *Letters*, Vol. VII, p. 539.

with practical matters, the character Dora can be read as satirical exaggeration of Maria Beadnell, and Dora's general ineptitude reflects Dickens's criticism of his wife Catherine. In the novel Agnes Wickfield represents the womanly ideal Dickens praised in his real-life sister Fanny and late sister-in-law Mary Hogarth.[9] One-dimensional as they are, Dickens's characterizations of Dora and Agnes are but part of the novel's larger, generally more realistically rendered, gallery of female characters. David's search for manliness depends heavily upon his relationships with all these women. The values the supportive women stress for him are manly: firmness of purpose and earnestness tempered by gentleness. These are the values that Dickens also posited with the honest poor and with both male and female children.

To help readers not well acquainted with Dickens's life and works or with the Victorian views of social/economic class, womanhood and childhood, I have focused on these biographical contexts for David Copperfield. But from its opening pages, the narrator invites us to think with him about larger questions of life's worth. David begins by wondering about the value of his life as he sets the task for what he has yet to write: 'Whether I shall turn out to be the hero of my own life, or whether that station will be held by anybody else, these pages must show' (Chapter 1). The question is one of self-respect and self-satisfaction. The self-respect is fundamentally a question of whether David has become his own man; the self-satisfaction of his status as gentleman and successful author. We can take David's first words as the fictional autobiographer's teasing assurance that he knows what he is looking for and will find in his story. Thus, the conditional 'whether' gets predicated by the vague assertion, 'these pages must show'.

Concepts of manliness and heroism were important topics to Victorians. Historians, biographers and historical novelists searched the past for heroic models. Victorian England redefined its specifications for heroic models, and both Dickens's and David's stories incorporate and endorse contemporary expectations of the hero and gentleman. David's chronicle of beginning and going on with life on his 'own account' is certainly a fictional version of Dickens's self-determination and phenomenal success, a story welcome to an age which put high moral value on the earnestness of such 'resolution'. More than a decade before Dickens wrote his novel, his friend Thomas Carlyle had insisted that heroes of all ages must evince strong moral character coupled with hard work.[10] In Self-Help, one of the century's best sellers and earliest versions of self-improvement non-fiction, clergyman and educator Samuel Smiles applied the Carlylean work ethic to his account of numerous men who succeeded in becoming gentlemen, if not heroes. Although Dickens is never his specific subject, Smiles in his final chapter, 'Character—The True Gentleman' (pp. 26–7), well delineates Victorian moral parameters that a decade earlier were David's measures for success.

At the beginning of the twentieth century, novelist and social commentator

9 The best biographical and critical study of women in Dickens's life and fiction is Michael Slater's *Dickens and Women* (Palo Alto, Calif.: Stanford University Press, 1983).
10 See *On Heroes and Hero-Worship, and the Heroic in History*, ed. Carl Niemeyer (Lincoln, Nebr.: University of Nebraska Press: 1966), where Carlyle made the case for the heroic priest, prophet, poet and man-of-letters.

George Gissing well situated Dickens as embodying nineteenth-century male and class aspiration:

> To say that he was twenty in the year 1832 is to point more significantly the period of his growth into manhood. At least a year before the passage of that Reform Bill which was to give political power to English capitalism [. . .] Dickens had begun work as a shorthand writer, and as journalist. [. . .] In short, Dickens's years of apprenticeship to life and literature were those which saw the rise and establishment of the Middle Class, [. . .] of the new power in political and social England which owed its development to coal and steam and iron mechanism. By birth superior to the rank of proletary,[11] inferior to that of capitalist, this young man, endowed with original genius, and with the invincible vitality demanded for its exercise under such conditions, observed in a spirit of lively criticism [. . .] the class so rapidly achieving wealth and rule. [. . . He] could not forget (the great writer could never desire to forget) a miserable childhood imprisoned in the limbo of squalid London; his grudge against this memory was in essence a *class* feeling: to the end his personal triumph gratified him, however unconsciously, as the vindication of a social claim.[12]

David Copperfield brings together many factual personal experiences, social conditions, attitudes and issues of early Victorian England. Had Dickens remained a journalist, or even been only an actor as he once intended, or had written only his major novels and shorter fiction, he would have achieved wide and lasting recognition. His phenomenal energy persisted as he grew older, and during the last two decades of his life Dickens entertained himself and others with amateur theatricals and very popular and profitable public readings adapted from his writing. Dickens expressively enacted and reflected the life around him. Dickens the performer emerges from Dickens the novelist to stage the life and drama (sometimes melodrama) of his characters and stories.

Influential essayist, historian and philosopher, Thomas Carlyle was a good friend of Dickens, and in later years Dickens dedicated one book (*Hard Times*) to him and drew heavily upon Carlyle's history of the French Revolution for another (*A Tale of Two Cities*). Carlyle's strong views on the question of heroism in the earlier 1840s provide a contextual template for today's reader encountering David's opening lines about being the hero of his own life. In his lecture series 'On Heroes and Hero-Worship' (1841) and in his scathing examination of England in *Past and Present* (1843), Carlyle imposed strong moral imperatives for effective modern heroism. The hero has 'the power of articulate Thinking; [. . .] existence has become articulate, melodious by him: he first has made Life alive!'[13] Carlyle

---

11   The proletariat, or working class.
12   *Charles Dickens: A Critical Study* (London: Gresham Publishing, 1903), pp. 1–2.
13   *On Heroes and Hero-Worship*, p. 21.

defined the hero as seer and prophet, and he gave separate lectures on the hero as poet, as priest and as man of letters (deliberately excluding contemporary writers). To Carlyle, 'The Writer of a Book, is not he a Preacher preaching not to this parish or that, on this day or that, but to all men in all times and places?'[14] In *David Copperfield* this work ethic takes most simplistic form in David's resolution to put metaphoric axe in hand and hew his way through a looming forest of difficulty (**p. 133**). Considered more fully in light of the novel's framing question about heroism, it is precisely the Carlylean emphasis upon work that David endorses. Carlyle had hailed the heroic man of letters as someone 'uttering-forth, in such way as he has, the inspired soul of him; all that a man, in any case can do. I say *inspired*; for what we call "originality," "sincerity," "genius," the heroic quality we have no good name for, signifies that.'[15] So goes the professional life of the fictional fictionist/autobiographer, David Copperfield.

Dickens's fiction presents an individualized view of the Victorian world, and this is particularly true of *David Copperfield*. England in the years of Dickens's young manhood and adulthood (1830–49) was undergoing a vibrant period of growth and change, and the writers benefited enormously from technical progress in publishing and especially from an increasing number of readers. Small wonder, then, that in searching for a title Dickens worked through more than a dozen variants such as 'The Copperfield Survey of the World As It Rolled'. Even a public advertisement appearing a month before publication of the new novel's first number retained the trial-title promise of a 'survey' (see Frontispiece). But even with the more modest scope of the title character's history, adventures, experience and observation, the novel's view of life is large, eccentric and spectacular, sometimes sordid, but seldom at rest, for its story is about life's dislocations, gains and losses.

David Copperfield, both as major literary work and document of mid-nineteenth-century values and issues, shines in the lustre of a larger literary galaxy. Like *Copperfield*, Charlotte Brontë's *Jane Eyre* (1847), Alfred Lord Tennyson's *In Memoriam* (1850) and William Wordsworth's posthumously published *Prelude* (1850) use the fictional autobiographer's viewpoint for recalling times of personal crisis, conditions of great suffering, and moments of comfort and joy. Each work deals with a crisis of moral and authorial confidence. *Jane Eyre* most resembles Dickens's novel because it so vividly dramatizes a child's suffering at the hands of cruel relations and harsh teachers, overlays childhood imaginings with adult understanding, and in its adult perspective asserts moral self-confidence. We can read *Jane Eyre* as a declaration of female imaginative independence and, as such, a powerful counterstatement to David's male perspective. *In Memoriam*, a long elegy comprised of 131 separate parts, charts the uneven course of the impact the sudden death of a beloved friend has upon the narrator. Similarly, the much longer *Prelude* deals with many losses as it surveys, retrospectively, the growth of a poet's mind. The nature and power of memory and imagination are central subjects in all these works. Such moments in David's story, as his account of a

---

14 *On Heroes and Hero-Worship*, p. 159.
15 *On Heroes and Hero-Worship*, p. 155.

great storm at sea, have their counterparts, climactically and climatologically, in these writings of Brontë, Tennyson and Wordsworth. Loves lost and found, friends and conditions helpful or hostile, loom large in the autobiographers' recollections. However familiar we may be with these literary relatives of *David Copperfield*, the point to recognize is that in each instance the form of autobiographical narration provided a literary form for self-assessment, for explaining formative (for good or ill) conditions of nineteenth-century life, and for validating the means and ends of writing itself. Brief extracts from *Jane Eyre, In Memoriam* and the *Prelude* situate *David Copperfield* in the literary context of fictional autobiography. Romantic and Victorian writers forged connections between past and present, individual and community, however fleeting and uncertain those connections might be. By the middle of the nineteenth century there was a growing sense of personal dislocation in the face of widening social and economic class chasms. In *David Copperfield* class and gender roles and distinctions are often troubled, and David at moments in the telling of his tale finds himself poised powerless between his past and present.

Chronology

Bullet points denote events in Dickens's life; asterisks denote selected historical and literary events.

1812
- Charles Dickens (CD) born (7 February) in Portsmouth
* England at war with America; Prince of Wales serving as Regent

1815
* Wellington defeats Napoleon at Waterloo; Jane Austen, *Emma*

1817
- Dickens family moves to Chatham, near Rochester, site of CD's happiest earlier years and near Gadshill, his principal residence 1860–70
* Sir Walter Scott, *Rob Roy*

1820
* Death of George III; Regent Prince becomes George IV

1822
- Dickens family moves to London

1824
- CD leaves school and works for about six months at Warren's blacking factory; his father imprisoned for debt

1825
- CD attends Wellington House Academy
* First passenger railway

1827
- CD leaves school and works as solicitor's clerk

1829
- CD, self-taught shorthand, becomes reporter and works as clerk at Doctors' Commons

1830
- CD in love with Maria Beadnell, a prototype for Dora Spenlow in *David Copperfield*
* George IV succeeded by William IV

1831
- CD employed as Parliamentary reporter

1832
* First Reform Bill

1833
- Relationship with Maria Beadnell ends; CD publishes first sketch, 'A Dinner at Poplar Walk', later collected in *Sketches by Boz*

1834
- CD becomes reporter for *The Morning Chronicle*, meets Catherine Hogarth
* New Poor Law; Thomas Carlyle, *Sartor Resartus*

1836
- CD marries Catherine Hogarth; *Sketches by Boz, First Series*; begins monthly parts of *Pickwick Papers*; *Sketches by Boz, Second Series*; meets John Forster (attorney and man of letters, later first biographer of CD)

1837
- Begins monthly parts of *Oliver Twist* (in *Bentley's Miscellany*); concludes *Pickwick Papers*
* William IV succeeded by Victoria; Thomas Carlyle, *The French Revolution*

1838
- Begins monthly parts of *Nicholas Nickleby*; concludes *Oliver Twist*
* Publication of The People's Charter and National Petition, a workers' effort persisting in the 1840s, to require annual Parliaments, universal male suffrage, equal electoral districts, secret ballot, removal of property qualification but payment for members of Parliament

1839
- Concludes *Nicholas Nickleby*

1840
- Weekly numbers of *The Old Curiosity Shop* (in CD's magazine, *Master Humphrey's Clock*)

1841

- Weekly numbers of *Barnaby Rudge* (in CD's magazine, *Master Humphrey's Clock*)
* Thomas Carlyle's *On Heroes, Hero-Worship, and the Heroic in History*

1842

- CD and wife visit America, where he was well known but criticized for speaking in favour of international copyright. *American Notes*; begins monthly parts of *Martin Chuzzlewit* (which would later draw on his American experiences)

1843

- *A Christmas Carol*
* Thomas Carlyle, *Past and Present*

1844

- CD and family live in Italy for a year (July 1844–June 1845); concludes *Martin Chuzzlewit*; *The Chimes* (second Christmas book)

1845

- *The Cricket on the Hearth* (third Christmas book); leads amateur theatrical company, begins autobiography (surviving fragment published in John Forster's 1872 CD biography) that he draws on directly for early parts of *David Copperfield*

1846

- *The Battle of Life* (fourth Christmas book), *Pictures from Italy* (appearing first in *Daily News*, edited briefly by CD); begins monthly parts of *Dombey and Son*
* Irish famine

1847

- CD works with Angela Burdett Coutts to establish and help manage home for fallen women, writes 'An Appeal' to prospective residents
* William Makepeace Thackeray, *Vanity Fair* (concludes serially in 1848), Charlotte Brontë, *Jane Eyre*; Emily Brontë, *Wuthering Heights*

1848

- Concludes *Dombey and Son*; publishes *The Haunted Man* (fifth Christmas book)
* Revolutions in Europe

1849

- Begins monthly parts of *David Copperfield* in May

1850
- Establishes weekly magazine *Household Words*; concludes *David Copperfield* in November; attends unauthorized stage adaptation of *David Copperfield*
- * Australian Colonies Act; William Wordsworth (posthumously), *The Prelude*; Alfred Lord Tennyson, *In Memoriam*

1851
- Begins *A Child's History of England* (to run occasionally in *Household Words* until 1853); deaths of father, John Dickens (prototype for *Copperfield*'s Mr Micawber), and infant daughter, Dora (born during that novel's serialization, she shared the name of David's first wife)
- * Great Exhibition (Crystal Palace) in London

1852
- Begins monthly parts of *Bleak House*
- * Death of the Duke of Wellington, hero of Waterloo and later Prime Minister

1853
- First public reading (for charity) of *A Christmas Carol*; concludes *Bleak House*

1854
- Weekly parts of *Hard Times* (in *Household Words*)
- * Crimean War begins

1855
- Begins monthly parts of *Little Dorrit*

1856
- * End of Crimean War

1857
- Completes *Little Dorrit*
- * Thomas Hughes, *Tom Brown's Schooldays*

1858
- CD performs public readings from his works for profit; separates from wife

1859
- Weekly parts of *A Tale of Two Cities* (in CD's magazine *All the Year Round*, which succeeded *Household Words*)
- * Charles Darwin, *On the Origin of Species by means of Natural Selection*; George Eliot, *Adam Bede*; Samuel Smiles, *Self-Help*

1860
- After rereading *David Copperfield* to avoid repetition, CD begins monthly parts of *Great Expectations* in his magazine *All the Year Round*

1861
- Concludes *Great Expectations*; first public reading from *David Copperfield*
* Death of Prince Albert; beginning of American Civil War

1864
- Begins monthly parts of *Our Mutual Friend*

1865
- Completes *Our Mutual Friend*; survives train derailment when returning from France with actress Ellen Ternan
* End of American Civil War

1867
- Triumphant reading tour of America (November–May 1868); adds preface to *David Copperfield* for collected edition of works
* Second Reform Bill further extends voting franchise but, like the 1832 Reform Bill, was a political compromise

1870
- Farewell reading tour in England; begins but completes only six of projected twelve monthly parts of *The Mystery of Edwin Drood*; dies 9 June, buried in Westminster Abbey

1872
- First disclosure of Dickens's childhood labour and father's imprisonment for debt in John Forster's *The Life of Charles Dickens*. Subsequent volumes of this biography in 1873, 1874

Contemporary Documents

From **Charles Dickens, 'Autobiographical Fragment'** (composed in mid-1840s), published in John Forster, *The Life of Charles Dickens*, vol. 1 (London: Chapman & Hall, 1872), pp. 47–70

Dickens never provided his family with the facts of his own early life, and in the fictional autobiography David draws a curtain on painful childhood experiences. It was not until after Dickens's death in 1870 that all his family and the public knew the secret of his life-long humiliation over having been sent to work in a blacking factory as a child. Dickens had begun and abandoned an autobiography in the 1840s, entrusting a now-lost fragment of it to his friend and ultimate biographer, John Forster. These extracts from the autobiography deal with the subject of Dickens's childhood labour in a shoe blacking factory, and his account of that experience closely parallels David Copperfield's recollection of similar servitude with a firm of wine merchants (see **pp. 59–62, 65–8**, for critical assessments of the psychological, biographical and critical importance of Dickens's long-kept secrets).

[A relative] proposed that I should go into the blacking-warehouse, to be as useful as I could, at a salary, I think, of six shillings a week. I am not clear whether it was six or seven. [. . .] At any rate the offer was accepted very willingly by my father and mother, and on a Monday morning I went down to the blacking-warehouse to begin my business life.

It is wonderful to me how I could have been so easily cast away at such an age. It is wonderful to me, that, even after my descent into the poor little drudge I had been since we came to London, no one had compassion enough on me–a child of singular abilities, quick, eager, delicate, and soon hurt, bodily or mentally–to suggest that something might have been spared, as certainly it might have been, to place me at any common school. [. . .] My father and mother were quite satisfied. They could hardly have been more so if I had been twenty years of age, distinguished at a grammar-school, and going to Cambridge. [. . .]

No words can express the secret agony of my soul as I sunk into this companionship; compared these every-day associates with those of my happier childhood; and felt my early hopes of growing up to be a learned and distinguished man, crushed in my breast. The deep remembrance of the sense I had of being utterly neglected and hopeless; of the shame I felt in my position; of the misery it was to my young heart to believe that, day by day, what I had learned, and thought, and delighted in, and raised my fancy and my emulation up by, was passing away from me, never to be brought back any more; cannot be written. My whole nature was so penetrated with the grief and humiliation of such considerations, that even now, famous and caressed and happy, I often forget in my dreams that I have a dear wife and children; even that I am a man; and wander desolately back to that time of my life. [. . .]

My own exclusive breakfast, of a penny cottage loaf and a pennyworth of milk, I provided for myself. I kept another small loaf, and a quarter of a pound of cheese [. . .] to make my supper on when I came back at night. They made a hole in the six or seven shillings. [. . .] I suppose my lodging was paid for, by my father. [. . .] I certainly had no other assistance whatever. [. . .] No advice, no counsel, no encouragement, no consolation, no support, from any one I can call to mind, so help me God. [. . .]

I was so young and childish, and so little qualified–how could I be otherwise?– to undertake the whole charge of my own existence [. . .]

I know I do not exaggerate, unconsciously and unintentionally, the scantiness of my resources and the difficulties of my life. I know that if a shilling or so were given me by any one, I spent it in a dinner or a tea. I know that I worked, from morning to night, with common men and boys, a shabby child. I know that I tried, but ineffectually, not to anticipate my money, and to make it last the week through [. . .]. I know that I have lounged about the streets, insufficiently and unsatisfactorily fed. I know that, but for the mercy of God, I might easily have been, for any care that was taken of me, a little robber or a little vagabond.

But I held some station at the blacking warehouse too. Besides that my relative at the counting-house did what a man so occupied, and dealing with a thing so anomalous, could, to treat me as one upon a different footing from the rest, I never said, to man or boy, how it was that I came to be there, or gave the least indication of being sorry that I was there. That I suffered in secret, and that I suffered exquisitely, no one ever knew but I. How much I suffered, it is, as I have said already, utterly beyond my power to tell. No man's imagination can overstep the reality. But I kept my own counsel, and I did my work. I knew from the first that, if I could not do my work as well as any of the rest, I could not hold myself above slight and contempt. I soon became at least as expeditious and as skillful with my hands, as either of the other boys. [. . .]

My rescue from this kind of existence I considered quite hopeless, and abandoned as such, altogether; though I am solemnly convinced that I never, for one hour, was reconciled to it, or was otherwise than miserably unhappy. [. . .]

[. . .] My father said, I should go back no more, and should go to school. I do not write resentfully or angrily: for I know how all these things have worked together to make me what I am; but I never afterwards forgot, I never shall forget, I never can forget, that my mother was warm for my being sent back.

From that hour until this at which I write, no word of that part of my childhood which I have now gladly brought to a close has passed my lips to any human being. I have no idea how long it lasted; whether for a year, or much more, or less.[1] From that hour, until this, my father and my mother have been stricken dumb upon it. I have never heard the least allusion to it, however far off and remote, from either of them. I have never, until I now impart it to this paper, in any burst of confidence with any one, my own wife not excepted, raised the curtain I then dropped, thank God.[2]

Until old Hungerford market was pulled down, until old Hungerford-stairs were destroyed[3] and the very nature of the ground changed, I never had the courage to go back to the place where my servitude began. I never saw it. I could not endure to go near it. For many years when I came near to Robert Warren's in the Strand,[4] I crossed over to the opposite side of the way, to avoid a certain smell of the cement they put upon the blacking-corks, which reminded me of what I was once. [. . .] My old way home by the borough made me cry, after my eldest child could speak.

In my walks at night I have walked there often, since then, and by degrees I have come to write this. It does not seem a tithe of what I might have written, or of what I mean to write.

From **Charles Dickens, 'An Appeal to Fallen Women'** (1847) in Edgar Johnson, ed., The Heart of Charles Dickens (New York: Duell, Sloan & Pearce, 1952), pp. 97–100

Throughout his life Dickens engaged in good works such as the assistance he gave Angela Burdett Coutts, the richest woman in England apart from the Queen, in establishing a shelter for fallen women. As Dickens explained to Miss Coutts, the purpose of the home was 'to appeal to them by means of affectionate kindness and trustfulness, – but firmly, too. To improve them by education and example – establish habits of the most rigid order, punctuality, and neatness – but to make as great a variety in their daily lives as their daily lives will admit of – and render them an innocently cheerful Family while they live together there. On the cheerfulness and kindness all our hopes rest.' The 'Appeal' he authored for distribution to prospective residents of the shelter resounds with the hopefulness for a better life that Dickens would later envision for the fallen Little Em'ly in David Copperfield (**pp. 129–31, 141–3** and **157–62**; also Alexander Welsh's discussion of fallen women in the novel, **pp. 65–8**).

1 Although the exact dates are not known, the twelve-year-old Dickens worked at the blacking factory for about six months in early 1824.
2 At the conclusion of Chapter 14, David Copperfield says that 'a curtain had for ever fallen on my life at Murdstone and Grinby. [. . .] No one has ever raised that curtain since. [. . .] I have lifted it for a moment, even in this narrative, with a reluctant hand, and dropped it gladly.'
3 Stairs to the river removed with improved embankment of the Thames.
4 The blacking warehouse where Dickens had worked as a child belonged to this firm.

Think for a moment what your present situation is. Think how impossible it is that it ever can be better if you continue to live as you have lived, and how certain it is that it must be worse. You know what the streets are; you know how cruel the companions that you find there are; you know the vices practised there, and to what wretched consequences they bring you, even while you are young. Shunned by decent people, marked out from all other kinds of women as you walk along, avoided by the very children, hunted by the police, imprisoned, and only set free to be imprisoned over and over again–reading this very letter in a common gaol you have already dismal experience of the truth.

But to grow old in such a way of life, and among such company–to escape an early death from terrible disease, or your own maddened hand, and arrive at old age in such a course–will be an aggravation of every misery that you know now, which words cannot describe. Imagine for yourself the bed on which you, then an object terrible to look at, will lie down to die. Imagine all the long, long years of shame, want, crime, and ruin that will arise before you. And by that dreadful day, and by the judgment that will follow it, and by the recollection that you are certain to have then, when it is too late, of the offer that is made to you now, when it is NOT too late, I implore you to think of it and weigh it well.

There is a lady in this town who from the windows of her house has seen such as you going past at night, and has felt her heart bleed at the sight. She is what is called a great lady, but she has looked after you with compassion as being of her own sex and nature, and the thought of such fallen women has troubled her in her bed.

She has resolved to open at her own expense a place of refuge near London for a small number of females, who without such help are lost for ever, and to make a HOME for them. In this home they will be taught all household work that would be useful to them in a home of their own and enable them to make it comfortable and happy. In this home, which stands in a pleasant country lane and where each may have her little flower-garden if she pleases, they will be treated with the greatest kindness: will lead an active, cheerful, healthy life: will learn many things it is profitable and good to know, and being entirely removed from all who have any knowledge of their past career will begin life afresh and be able to win a good name and character.

And because it is this lady's wish that these young women should not be shut out from the world after they have repented and learned to do their duty there, and because it is her wish and object that they be restored to society–a comfort to themselves and it–they will be supplied with every means, when some time have elapsed and their conduct shall have fully proved their earnestness and reforma-tion, to go abroad, where in a distant country they may become the faithful wives of honest men, and live and die in peace. [. . .]

From **Charles Dickens, *A Christmas Carol*** (1843) in *Christmas Books by Charles Dickens* (New York: Charles Scribner's Sons, 1911), pp. 9–98

In this first and best known of his five Christmas books published just a few years before he wrote the autobiographical fragment and six years before *Copperfield*, Dickens pictured childhood as a time of great joy in itself. The Ghost of Christmas Past, the first of three spirits to visit, carries Scrooge back to the scenes of his childhood. What the spirit forces Scrooge to recall are the sorts of treasured childhood experience that more voluntarily David Copperfield recalls as fictional autobiographer. Only after frightening reminders of how Scrooge has become an embittered and joyless person does he get the point and change his ways. This short excerpt includes a vision in which Scrooge recalls lonely days in school. Dickens describes the place as though it were the blacking factory of his childhood. More broadly, the story of Scrooge anticipates *David Copperfield* by valuing memory as the means for holding evident and dear life's experiences and as the agent for moral renewal. Scrooge vows to 'live in the Past, the Present, and the Future', and that is exactly what David the writer attempts, especially in the several chapters (**pp. 134–5, 148–50**) where by using the present tense he treats the past as though it were literally present before his eyes. Ultimately, David's adult happiness comes in new relationships with old loves and friends, especially Agnes Wickfield. One of the most telling lines in all of Dickens's writing is the one concerning Scrooge at the end of this extract: 'His own heart laughed: and that was quite enough for him.' Good humour for Dickens is amiable and sociable, a sign of the good heart. In *David Copperfield* such capacity for feeling distinguishes the stern Murdstone, self-centred Uriah Heep and James Steerforth from David who finally values the good cheer of the Micawbers, Peggottys and Mr Dick and can laugh also at some of his earlier *naïveté*.

It was a strange figure – like a child: yet not so like a child as like an old man, viewed through some supernatural medium, which gave him the appearance of having receded from the view, and being diminished to a child's proportions. Its hair, which hung about its neck and down its back, was white as if with age; and yet the face had not a wrinkle in it, and the tenderest bloom was on the skin. The arms were long and muscular; the hands the same, as if its hold were of uncommon strength. Its legs and feet, most delicately formed, were, like those upper members, bared. It wore a tunic of the purest white; and round its waist was bound a lustrous belt, the sheen of which was beautiful. It held a branch of fresh green holly in its hand; and, in singular contradiction of that wintry emblem, had its dress trimmed with summer flowers. But the strangest thing about it was, that from the crown of its head there sprung a bright clear jet of light, by which all this was visible; and which was doubtless the occasion of its using, in its duller moments, a great extinguisher for a cap,[1] which it now held under its arm. [. . .]

"Who, and what are you?" Scrooge demanded.

"I am the Ghost of Christmas Past."

"Long past?" inquired Scrooge: observant of its dwarfish stature.

"No. Your Past." [. . .]

He then made bold to inquire what business brought him there.

"Your welfare!" said the Ghost.

Scrooge expressed himself much obliged, but could not help thinking that a night of unbroken rest would have been more conducive to that end. The Spirit must have heard him thinking, for it said immediately:

"Your reclamation, then. Take heed!"

It put out its strong hand as it spoke, and clasped him gently by the arm.

"Rise! and walk with me!" [. . .]

"You recollect the way?" inquired the Spirit.

"Remember it!" cried Scrooge with fervour – "I could walk it blindfold."

"Strange to have forgotten it for so many years!" observed the Ghost. "Let us go on."

They walked along the road; Scrooge recognising every gate, and post, and tree; until a little market-town appeared in the distance, with its bridge, its church, and winding river. Some shaggy ponies now were seen trotting towards them with boys upon their backs, who called to other boys in country gigs and carts, driven by farmers. All these boys were in great spirits, and shouted to each other, until the broad fields were so full of merry music, that the crisp air laughed to hear it.

"These are but shadows of the things that have been," said the Ghost. "They have no consciousness of us."

The jocund travellers came on; and as they came, Scrooge knew and named them every one. Why was he rejoiced beyond all bounds to see them! Why did his cold eye glisten, and his heart leap up as they went past! [. . .]

The Spirit touched him on the arm, and pointed to his younger self, intent upon his reading. Suddenly a man, in foreign garments; wonderfully real and distinct to look at: stood outside the window, with an axe stuck in his belt, and leading an ass laden with wood by the bridle.

"Why, it's Ali Baba!" Scrooge exclaimed in ecstasy. "It's dear old honest Ali Baba."[2] To hear Scrooge expending all the earnestness of his nature on such subjects, in a most extraordinary voice between laughing and crying; and to see his heightened and excited face; would have been a surprise to his business friends in the city, indeed. [. . .]

"I will honour Christmas in my heart, and try to keep it all the year. I will live in the Past, the Present, and the Future. The Spirits of all Three shall strive within me. I will not shut out the lessons that they teach." [. . .]

---

1 Metal candle snuffers were in the shape of conical hats.
2 The recollection of childhood reading recurs in *Copperfield*, and twice David refers to the *Arabian Nights* as a source of pleasure (pp. 95, 102, extracts 4 and 5). The first spirit conducts Scrooge's return to school days, first love, boyhood employment with the jolly Fezziwig.

Scrooge was better than his word. He did it all, and infinitely more. [. . .] He became as good a friend, as good a master, and as good a man, as the good old city knew, or any other good old city, town, or borough, in the good old world. Some people laughed to see the alteration in him, but he let them laugh, and little heeded them; for he was wise enough to know that nothing ever happened on this globe, for good, at which some people did not have their fill of laughter in the outset; and knowing that such as these would be blind anyway, he thought it quite as well that they should wrinkle up their eyes in grins, as have the malady in less attractive forms. His own heart laughed: and that was quite enough for him.

From **Samuel Smiles, *Self-Help*** (London: John Murray, 1859), Chapter 13, pp. 321–40

Victorians argued that moral character, and not circumstance of birth, best defined both hero and gentleman. These extracts from the last chapter of Smiles's best-selling book of 1859 show that the moral lessons David Copperfield learns and applies were precisely those Smiles would later describe and prescribe for men of the time. In *David Copperfield*, model male morality is notably absent in both David's idol, Steerforth, and his lowly nemesis, Uriah Heep. But David himself, with heart finally disciplined and earnestness applied, writes the story that, with Smiles's subsequent moral directive, exemplifies the nineteenth-century sense of a gentleman. Smiles's concerns – moral motive force, conduct informed by both feeling and knowledge, integrity and self-respect – and the importance given to the question of how well a man exercises power over subordinates, namely women and children, are principal criteria both for David's self-assessment and for his first readers' judgements of him.

CHARACTER—THE TRUE GENTLEMAN

[. . .] Character is human nature in its best form. It is moral order embodied in the individual. Men of character are not only the conscience of society, but in every well-governed State they are its best motive power; for it is moral qualities in the main which rule the world. Even in war, Napoleon said the moral is to the physical as ten to one. The strength, the industry, and the civilization of nations – all depend upon individual character; and the very foundations of civil security rest upon it. [. . .]

Though a man have comparative little culture, slender abilities, and but small wealth, yet, if his character be of sterling worth, he will always command an influence, whether it be in the workshop, the counting-house, mart, or the senate. [. . .]

That character is power is true in a much higher sense than that knowledge is power. Mind without heart, intelligence without conduct, cleverness without goodness, are powers in their way, but they may be powers only for mischief. We may be instructed or amused by them; but it is sometimes as difficult to admire them as it would be to admire the dexterity of a pickpocket or the horsemanship of a highwayman.

Truthfulness, integrity, and goodness – qualities that hang not on any man's breath – form the essence of manly character. [. . .] He who possesses these qualities, united with strength of purpose, carries with him a power which is irresistible. He is strong to do good, strong to resist evil, and strong to bear up under difficulty and misfortune. [. . .]

The True Gentleman is one whose nature has been fashioned after the highest models. It is a grand old name, that of Gentleman, and has been recognized as a rank and power in all stages of society. [. . .] To possess this character is a dignity of itself, commanding the instinctive homage of every generous mind, and those who will not bow to titular rank will yet do homage to the gentleman. His qualities depend not upon fashion or manners, but upon moral worth – not on personal possessions, but on personal qualities. The Psalmist briefly describes him as one "that walketh uprightly, and worketh righteously, and speaketh the truth in his heart."

The gentleman is eminently distinguished for his self-respect. He values his character – not so much of it only as can be seen of others, but as he sees it himself; having regard for the approval of his inward monitor. [. . .]

Riches and rank have no necessary connexion with genuine gentlemanly qualities. The poor man may be a true gentleman – in spirit and in daily life. He may be honest, truthful, upright, polite, temperate, courageous, self-respecting, and self-helping – that is, be a true gentleman. The poor man with a rich spirit is in all ways superior to the rich man with a poor spirit. [. . .]

There are many tests by which a gentleman may be known; but there is one that never fails – How does he *exercise power* over those subordinate to him? How does he conduct himself towards women and children? How does the officer treat his men, the employer his servants, the master his pupils, and men in every station those who are weaker than himself? The discretion, forbearance, and kindliness with which power in such cases is used may indeed be regarded as the crucial test of gentlemanly power. [. . .]

From **William Wordsworth, *The Prelude*** (1850), ed. Ernest De Selincourt (Oxford: Oxford University Press, 1959)

Romantic and Victorian writers placed a new stress on moments and acts of connection between people and external nature.[1] Wordsworth's point here is

1 Literary historians generally date the Romantic period in English literature from the early 1790s to the early 1830s; the Victorian from the early 1830s to 1900. Literature of the later nineteenth and earlier twentieth centuries continued to examine such central premises of Romanticism as this celebration of nature, and thus we can realize how confining the traditional dating of literary and historical periods can be.

that, however brief, emotionally intense and enlightening 'spots of time' remain in our consciousness. In *The Prelude*, which traces the growth of the poet's mind, the process of remembering, as much as any specifically remembered incident, empowers the autobiographer with a 'renovating virtue'. Similarly, David Copperfield remarks, 'I think the memory of most us can go farther back . . . than many of us suppose; just as I believe the power of observation in numbers of very young children to be quite wonderful for its closeness and accuracy' (**p. 91**). The novel is filled with many closely described 'spots of time', and a number of them pair verbal descriptions with full-page illustrations. In several later chapters with titles including the word 'Retrospect', David turns from past to present tense to emphasize how particular parts of his earlier life remain actively present before his eyes (**pp. 129–31, 141–3** and **157–62**). The longer passage here extracted from *The Prelude* shares the larger theme of Dickens's novel which frankly acknowledges mistakes and misdirections in a life story morally dependent upon various good influences, particularly those of beloved women. Wordsworth speaks in this passage of his dear sister; for David Copperfield it is his sister-like friend and ultimate wife, Agnes Wickfield, who patiently admonishes and constantly supports him.

[. . .] There are in our existence spots of time,
That with distinct pre-eminence retain
A renovating virtue, whence, depressed
By false opinion and contentious thought,
Or aught of heavier or more deadly weight,
　　[. . .] Such moments
Are scattered everywhere, taking their date
From our first Childhood. (Book 12, 208–25)

[. . .] Share with me, Friend! the wish
That some dramatic tale endued with shapes[2]
Livelier, and flinging out less guarded words
Than suit the Work we fashion, might set forth
What then I learned, or think I learned, of truth,
And the errors into which I fell, betrayed
By present objects, and by reasonings false
From their beginnings, inasmuch as drawn
Out of a heart that had been turned aside
From Nature's way by outward accidents,
And which was thus confounded, more and more
Misguided and misguiding. [. . .]

2　The 'friend' is Wordsworth's sister, Dorothy. With the term 'endued', meaning pervaded or permeated, Wordsworth stresses the intensity or density of his literary work. In Romantic theory, the natural world is itself deeply imbued with significance which the artist not only struggles to apprehend but also to incorporate in writing, painting or music.

[. . .] Then it was —
Thanks to the bounteous giver of all Good!
Thanks to the beloved Sister in whose sight
These days were passed, now speaking in a voice
Of sudden admonition – like a brook
That did but cross a lonely road, and now
Seen, heard, and felt, and caught at every turn,
Companion never lost through many a league –
Maintained for me a saving intercourse
With my true self
[. . .] She in the midst of all preserved me still
A Poet, made me seek beneath that name,
And that alone, my office upon earth. (Book 11, 282–93, 333–48)

From **Charlotte Brontë, *Jane Eyre*** (1847) (Edinburgh: John Grant, 1924) pp. 135, 153–4 and 180–2

> *David Copperfield*, the classic nineteenth-century male fictional autobiography, has a female counterpart in *Jane Eyre*. In these excerpts Jane the autobiographer directly addresses the reader to explain her focus on meaningful memory, and later, in a powerful feminist manifesto, she asserts her rights for gender equality. As does Jane, David Copperfield makes determined resolution to move on in life (**pp. 107–11** and **132–3**) and as he proceeds nonetheless experiences, as does Jane, continuing restlessness and uncertainty (**pp. 128–9, 139–40** and **156–7**).

Hitherto I have recorded in detail the events of my insignificant existence: to the first ten years of my life, I have given almost as many chapters. But this is not to be a regular autobiography: I am only bound to invoke memory where I know her responses will possess some degree of interest; therefore I now pass a space of eight years almost in silence: a few lines only are necessary to keep up the links of connection. [Ch. 10]

[. . .]

Reader, though I look comfortably accommodated, I am not very tranquil in my mind [. . .] It is a very strange sensation to inexperienced youth to feel itself quite alone in the world, cut adrift from every connection, uncertain whether the port to which it is bound can be reached, and prevented by many impediments from returning to that it has quitted. The charm of adventure sweetens that sensation, the glow of pride warms it; but then the throb of fear disturbs it [. . .] [Ch. 11]

[. . .]

[It was when I] looked out afar over sequestered field and hill, and along the dim sky-line – that then I longed for a power of vision which might overpass that limit; which might reach the busy world, towns, regions full of life I had heard of but never seen: that then I desired more of practical experience than I possessed, more of intercourse with my kind, of acquaintance with variety of character, than was here within my reach. [. . .]

Who blames me? Many, no doubt, and I shall be called discontented. I could not help it: the restlessness was in my nature; it agitated me to pain sometimes. Then my sole relief was to walk along the corridor of the third story, backwards and forwards, safe in the silence and solitude of the spot and allow my mind's eye to dwell on whatever bright visions rose before it – and certainly they were many and glowing; to let my heart be heaved by the exultant movement, which, while it swelled it in trouble, expanded it, with life; and, best of all, to open my inward ear to a tale that was never ended – a tale my imagination created, and narrated continuously; quickened with all incident, life, fire, feeling, that I desired and had not in my actual existence.

It is vain to say human beings ought to be satisfied with tranquillity: they must have action; and they will make it if they cannot find it. Millions are condemned to a stiller doom than mine, and millions are in silent revolt against their lot. Nobody knows how many rebellions besides political rebellions ferment in the masses of life which people earth. Women are supposed to be very calm generally: but women feel just as men feel; they need exercise for their faculties and a field for their efforts as much as their brothers do; they suffer from too rigid a restraint, too absolute a stagnation, precisely as men would suffer; and it is narrow-minded in their more privileged fellow-creatures to say that they ought to confine themselves to making puddings and knitting stockings, to playing on the piano and embroidering bags. It is thoughtless to condemn them, or laugh at them, if they seek to do more or learn more than custom has pronounced necessary for their sex. [Ch. 12]

From **Alfred Tennyson, *In Memoriam*** (1850) W. J. Rolfe, ed., *The Complete Poetical Works of Tennyson* (Boston, Mass.: Houghton Mifflin, 1898), pp. 162–98

David Copperfield, The Prelude and *Jane Eyre* all chart passages of life from childhood through educative childhood and youth to adulthood, from which the central characters recollect and evaluate significant parts of their earlier lives. *In Memoriam*, an elegy comprised of 131 numbered sections of various lengths compacted into a fictional three-year chronology, deals with but one period of Tennyson's life, the years following the death of his friend Arthur Henry Hallam, as the poet struggled to find purpose and meaning in his own life. The pertinence of the following *In Memoriam* lines to *David Copperfield* is in their assurance that revisiting one's loves and losses in acts of recollective writing results in affirmative self-renewal. David the novelist confesses the pain of writing parts of his story; David the character suffers losses of loved ones and ultimately rediscovers vital life around him. This new consciousness (**pp. 156–7**) resembles that which Tennyson describes in section 119, because David, too, finds 'great nature' speaking to and soothing him.

5

I sometimes hold it half a sin
   To put in words the grief I feel;
   For words, like Nature, half reveal
And half conceal the Soul within.

But, for the unquiet heart and brain,
   A use in measured language lies;
   The sad mechanic exercise,
Like dull narcotics, numbing pain.

In words, like weeds, I'll wrap me o'er,
   Like coarsest clothes against the cold:
   But that large grief which these enfold
Is given in outline and no more.

27
[. . .]

I hold it true, whate'er befall;
   I feel it, when I sorrow most;
   'Tis better to have loved and lost
Than never to have loved at all.

119

Doors, where my heart was used to beat
   So quickly, not as one that weeps
   I come once more; the city sleeps;
I smell the meadow in the street;

I hear a chirp of birds; I see
   Betwixt the black fronts long-withdrawn
   A light-blue lane of early dawn,
And think of early days and thee,

And bless thee, for thy lips are bland,
   And bright the friendship of thine eye;
   And in my thoughts with scarce a sigh
I take the pressure of thine hand.

2

Interpretations

Critical History

Critical response to *David Copperfield* began with the monthly part publication between May 1849 and November 1850. As was Dickens's practice, he both composed and published from month to month, and the last monthly part included the preface that would head the first complete edition, which was comprised of the collected parts. Nineteenth-century reviews tended to be more summary than critical, but in reprinting representative passages they did provide some rationale for what they thought to be a work's strengths and weaknesses, and they are often good registers of the more general public reception. Reviews invariably reflected the editorial bias of the paper or magazine in which they appeared. Because of the prominence and number of Dickens's previous works, reviewers approached *David Copperfield* with clear expectations and, sometimes, prejudice, but by 1849–50, Dickens was England's principal novelist and was known worldwide.

Significant critical reassessment of *David Copperfield* came after his death in 1870, much of it influenced by John Forster's *The Life of Charles Dickens* (1872, 1874) which disclosed how *Copperfield* had concealed details of Dickens's own life (**pp. 20–2**). Forster had been one of the novel's earliest champions in an anonymous review in *The Examiner* (14 December 1850), and he reiterates that earlier high regard in critical assessment of *Copperfield* in the later biography (**pp. 42–3**). By and large, biographers and critics in the later nineteenth and early twentieth centuries continued to regard this as a wonderfully comic novel, peopled with some of Dickens's most memorable characters, and as a remarkable evocation of childhood. Thus the critical view tended to be appreciative, whether the commentary linked *Copperfield* most with the exuberant early Dickens novels or found in it hints of more sombre later works.

Edmund Wilson, at the beginning of his landmark essay, 'Charles Dickens: The Two Scrooges' (1941), well describes the general state of earlier Dickens criticism, and his comments certainly apply to the critical reception of *David Copperfield*.

Of all the great English writers, Charles Dickens has received in his own country the scantiest serious attention from either biographers, scholars, or critics. He has become for the English middle class so much one of the articles of their creed – a familiar joke, a favorite dish, a Christmas ritual – that it is difficult for British pundits to see in him the great artist and social critic that he was. Dickens had no university education, and the literary men from Oxford and Cambridge, who have lately been sifting fastidiously so much of the English heritage, have rather snubbingly let him alone.[1]

Wilson's study charts the psychological and sociological dimensions of Dickens's life and work, and Wilson finds Dickens a great artist and social critic. He explores the biographical basis for Dickens's ever self-expressive writing and for his life-long critical attacks upon the social system. In the 1930s Freudian psychology and Marxian social theory were strongly influencing literary biography and criticism and that influence is clear in Wilson's work, even though his incisive essay keeps the subject Dickens, not Freud or Marx; 'the work of Dickens' whole career was an attempt to digest [. . .] early shocks and hardships, to explain them to himself, to justify himself in relation to them, to give an intelligible and tolerable picture of a world in which such things could occur' (pp. 8–9). Wilson, however, does not find *Copperfield* 'one of Dickens' deepest books', and in so thinking, even as he calls for newly serious study of Dickens, fails to look closely at this novel. Unlike many critics who follow him, Wilson sees David as 'too candid and simple to represent Dickens himself; and though the blacking warehouse episode is utilized, all the other bitter circumstances of Dickens' youth were left out' (p. 37).

As then the most complete and critically astute biography since Forster's eighty years earlier, Edgar Johnson's *Charles Dickens: His Tragedy and Triumph* (1952) supplies much informative reinforcement for Wilson's arguments about the importance of Dickens's childhood experience and the force of his social commitment. Like Wilson, Johnson continues to celebrate *David Copperfield* 'as the most enchanting' of Dickens's novels, but he stresses 'its cardinal significance to the psychologist and biographer' (pp. 677–8). As both the massive Pilgrim Edition of Dickens's letters and definitive Clarendon editions of his novels began to appear in the 1960s,[2] a wealth of new information became available for biographers, critics and general readers. Before the mid-twentieth century, much literary criticism centred biographically on the relation of authors' works and lives, or historically located writers and books in such periods as Romantic and Victorian, or such genres as the novel. For an understanding of fresh directions in modern criticism of *David Copperfield*, it is good to start with J. Hillis Miller and James Kincaid. Acknowledging, especially, Wilson's earlier work but setting for himself the task of assessing 'the specific quality of Dickens' imagination in the

1   Edmund Wilson, 'Charles Dickens: The Two Scrooges', *The Wound and the Bow* (New York: Oxford University Press, 1965), p. 3.
2   Both series are from Oxford: Clarendon Press. The volumes of letters most pertinent to *David Copperfield* are V (1981) and VI (1988), with Dickens's letters during the years in which he conceived and produced the novel. The Clarendon edition of *David Copperfield*, edited by Nina Burgis, was published in 1981 and identifies all textual variants from manuscript, corrected proofs, and the editions over which Dickens had control.

totality of his work', Miller 'reverses the usual causal sequence between the psychology of an author and his work' in order to see 'literature not as the mere symptom or product of a pre-existent psychological condition, but as the very means by which a writer apprehends and, in some measure, creates himself'.[3] As 'personal history' narrated by a fictional autobiographer, *David Copperfield* is an artificially but artistically constructed 'self-making' in which Miller finds 'repeated references to a very different kind of unifying presence, a presence external to the hero, guiding his life, and casting into any moment of time foreshadowings, presentiments of the future, and echoes of the past. [. . .] The hero has not made his own life and given himself a developing identity through the psychological power of memory; his destiny and identity and those of other people have been made by a metaphysical power, the power of divine Providence' (pp. 155–6). I quote Miller at this length here simply to show the seriousness with which he takes this novel (see below **pp. 44–6**). Published a decade later than Miller's book and examining 'Dickens's techniques as a humorist [. . .] to understand the individual novels better by more sharply defining our reaction to them', James Kincaid's study contributes greatly to our broad understanding of Dickens, and poses important questions concerning the function of rhetorically subversive humour in *David Copperfield*.[4]

Q. D. Leavis furthers 'The Case for a Serious View of *David Copperfield*' by examining the novel's thematic coherence and 'underlying psychological veracity [. . .] characteristic of Dickens's development as a novelist'. Over the last quarter of the twentieth century and carrying on today, literary criticism incorporates new interests and methods as it draws upon literary and social theory to conceptualize genre and form, historical and social context and impact. Close reading of such novels as *David Copperfield* considers theoretically what sort of novel it is, what it reveals or conceals about literary authorship and about class and gender-based authority, the relationship of fictional autobiography to autobiography. To the New Historicist (distinct from the earlier biographer or literary historian who too often dealt with only great lives, works and events), *Copperfield* is one of many documents illustrating everyday conditions and the value of mid-Victorian culture. As a case in point, William J. Palmer points out the prominent topicality of shipwreck in this novel both as economic reality and as metaphor for damaged lives (**pp. 52–5**). Feminist and gender study both deal with (among other things) the social construction of male and female roles and values. Mary Poovey closely scrutinizes the novel's assertive but problematic class and gender hierarchies in terms of the gender and class power relationships endemic to the age (**pp. 59–62**). Alexander Welsh, like Poovey, is interested in male power exercised by both David and Dickens in their acts of authorship (**pp. 65–8**). Turning to the situation of children and the value Dickens finds in childhood through 'Trials of Maturity', Malcolm Andrews reconsiders the novel's often praised rendering of 'Children and the Childlike' (**pp. 55–8**). Turning

---

3   *Charles Dickens: The World of His Novels* (Cambridge, Mass.: Harvard University Press, 1958), p. viii.
4   *Dickens and the Rhetoric of Laughter* (Oxford: Clarendon Press, 1971), p. 2.

from the good and the heroic to their opposites, Juliet John reminds us of Dickens's inveterate theatricality as she considers the 'Byronic Baddies, [and] Melodramatic Anxieties' of *David Copperfield*, a study helpful to readers interested in the novel's characterization of both the aristocratic James Steerforth and the lowly worm Uriah Heep (**pp. 62–5**).

A different strain of modern criticism concerns the relationship of the novel to various stage and film adaptations. The animation of film, often based on the novel's original illustration, helps the viewer/reader to better recognize the inherent relationship of forty original illustrations to Dickens's highly pictorial writing. In a recent study, Robert Patten rightly stresses the importance of this combination: the illustrations 'image multiple points of view, times, identities, relationships, potential plots; they interact with all kinds of cues in the text [. . .] and enlighten, light up, elucidate, and embellish the subject, and by doing so [. . .] render both luminous and illustrious the work they share with the letterpress.'[5] In the last decade of his life, Dickens demonstrated the novel's performative quality when he delighted large audiences with one-man theatrical readings based on the book. Later stage and film adaptations much depend on the novel's illustration for casting and costuming of characters and for staging key scenes. Readers need to keep in mind that the superbly illustrated novel combines words and pictures to achieve pictorial and dramatic effects that carry forward in stage and screen versions. This sourcebook provides materials about the novel in performance (**pp. 72–81**) and later it includes several of the illustrations as textual extracts (**pp. 88, 94, 113, 119, 149** and **162**). Critical discussion of the illustrations, such as Stephen Lutman's (**pp. 68–70**), and reviews, such as Robert Giddings's (**pp. 80–1**) of recent films, help readers to understand these fundamental components of the novel.

This Sourcebook's selections represent but a sample of sound and useful criticism. Separately, and also in relation to one another, these commentaries can help us to understand why *David Copperfield* continues to be one of the world's most read and admired novels, how it works as literature, and what themes and topics it projects from Dickens's world to ours. It is a work of its time and for all time. Childhood experienced and remembered, individual fears and desires, family and larger social relationships, rightness or wrongness of intention and action – these are human issues upon which *David Copperfield* provides perspective and challenges new generations of critics and readers to reconsider.

---

5   'Illustration and Storytelling in *David Copperfield*'. *The Victorian Illustrated Book*, ed. Richard Maxwell (Charlottesville, Va.: University of Virginia Press, 2002), p. 121.

Early Critical Reception

From **[H. F. Chorley], 'The Personal History of David Copperfield'**, *The Athenaeum*, 23 November 1850, pp. 1209–11

The novel had appeared serially from May 1849, and was published in single-volume form in November 1850. Noting how it fulfils reader expectations based on Dickens's previous writing, Chorley begins by also pointing out the book's particular appeal. His praise for the genial humour, perspective on childhood and young love, and many memorable characters reflects strengths recognized by Dickens's first readers.

[. . .] That this is in many respects the most beautiful and highly finished work which the world has had from the pen of Mr Dickens, we are strongly of opinion. It has all the merits to which the author already owes a world-wide popularity; with some graces which are peculiar to itself – or have been but feebly indicated in his former creations. In no previous fiction has he shown so much gentleness of touch and delicacy of tone, – such abstinence from trick in what might be called the level part of the narrative, – so large an amount of refined and poetical yet simple knowledge of humanity. The Chronicler himself is one of the best heroes ever sketched or wrought out by Mr Dickens. Gentle, affectionate and trusting, – his fine observation and his love of reverie raise David Copperfield far above the level of sentimental lovers or hectoring youths whose fortunes and characters are too often in works of this sort made axles on which the action and passion of the story turn. The loving, imaginative child – with his childish fancies perpetually reaching away towards heights too high for childhood to climb – his rapid and sympathetic instincts for enjoyment – his quick sense of injustice, – his tremulous foresight of coming griefs, – the boy seduced by the fascinating qualities of a dangerous friend, – the youth's boy-love for his child-wife, – that love itself never faltering even to the end, yet by a fine instinctive information leading his mind to dim glimpses of a higher domestic happiness at which he might have aimed, – all these are outlined, filled in and coloured without one stroke awry or one

exaggerated tint to mar the portraiture. [. . .] – Then, over all there hangs that
mournful sentiment which, being the natural accompaniment of all personal
reviews of the past, never in its saddest expressions takes the tone of sentimental-
ism; but follows the narrative like a low, sweet – and true – music: – beginning
with the narrator's first look out on his father's cold grave in the churchyard
against which every night his mother's door is barred, and only ending with the
last line that chronicles the gains, the trials and the losses of a life.

To lovers of higher excitement – who have no relish for these natural truths –
the tale before us will be less pleasing than many another written by Mr. Dickens,
exactly for the reason which makes us like it better. As an autobiography –
the story of a life – *David Copperfield* is – properly – more than usually desti-
tute of defined and artistic plot. The looseness of texture as a story, however,
is, on the one hand, imperfectly, sought to be designed by afterthoughts, – on
the other, rendered more apparent by one or two strained incidents and forced
scenes. [. . .]

There is one other scene on which we have to remark in the way of objection to
make. [. . .] The scene to which we allude is one of the most awful, elaborate and
powerfully descriptive in the book: – that of the great storm in which the injured
lover and the seducer perish within a hand's breadth of each other, close to the
devastated home. That moral calamity never takes the forms of such fantastic
combination, who shall dare to say? That Doom and Horror are never sym-
phonized as in all the careful preparations made for the catastrophe by Mr. Dickens, few will be prepared to assert. But the novelist is bound when wielding the
thunderbolt to spare us the crucible and the laboratory: – for his own sake, as an
artist, to conceal, not display, his recourse to forced expedients for the purpose of
administering poetical justice – whether it shape itself into the vengeance of
annihilation or into the vengeance of forgiveness. In spite of the amazing descriptive power here exhibited – a power that deafens as it were with the sounds and
the assaults of wave and wind – in spite of the wonderful force given by accumulation of detail – we cannot divest ourselves of an impression of stage-effect; of that
of a punishment elaborately adjusted by Man – rather than bursting on us with
the terrible unexpectedness of the thunders of retribution. [. . .] In reference to a
book which is so full of wholesome and beautiful things, we should scarcely have
cared to urge this point of objection, were there not in it so many signs of the
mellowing and ripening processes through which successful and experienced
genius passes having already taken place with Mr. Dickens. We do not demand
from him a sacrifice of that exaggeration in which his forte lies, so much as
a distribution of it. We would not yield up any characteristics of so keen an
observer, so capital a narrator as Mr. Dickens; – only bring them into a greater
harmony one with the other, and himself into a better agreement with
himself. [The remainder of the review consists of representative passages from the
novel.]

From **[Margaret Oliphant], 'Charles Dickens'**, *Blackwood's Edinburgh Magazine*, April 1855, pp. 451–2

Margaret Oliphant recognizes the issues of social class in Dickens's writings pertaining both to his fictional world and to Dickens himself. The class-consciousness is one way of accounting for his great popularity, claims Oliphant, but not until more than a century later did critics more thoroughly discuss class issues and values in Dickens (see Poovey and Welsh, **pp. 59–62** and **65–8**).

We men and women of to-day are very limited people, with all our sciences and knowledges; and instead of standing on one broad common ground as human creatures, brothers and sisters to each other, we are all, more or less, inhabitants of such and such a street, keeping so many servants, and paying such a rent for our houses. That one of us who has five thousand a year has perhaps great respect for the other one who has five hundred; and he, in his turn, recognizes, without hesitation, the excellent qualities of his poor clerk who has but fifty. What then? "We are a different class of society," say respectively these respectable gentlemen. They are both potentates in their way – enviable, sufficient, well-appointed Englishmen, whose incomes, and honours, and appearances, are part of their identity, and who, neither of them, could well recognize the naked primitive creature who only *wears* these vestments of social position for himself. This living centre of their greatness is certainly the foundation of all, and the first object of care and tenderness. [. . .]

It does not need this argument, or any other save his own great gifts and powers, to account for the power of Mr. Dickens; nevertheless, we cannot but express our conviction that it is to the fact that he represents a class that he owes his speedy elevation to the top of the wave of popular favour. He is a man of very liberal sentiments – an assailer of constituted wrongs and authorities – one of the advocates in the plea of Poor *versus* Rich, to the progress of which he has lent no small aid in his day. But he is, notwithstanding, perhaps more distinctly than any other author of the time a *class* writer, the historian and representative of one circle in the many ranks of our social scale. Despite their descents into the lowest class, and their occasional flights into the less familiar ground of fashion, it is the air and the breath of middle-class respectability which fills the books of Mr. Dickens. [. . .] Home-bred and sensitive, much impressed by feminine influences, swayed by the motives, the regards, and the laws which were absolute to their childhood, Mr. Dickens' heroes are all young for a necessity. Their courage is of the order of courage which belongs to women. They are spotless in their thoughts, their intentions, and wishes.

From **John Forster, *The Life of Charles Dickens*** (London: Chapman & Hall, 1874), Vol. II, pp. 21–36

Forster had written a review of *Copperfield* while the novel was still appearing as a serial, but did not reveal his knowledge of the use Dickens made of his fragmentary autobiography and how he had modelled much of Mr Micawber upon his father. When he did so in his very popular biography of Dickens, he continued to celebrate the book as comic masterpiece, and he urged readers to discriminate between the fictional life of David and the life of Dickens.

Dickens never stood so high in reputation as at the completion of *Copperfield*. The popularity it obtained at the outset increased to a degree not approached by any previous book excepting *Pickwick*,[1] [. . .] If the power was not greater than in *Chuzzlewit*,[2] the subject had more attractiveness; there was more variety of incident, with a freer play of character; and there was withal a suspicion, which though general and vague had sharpened interest not a little, that underneath the fiction lay something of the author's life. How much, was not known by the world until he had passed away.

To be acquainted with English literature is to know that, into its most famous prose fiction, autobiography has entered largely in disguise, and that the characters most familiar to us in the English novel had originals in actual life. [. . .] We have seen in what way Dickens was moved or inspired by the rough lessons of his boyhood[3] and the groundwork of the character [Wilkins Micawber] was then undoubtedly laid; but the rhetorical exuberance impressed itself upon him later, and from this, as it expanded and developed in a thousand amusing ways, the full-length figure took its great charm. Better illustration of it could not perhaps be given than by passages from letters of Dickens, written long before Micawber was thought of, in which this peculiarity of his father found frequent and always agreeable expression. [. . .] It is proper to preface them by saying that no one could know the elder Dickens without secretly liking him the better for these flourishes of speech, which adapted themselves so readily to his gloom as well as to his cheerfulness, that it was difficult not to fancy that they had helped him considerably in both, and had rendered more tolerable to him [. . .] the shade and sunshine of a chequered life. . . . [I]t delighted Dickens to remember that it was of one of his connections his father wrote a celebrated sentence; "And I must express my tendency to believe that his longevity is (to say the least of it) extremely problematical." [. . .] There was a laugh in the enjoyment of all this, no doubt, but

---

1 Despite its very favourable critical reception, *Copperfield*, selling an average of 20,000 copies during the serial publication, did not sell nearly as well as the 30,000 monthly part average for *Dombey and Son* which preceded it. Robert L. Patten, *Charles Dickens and His Publishers* (Oxford: Clarendon Press, 1978), p. 208.
2 *Martin Chuzzlewit* (1842–44) marked a turning point in Dickens's career because it centred on an organizing theme, pride.
3 Forster here reminds readers of the revelation he made of Dickens's autobiographical fragment in volume one of this biography.

with it much personal fondness; and the feeling of the creator of Micawber as he thus humoured and remembered the foibles of his original qualities.

[. . .] The character of the hero of the novel finds indeed his right place in the story he is supposed to tell, rather by unlikeness than by likeness to Dickens, even where intentional resemblance might seem to be prominent. Take autobiography as a design to show that no man's life may be as a mirror of existence to all men, and the individual career becomes altogether secondary to the variety of experiences received and rendered back in it. This particular form in imaginative literature has too often led to the indulgence of mental analysis, metaphysics and sentiment, all in excess: but Dickens was carried safely over these allurements by a healthy judgment and sleepless creative fancy; and even the method of his narrative is more simple here than it generally is in his books. [. . .]

That the incidents arise easily, and to the very end connect themselves naturally and unobtrusively with the characters of which they are a part, is to be said perhaps more truly of this than of any other of Dickens's novels. There is a profusion of distinct and distinguishable people, and a prodigal wealth of detail; but unity of drift or purpose is apparent always, and the tone is uniformly right. By the course of events we learn the value of self-denial and patience, quiet endurance of unavoidable ills, strenuous effort against ills remediable; and everything in the fortunes of the actors warns us, to strengthen our generous emotions and to guard the purities of home. It is easy thus to account for the supreme popularity of *Copperfield*, without the addition that it can hardly have had a reader, man or lad, who did not discover that he was something of a Copperfield himself. Childhood and youth live again for all of us in its marvellous boy-experiences. Mr. Micawber's presence does not prevent my saying that it does not take the lead of other novels in humorous creation; but in the use of humour to bring out prominently the ludicrous in any object or incident without excluding or weakening its most enchanting sentiment, it stands decidedly first. It is the perfection of English mirth.

Modern Criticism

From **J. Hillis Miller, 'David Copperfield'**, Charles Dickens: The World of His Novels (Cambridge, Mass.: Harvard University Press, 1958), pp. 150–9

For Miller the novel's organizing spiritual thread is David's personal search for that person who will give purpose and sustenance to his being. Memory is not simply what he recollects but his imaginative act of putting together the earlier parts of his life. We see this most clearly when David moves from past to present tense in what he calls 'Retrospect' (**pp. 129–31, 141–3** and **157–68**). Like many more recent critics, Miller finds the novel more complex than it may appear, and he points to worldly and other-worldly powers; he cites, especially, Agnes and Providence as forces which control David. We can see this in David's final words about her (**p. 162**).

[. . . T]hough the past can never be fully recaptured, nevertheless all David's memories hang together to form a whole, the integrated continuum of his past life as it has led by stages up to his present condition. All David's memories are linked to one another. Any one point radiates backward and forward in a multitudinous web connecting it to past and future. [. . .]

[. . . T]his novel has a duration and a coherence denied to all the third-person narratives among Dickens' novels. The spiritual presence of the hero organizes all these recollected events, through the powerful operation of association, into a single unified pattern which forms his destiny. At first David, as a child, can only experience isolated fragments of sensation, without possessing any power to put these together to form a coherent whole: "I could observe, in little pieces, as it were; but as to making a net of a number of these pieces, and catching anybody in it, that was, as yet, beyond me" (Ch. 1). But in the end the protagonist can boast that he has fabricated his own destiny by living through these experiences, and holding them together with the magnetic field of his mind. Without his organizing presence the world might fall back into disconnected fragments.

However, there are also throughout the novel repeated references to a very different kind of unifying presence, a presence external to the hero, guiding his life, and casting into any moment of time foreshadowings, presentiments, of the future, and echoes of the past. This providential spirit has determined the cohesion of events and their inalterable necessity. The hero has not made his own life and given himself a developing identity through the psychological power of memory; his destiny and identity and those of other people have been made by a metaphysical power, the power of divine Providence. [. . .]

David has, during his childhood of neglect and misuse, been acutely aware of himself as a gap in being. He has seemed to himself to be "a blank space . . ., which everybody overlooked, and yet was in everybody's way" (Ch. 8), "cast away among creatures with whom I had no community of nature" (Ch. 9), "a somebody too many" (Ch. 8). Even after his marriage to Dora he has felt, in a phrase which is repeated again and again in the novel, an "old unhappy loss or want of something never to be realised" (Ch. 58). After he is married to Dora, he wishes that his child-wife "had had more character and purpose, to sustain me, and improve me by; had been endowed with power to fill up the void which somewhere seemed to be about me" (Ch. 44). The center of David's life, then, is the search for some relationship to another person which will support his life, fill up the emptiness within him, and give him a substantial identity. And the turning point of his destiny is his recognition that it is Agnes who stands in that relation to him: ". . . without her I was not, and I never had been, what she thought me" (Ch. 58); "What I am, you have made me, Agnes" (Ch. 60). After this recognition, he must "discipline" his "undisciplined heart" (Ch. 48) by renouncing any claim on Agnes, and, through that renunciation, become worthy of possessing her at last as his wife. David in the end has altogether escaped from his initial condition of emptiness and nonbeing, when his life was "a ruined blank and waste" (Ch. 58). He stands in an unmediated relation to that which is the source of his being and the guarantee of the solidity of his selfhood: "Clasped in my embrace, I held the source of every worthy aspiration I had ever had; the centre of myself, the circle of my life, my own, my wife; my love of whom was founded on a rock!" (Ch. 62). [. . .] David has that relation to Agnes[1] which a devout Christian has to God, the creator of his selfhood, without whom he would be nothing.

But has David chosen these roles for Agnes and himself, or has he simply assented to them passively? If the former is the case, then David's existence is returned in a way to the same emptiness, since he has no power in himself to validate Agnes as his human goddess. And if the latter possibility is the case, then David is a mere puppet, manipulated by his destiny. Dickens contrives to have it both ways for David, and in having it both ways he achieves the only satisfactory solution to his problem. On the one hand, since David has been for so long ignorant of the place Agnes has in his life, and has finally discovered it for himself, he can say truthfully: "I . . . had worked out my own destiny" (Ch. 62). And, on the other hand [. . .] Agnes has been all along secretly destined for him by a benign Providence. [. . .]

---

1 Agnes Wickfield, in whose home he lodges while in school at Canterbury and who he later discovers to be his 'good angel'.

But at the time David cannot understand the divine hints, and is left to work out his own destiny. It is only long afterward, in the perspective of his total recollection of his life, that David can understand these moments and give them their true value. Only then can he see that it is not so much his own mind as the central presence of Agnes which organizes his memories and makes them a whole: "With the unerring instinct of her noble heart, she touched the chords of my memory so softly and harmoniously, that not one jarred within me; I could listen to the sorrowful, distant music, and desire to shrink from nothing it awoke. How could I, when, blended with it all, was her dear self, the better angel of my life?" (Ch. 60). David, then, has both made himself and escaped the guilt which always hovers, for Dickens, over the man who takes matters into his own hands.

From **Q. D. Leavis, 'Dickens and Tolstoy: The Case for a Serious View of *David Copperfield*'** in F. R. Leavis and Q. D. Leavis, *Dickens the Novelist* (New York: Pantheon Books, 1970), pp. 43–85

The centenary of Dickens's death in 1970 occasioned many reconsiderations of his life and work, and one of the most important studies was by British critics F. R. and Q. D. Leavis. The Leavises regard 'the trend of American criticism of Dickens, from Edmund Wilson onwards, as being in general wrong-headed', and argue that Dickens 'developed a fully conscious devotion to his art, becoming . . . a popular and fecund, but yet profound, serious and wonderfully resourceful practising novelist'. As Q. D. Leavis counters Edmund Wilson's views that '*Copperfield* is not one of Dickens's deepest books' (**p. 36**), she gives more pages to this novel than Wilson had given the whole of Dickens. She argues for the masterly construction of *Copperfield*, with high regard for the fictional auto-biographical form and also for Dickens's psychologically complex characteriza-tion of Dan Peggotty, faithful uncle of David's childhood playmate, Little Em'ly.

[. . .]
The masterly construction of *Copperfield* is the more surprising when one reflects that its only predecessor as an integrally conceived novel was *Dombey*, and that that broke down, changing direction and mode, with the death of little Paul, losing its previous steady focus on the theme.[1] *Copperfield* is only a year later but what an advance it shows in planning, complexity of conception and consistency from the first chapter right through to the schematic ending! (leaving out the last chapter, which provides a pantomime transformation scene – a concession to the reading-public which Dickens never again makes. There are no happy endings after *Copperfield*).

---

1   Paul Dombey, 'son' in *Dombey and Son*, who finds the world of business incomprehensible and dies as a prematurely aged child. His surviving sister, long ignored by her father, eventually wins his favour, and as the narrator comments, the story turns out finally to be one of 'Dombey and Daughter'.

[. . . David] is an innocent, by the circumstances of his childhood and upbringing, simply passive in being imprinted with the age's 'best' ideals of love, marriage, conduct of life and what is desirable in a woman. He is deliberately chosen to be representative, in order to examine current ideas; we should note that he is otherwise colourless, and impossible to visualize physically in any respect – seeing how gifted Dickens is at communicating personal characteristics and how naturally this comes to him, only concentration on this conception of his protagonist could have stopped Dickens from providing David with a full, vivid individuality. [. . .] It follows that David's relation to Dickens is nothing like what it has generally been alleged to be. [. . .]

[. . .] Not only is David's life not Dickens's past, but even though, as Forster[2] noted, the young male reader of his time naturally identified himself with David, there is no compulsion to identify with him uncritically as there is, for instance, for the reader of *Jane Eyre* to do so with the heroine. In fact, those critics who *do* identify C. D. with D. C. and complain that Dickens didn't realize that David was stupid not to see through Dora, or reprehensible not to blame himself, merely expose their inability to read what Dickens has offered them. Dickens had started to write his autobiography, it is true, and abandoned the project when he decided to write the novel instead; but this must have been because he *did* want to examine *impersonally* the experience of growing up in the first half of the 19th century, with the problems that a young man of that generation incurred, an examination needing the kind of objectivity that inheres in the novelist's art, but still one best exposed through the autobiographical form. [. . .]

[. . .] David's history is a model one in that buoyant era which believed or held that every man had the prospect of achieving comfort and respectability, even riches and distinction, at any rate happiness, if he would choose the path of thrift, austerity, perseverance in hard work, and self-improvement. This David does, and he accepts the reward that his society had given him to understand would then make him happy: domestic bliss which would be guaranteed by marriage with the incarnation of a feminine ideal he had been conditioned to accept as lovable. Dickens had done so too, and evidently had now reached the point of asking himself: Why then am I not contented? If society is right, what went wrong? Or was it the wrong prescription? What should it have been? These questions are explored through the history of David Copperfield. [. . .]

[. . . T]he artist – the truthteller, the psychological realist – is visible without any possibility of denial or conjecture in another aspect of the Emily episode – in the morbidity Dickens shows as powering the intense affection Daniel Peggotty has for his niece – another critical comment on what could pass as 'affection' and thus as admirable – though that might be acceptable to the Victorian reader as the touching devotion of one who stood in the relation of adopted father to Little Em'ly. But while Mr. Peggotty seems at first sight to offer the pattern of disinterested devotion to the winning child he had fostered, what emerges is a horribly

2   John Forster, Dickens's close friend and first biographer, who after the author's death published the autobiographical fragment (**pp. 20–2**).

possessive love that is expressed characteristically in heat, violence and fantasies, impressing us as maniacal. And Dickens doesn't attempt to disguise this; on the contrary, it is hammered home. Mr. Peggotty had no objection to his niece's marrying her cousin Ham, whom she doesn't love as much as her uncle and who, while not being a rival in her affections, will keep her in the family; but her elopement with Steerforth, even though marriage is what she intended, makes him aware of what he cannot face, that she loves Steerforth enough to leave home and uncle for him. Daniel Peggotty is shown driven by uncontrollable passion through Europe on foot to search for Emily, though without any clue as to her whereabouts, determined to find Emily and bring her home, ignoring the very relevant fact that she had preferred to give up that home in order to share Steerforth's life because she can do without her uncle. The Victorian reader understood that he was acting in the interests of Morality in rescuing Emily from a life of shame, but Dickens's attention is elsewhere, on putting into Daniel Peggotty's mouth words of a truly astonishing import:

> 'I'm a-going to seek my niece through the wureld. I'm a-going to find my poor niece in her shame and bring her back. . . . I'm a-going to seek her, fur and wide. . . . I began to think within my own self "What shall I do when I see her?" I never doubted her. On'y let her see my face – on'y let her heer my voice – on'y let my stanning afore her bring to her thoughts the home she had fled away from, and the child she had been – and if she had growed to be a royal lady, she'd have fell down at my feet. I know'd it well! Many a time in my sleep had I heerd her cry out, "Uncle!" and seen her fall like death afore me. Many a time in my sleep had I raised her up and whispered to her "Em'ly, my dear, I am come fur to bring forgiveness, and to take you home!" *He* was nowt to me now, Em'ly was all. I bought a country dress to put upon her; and I know'd that, once found, she would walk beside me over them stony roads, go wheer I would, and never, never, leave me more.'[3]

It is this genius, which cannot stop at the moralistic and sentimental but which burrows down below the superficial to find an underlying psychological veracity, that is characteristic of Dickens's development as a novelist. We may ask, How does Dickens know these truths? The awful conviction, the terrifying possessive passion Daniel Peggotty's words reveal, could hardly have been expected to pass even with unsophisticated readers as natural feelings creditable to a worthy uncle. Dickens's interest in morbid states and the strange self-deceptions of human nature, shown here in the compulsive fantasying, can never before have been so nakedly displayed. [. . .]

Thus from such strikingly forceful and absolutely original episodes in *Copperfield* alone [. . .] we can see that to Dickens it was the *meanings* of his mature novels which were important to him and the reason for his undertakings. The

---

3 See pp. 129–31 for more details of this key moment.

force of the language and the originality of conception and execution of such parts (in characterization, action and technique) prove that they were infinitely more the concern of the creative writer than the parts of these novels emanating from his concern (genuine though it was) for social welfare and ordinary morality.

From **James R. Kincaid, 'David Copperfield: Laughter and Point of View'**, *Dickens and the Rhetoric of Laughter* (Oxford: Clarendon Press, 1971), pp. 162–91

John Forster, in the 1872 volume of his biography of Dickens, hailed *David Copperfield* as the 'perfection of English mirth' (**p. 43**), an opinion largely shared by generations of readers. James Kincaid, on the other hand, sees this story as Dickens's 'farewell to comedy'; Kincaid means that Dickens was deepening and changing the direction of his comic vision, although Kincaid thinks this was a reluctant process. This extract, from a larger study of numerous subversive qualities in Dickens's humour, reconsiders the relationship of Dickens to his fictional narrator, and argues that he maintained a separate authorial presence from David's. Humour that embodied sociability and optimism in earlier Dickens writing here has a different significance. David is left melancholy and nostalgic, possessing a story in which the imaginative and ideal surrender to the pragmatic and real. A principal case in point is the novel's comic genius, Mr Micawber, who literally has no steady home or occupation in an asset-driven England, and thus he, like countless real-life speculators, ends up emigrating to Australia.

[. . .] *David Copperfield* is no comedy, but a farewell to comedy. It is, in fact, the most reluctant farewell to comedy on record.

For David is extremely sensitive to the comic vision; he is born in the midst of gentleness and joy, and he never forgets that atmosphere. It is certainly his misfortune that the Murdstones enter his life, but it might also be said that it is equally unfortunate that he had enjoyed such an idyllic childhood before the murderers arrived. He is thrown directly from a rich and imaginative Eden into a mean and restricted cash-box version of reality. He leaves for Yarmouth from a home which has nothing but joy and returns to a home which has none. No transition and no connection are ever established between these worlds, and as a result it is not possible for him to find in life either complete commercial rigidity or full imaginative joy. [. . .] David is always haunted by the sense of something missing, 'the old unhappy loss or want of something', and, like his mother, has the comic sense that things ought to be better, that one has a right to Eden. But the comic and commercial, the lovely and the firm, are never brought together, and David becomes something of a representative nineteenth-century man, for whom the realm of the imaginative, the spiritual, and the ideal is divorced from the realm of the pragmatic, the commercial, and the real.[1] And, in place of a resolution, he adopts a very representative operating principle: a self-congratulatory firmness, modified by a compensating sentimentality. One can say, of course, that he comes to terms with his world, but the price he is asked to pay is enormous.

He must, as he says so often, 'discipline' his heart.[2] It has struck many readers that this is a terribly reductive formula for a humane and responsive existence, that it is priggish, escapist, ugly, and narrow, that it denies the values that count—those of Dora, the Micawbers, and Mr. Dick—and that this 'disciplining' is partly a euphemism for desensitizing, falsifying, sentimentalizing. All these charges are true; they are fully supported by the novel. But it is equally true that the novel is never ironic in the sense of attacking its hero; it is never critical of David's decisions. But it is very sad about them. *David Copperfield*'s famous tone of melancholy is created by more than its bittersweet reminiscences; it is perhaps more to the point that these are reminiscences of defeat, of a world now lost. David's course, from joy to a pain so intense that it admits of no escape but only of more or less inadequate evasion, is one which is at the centre of the experience of the last two centuries. Indeed, it helps explain the novel's immense and continuing popularity. The primary means of the attempted escape are also common ones: the important comic values are denied, and trivial antithetical values are loudly proclaimed. David tries very hard to turn his novel into a celebration of prudence, distrust, discipline, rigid and unimaginative conduct, and the commonest sense. It is a cause both of his pain and of the novel's greatness that he has terrible difficulty ever accepting these values; their inadequacy and irrelevance are signalled over and over again. [. . .]

[. . .] Laughter is used to establish values, themes, and, paradoxically, the atmosphere of melancholy. *David Copperfield* is one of the funniest of Dickens's novels but also one of the saddest; for all of the fun is enlisted on the side of forces which are finally extinguished.

The crucial issue, then, is related to the technical one of point of view: the relation of the novel's established values to those gradually accepted by David and the control of our attitude towards both sets of value. It seems to me essential that we recognize that David is, in many key ways, neither the voice of the author nor the voice of the novel. In any case, there are three clearly distinguished stages in the novel, in which the conditions of David's life, the values suggested, and the rhetorical techniques all shift radically and significantly:

i. *Childhood joy.* Chapters 1–3. This section, though quite short, is extremely important in that it establishes an image of Eden which is never absent from David's mind but which is realized later only in tantalizingly brief snatches. The laughter in this section not only supports

1 On this point, see Samuel Smiles (pp. 26–7).
2 [Kincaid's note.] For a reading of the novel which accepts this phrase as an adequate statement of the theme see Gwendolyn B. Needham, 'The Undisciplined Heart of David Copperfield', *Nineteenth-Century Fiction*, ix (1954), 81–107. Several interpretations of the novel which start from an autobiographical premise are also associated with the notion of developing discipline and control; the best is by Edgar Johnson, *Charles Dickens: His Tragedy and Triumph* (New York: Simon & Schuster, 1952), pp. 677–90.

the comic values associated with David's happy childhood but, interestingly, encourages us to reject as harmless many of the threats which will later become more precisely defined and much more dangerous.

ii. *Isolation and fear*. Chapters 4–13. This black period, the period of Murdstone, Creakle, and the warehouse, functions as a direct contrast to the first and makes impossible for David the openness, spontaneity, and trust necessary for comedy. The humour in this section is similar to that in *Oliver Twist*, acting as rhetoric of attack in order to demand our sympathy for and identification with David. It also begins to build, through Micawber, an alternate system.

These first thirteen chapters are the novel's most crucial ones in determining the character of the hero; they are also among the finest in English literature in forming a complete fusion with their subject and creating a total imaginative identification with the child [. . .] These chapters urge us to identify with David, to sympathize with a value structure, and then to recognize that the two will likely never come together. The rest of the novel can be seen as the development of these dichotomies and of this rhetoric of frustration and melancholy.

iii *Fantasy and firmness*. Chapters 14–64. The remaining chapters explore David's attempts to deal with the hostile world about him, his dependence upon fantasy, and his pathetically ironic drift towards Murdstonean firmness and sentimentality. Laughter here is asked continually to reinforce the comic value system, identify the split between this system and the hero, and try to heal it. It trails off altogether as David moves to Agnes and Micawber moves to Australia. The impossibility of a comic society must finally, and sadly, be admitted.

[. . .]

The basic pattern of the novel, then, has been established. Only the outcasts are loyal and open to David; those in power are rigid and hostile. The boy then moves, in the rest of the novel, to look for an opening that is never there for long. Except for the comic joy of the outcasts, not available to him anyhow, he finds only the happy but dangerously flabby second childhood of the Wickfields or the hard, successful commercialism of Murdstone. The rest of his life can be seen as an attempt to combine the last two. Much of our laughter functions in this last section to remind us of the Eden David has lost, to show that the black world makes it impossible for him, and to suggest how limited his responses are.

He moves through a tragic marriage to the acceptance of simple notions of a disciplined heart, to a final union which seems to resolve none of the basic problems. He joins the firmly successful and the blurring escapists, the Agnes who is not only unable to stop Uriah Heep's subtle attacks on the Wickfield firm but who actually urges her father to enter into a partnership with Heep because she felt 'it was necessary for Papa's peace' (Ch. 25). Peace indeed! It is significant that those who are opposed to Murdstone are equally opposed to this sort of peace, and, when they are shipped off to Australia at the end, it is suggested, perhaps, that

52 INTERPRETATIONS

they are irrelevant to the mature David but more likely that they are incompatible with nineteenth-century England. The letters from Micawber keep coming, though, to remind us of what is missing, and the humour is used more and more to define a lost world and to point towards the ironic position David moves close to: a gentler version of Murdstone, who likewise doesn't know that the flowers will wither in a day or so.

From **William J. Palmer, 'Dickens and Shipwreck'**, *Dickens and New Historicism* (New York: St Martin's Press, 1997), pp. 49–100

> New historicism is a broad term describing the critical methodology of study informed by theoretical consideration of the relationships of literary and socio-economic history and of the need to regard literary productions as but one sort of historical documentation. Thus new historicism shifts our interest from great 'historical' events – reigns, wars, discoveries and inventions – to the messier hum and buzz of everyday life. Palmer challenges earlier assumptions that *David Copperfield*, as a fictional personal history, was an exception to Dickens's more broad-ranging, hard-hitting novelistic attacks on a number of social injustices, and he takes the book's literal and figurative attention to shipwreck as an extensive case in point. Noting the widespread loss of life and capital and consequent effect of shipwreck on so many Victorian lives, Palmer considers how Dickens metaphorically transfigures 'common knowledge into social historical myth'. Shipwrecks devastate the Peggottys, collective victims of disasters at sea, and their plight represents figuratively the moral and social condition of David's world. The 'Tempest' chapter (**pp. 150–5**) takes the life of Ham Peggotty, and this time disaster yokes in death the honest common man with the well-to-do deceiver, Steerforth (thus showing shipwreck classless). Dickens's description of the storm fuses it with the stormy mind and soul of David himself.

In a sense, *David Copperfield* is Dickens's most historical novel. Its historical consciousness is two-pronged. In its exorcism of the blacking factory episode and in its representation of Victorian marriage, it dwells more closely than any other of his novels on its author's personal history. But in its characterization of Steerforth and in the elaborate motif of shipwreck imagery that emerges out of that characterization, *David Copperfield* creates an intense commentary on England's class exploitation. It offers a harsh warning about the direction that the social history of the Victorian age is taking. *David Copperfield* is one of Dickens's most heteroglossic novels.[1] The voices of every class of Victorian society are represented, and those voices interact in terms of power relationships.

[. . .]

---
1 By 'heteroglossic' Palmer is designating this to be a novel containing many voices and perspectives.

For David, the up-coming shipwreck is "an event in my life . . . so awful" that it throws a "shadow over my childish days." But for Dickens it is the culmination of the structuring of his text, "indelible . . . bound by an infinite variety of ties to all that has preceded it, in these pages . . . from the beginning of my narrative." For David it is a culminating event in a life, but for Dickens it is the climax of a text, a word construct, "these pages." [. . .] [H]e defines the up-coming shipwreck as a rhetorical event, not a human event. It is a language apocalypse prepared for "from the beginning of my narrative" and "growing larger and larger as I advanced" and meticulously "fore-cast" throughout the writer's rhetorical construction of his text.

Thus Dickens's most memorable shipwreck narrative begins in a most uncharacteristic manner. The attention is deliberately diverted from the introduction of the shipwreck as event and directed toward Dickens's self-reflexive consciousness of the shipwreck as the culmination of the rhetorical structure of his text. In beginning this way, Dickens is making sure that his readers are aware of the text/subtext nature of David's narrative. *David Copperfield* is about navigating and surviving the shoals of Victorian life, but it is also about charting the voyage through a sea of words and the perils the writer must face before reaching the safe harbor of white at "The End" of his voyage. The very length and uncharacteristically parenthetical nature of David the narrator's introductory passage underlines the clear distinction Dickens is making between David's and his own interests in the upcoming scene. For David the text is an attempt to justify himself as "the hero of my own life," (Ch. 1), but, as this cunningly chosen moment of self-reflexive intrusion shows, the subtext is Dickens's own attempt to justify the writer's art as equally heroic. For Dickens, the ability to create a compelling and meaningful text out of a sea of words is heroic [. . .] in the Dickensian sense of imaginative alchemy as heroism.

To Dickens the metafictionist's credit, he, after this initial single paragraph of subtext intrusion, immediately relinquishes the stage to his primary text narrator, but the layered identity of this crucial scene has been established. After this intrusion, the scene moves back into David's voice. The reader, however, has been alerted to listen to what the waves are saying beneath the surface of that primary text voice. For example, the shipwreck is described by David as a lasting "association between it and a stormy wind, or the lightest mention of a sea-shore, as strong as any of which my mind is conscious. As plainly as I behold what happened, I will try to write it down." As the evidence of Dickens's canon demonstrates, the fact and the symbolic possibility of shipwreck is certainly an "association . . . as strong as any of which" Dickens's "mind is conscious." [. . .]

Throughout this shipwreck scene, beginning with his intrusive opening, Dickens forms an elaborate imagery of apocalypse, of the storm at sea and the wrecking of the ship and of the sea's destruction of human life, as representative of the manner in which the Victorian social process has plunged human values into the depths of darkness, has ripped asunder Victorian moral life. While this apocalyptic shipwreck is occurring, the writer can only stand upon the beach and describe the destruction. This shipwreck scene in *David Copperfield* is, on the level of his meta-fictional subtext,[2] a grudging admission of the writer's relative helplessness in the face of the terrible problems in his society, in the face of England's rapidly deteriorating condition. From this point on in his novels, Dickens will portray in increasingly desolate terms the manner in which the Victorian social process batters and drowns the better nature, the best intentions, the romantic dreams of the individual. In the shipwreck scene in *David Copperfield*, Dickens presents his first and most violent (as well as most passionately constructed) of a series of apocalyptic nightmares revealing the fragility and moral desolation of Victorian society.

[. . .]

[. . .] What is happening to the world in this shipwreck scene, to both David's Yarmouth world and Dickens's Victorian world, has overreached the normal articulative power of words. Thus, the subtext's observer/writer is frustrated in yet another way. The apocalyptic desolation of his world has gone so far with such violence that he can no longer even describe it, much less do anything about it, he simply hasn't powerful enough words at his disposal and he must resort to words of indeterminate magnification, meaningless words such as "infinitely," "unspeakable," and "inconceivable."

But the subtext's narrator is not alone in his utter helplessness. In the real shipwreck of the primary text, the waves rolling over the foundering ship "carried men, spars, casks, planks, bulwarks, heaps of such toys, into the boiling surge." Caught in the shipwreck of Victorian life, the writer, and all men, are but "toys" helpless in the grip of the dehumanized, materialistic surge.

The shipwreck scene from *David Copperfield* ends with the whole community standing on the shore watching the ship go down:

> I found bewailing women whose husbands were away in herring or oyster boats, which there was too much reason to think might have foundered before they could run in anywhere for safety. Grizzled old sailors were among the people, shaking their heads, as they looked from water to sky, and muttering to one another; ship-owners, excited and uneasy; children, huddling together, and peering into older faces; even stout mariners, disturbed and anxious, leveling their glasses at the sea from behind places of shelter, as if they were surveying an enemy.[3]

The whole community, from the "bewailing women" to the "old sailors" to "ship-owners" to "children" to "stout mariners," is out to bear witness to this shipwreck, to join David the narrator and Dickens the meta-narrator as they stand helplessly on the shore observing the apocalypse. All segments of society, every gender and generation is represented. The shipwreck scene's tableau is

2 Palmer, like many recent critics, finds *David Copperfield* to be, in part, a fiction about fiction, or 'meta-fiction'. See also Welsh's consideration of David as a 'novelist's novelist' (pp. 65–8).
3 See pp. 150–5.

perfect for articulating the point that Dickens, with his doubled narrator, is intent on making: The whole community, all of Yarmouth society, stands and watches as the world falls apart before its eyes. The whole community, especially the writer, stands helpless on the shore as its world deconstructs.

From **Malcolm Andrews, 'Children and the Childlike'** and **'The Trials of Maturity'**, *Dickens and the Grown-up Child* (London: Macmillan, 1994), pp. 135–71

> Dickens's celebration of childhood in *David Copperfield* and in so much of his other writing has prompted some readers to complain that he never grew up, and that he sentimentalized childhood in such works as *Oliver Twist*, *Nicholas Nickleby* and *Bleak House* where he most comprehensively addressed the plight of abandoned and abused children. Andrews devotes two chapters to *David Copperfield*, and these extracts provide some intriguing questions about what Andrews calls the novel's unresolved views of childhood and adulthood.

[. . .]

The story of David's growth to maturity much resembles a balance sheet of gains and losses and it is part of the aim of this chapter to audit David's account. To what extent is the child David lost in the adult David? To what extent does David himself see the two conditions as incompatible? [. . .]

[. . .]

The view that *David Copperfield* represents an allegory of cultural change in England is given some piquancy by Dickens's comment in 1849, soon after starting *Copperfield*: 'The world would not take another Pickwick from me, now; but we can be cheerful and merry I hope, notwithstanding, and with a little more purpose in us'.[1] 'The world' has clearly moved on in the twelve years since *Pickwick*, which was itself backdated nearly ten years. The rollicking, comic, picaresque adventure story would be wholly out of tune with the mood of the late 1840s: and indeed that incongruous older culture can only be smuggled into *Copperfield* in the form of those eighteenth-century novels (the legacy of David's feckless father) which are reserved for David's secret enjoyment. 'A little more purpose in us', is what Dickens suggests as now desirable. This is the new ethic. 'Purpose' is akin to 'earnestness', the taking of full, responsible control of one's life, the recognition of 'good purposes to be striven for'. The new ethic gave a distinct identity to the Victorian middle class, especially to its male representatives. [. . .]

---

1   [Andrews's note.] *The Letters of Charles Dickens* [Pilgrim Edition], V, 527.

This idea of earnestness is the single most important constituent of full moral and intellectual maturity in Victorian middle-class terms, particularly for men. So too is the assumption, without complaint, of the role of provider and principal support for the family. Masculine maturity was evaluated according to the dedication and efficiency shown in assuming these responsibilities. This involved a positive relish for the hardships of life, a profound belief in the nobility of work, both as the means to an economic end and as a moral end in itself. The child-figures in *David Copperfield* are, almost by definition in this scheme, those who are incapable of taking on life on these austere terms – the adolescent David, Dora ('not bred for a working life'), Clara, Emily, David's father, Mr Dick. To these one might add those magnificent examples of a lack of control over their lives, the Micawbers. All these characters seem impervious to the Victorian ethos of respectable earnestness. [. . .]

[. . .]

I have traced in outline the progress of David into early manhood, and suggested how that progress is largely determined by changing ideas in the second quarter of the nineteenth century about the relationship, where middle-class men are concerned, between childhood and maturity. I also suggested that at the end of the book there seems a curious discrepancy between the narrator David, whose sensitive responsiveness to experience links the man with his childhood self, and the dramatised adult David whose stuffy earnestness and 'disciplined heart' seem like a recoil from his childhood self. There is something not quite right about the whole process of maturity in David. It stems from that deep uncertainty about the relative status of childhood and adulthood that the present study has been exploring. The uncertainty is pervasively evident in this novel [. . .]. But Dickens is reflecting the ambivalent views of his changing culture, sharpened perhaps, but certainly not originating in his own experience of childhood and maturity. [. . .] *David Copperfield* is a celebration of the delayed but eventually successful passage to full maturity, presented as a fairly smooth progress from childhood to adulthood. I want to finish [. . .] by raising a large question mark over this rendering of his progress, and to argue that the relationship between childhood and adulthood remains unresolved beneath the apparent confirmation of a successful transition.

[. . .]

The story of David's life is one of discontinuity and overlap, of abruptly punctuated phases in his growing-up. William Lankford has written most perceptively of these convoluted narrative patterns. In recognising 'the tension between childish purity and adult discipline as sources of moral authority', he explores the way in which this tension influences the narrative design:

> This pattern of departure – retreat – return – departure continues throughout the action, serving to modulate temporal experience in the novel by

assimilating new experience to old, building a pattern of repetition and variation symbolically appropriate to a protagonist whose approach to new experience is so wary and whose attachment to the past is so deep.[2]

[. . .]

The older David is an accumulation of his experiences: the neglected child, the genteel scholar, the devoted friend of the Peggottys, the professional gentleman. One stage does not necessarily replace another as the bare narrative of his life might suggest. He is all of these people at once, and yet they are not integrated. The new starts in life might better be described as new layers: in other words, his development is not linear so much as stratified. A new way of life is deposited over its predecessor. [. . .] I suggested earlier that David managed, on two important occasions, conveniently to bury his childish past along with literal interments, those of his child-mother and his child-wife. This reinforced the impression that those past selves were well and truly dead. They remain as strata in his own fully formed psychological make-up, invisible and forgotten except when some seismic disturbance accidentally exposes a raw seam. A cross-section of David's psychological formation would be an interesting spectacle. But David himself sees his present as a natural seamless development from his past. Every now and then he turns round and looks down the diminishing, darkening road he has travelled so far on, and speculates on the selves he has left behind. To change the metaphor a little: as he pushes his way forward through the world, his discarded selves do not disappear; they continue to float about in his wake. They still exist vestigially in his present:

> That little fellow seems to be no part of me; I remember him as something left behind upon the road of life – as something I have passed, rather than have actually been – and almost think of him as of some one else (Ch. 18).

> When I tread the old ground, I do not wonder that I seem to see and pity, going on before me, an innocent romantic boy (Ch. 11).

Like the 'little fellow', the 'innocent romantic boy' seems to maintain an existence independent of his adult self. That particular child was unable to grow up, to complete his childhood. Some version of David Copperfield managed to make it through to adulthood, to adapt itself to the current version of ideal masculine maturity; but it was not one who could assimilate that childhood self satisfactorily. The adult David, or 'Trotwood', seems often to be one of the *child* David's fictional constructs, yet another imaginary projection from the child's literally fabulous repertoire of heroes – maybe Tom Jones Bowdlerised and retailored for

2   [Andrews's note.] ' "The Deep of Time": Narrative Order in *David Copperfield*', *ELH* 46 (1979), p. 461.

Victorian tastes.[3] To a boy who spent so much of his life rehearsing heroic roles – the most ambitious of which is this pious, reserved, professionally successful adult self – the famous opening of his autobiography is the best possible introduction: 'Whether I shall turn out to be the hero of my own life . . .' One never so keenly feels the factitious nature of the mature David as when his former self, with its wonderful authenticity of feeling, rises in his mind.

For the adult David asserts his maturity by distancing himself from his own childhood (and from most of his close childhood friends), as if it were in itself a manifestation of his disreputable past. [. . .] The adult narrator David who responds so strongly to the idea of the Devonshire girls and children's songs among the dry law-stationers is one in whom the spirit of childhood is very much alive. But there is little trace of this in the adult figure within the story who marries Agnes, wins fame as an author and presides over a family in his London drawing room.

The incompatibility between the two adult Davids may be partly resolved by reference to David's own writings, of which so little of any significance is said. Possibly in his novels David-in-the-story and David-the-narrator are integrated. A hint of this comes from one of the few descriptions of what his published fiction might consist of, or at least what went into the making of that fiction. He is walking in Highgate one evening, meditating on the novel then in progress, when he passes the Steerforth home:

> Coming before me on this particular evening that I mention, mingled with the childish recollections and later fancies, the ghosts of half-formed hopes, the broken shadows of disappointments dimly seen and understood, the blending of experience and imagination, incidental to the occupation with which my thoughts had been busy, it was more than commonly suggestive (Ch. 46).

Here, on his own and in the shadowy half-light of his meditations, many of the book's dualities seem to dissolve and the tensions ease. Childhood and later years, hopes and disappointments, experience and imagination, all are blended. There is no suggestion of mutual exclusiveness such as the novel has forced upon the growing David. The divisions and dualities that shaped the uneven, changing course of David's growth to maturity may well be resolved in his fiction: but this cannot be claimed for his autobiography.

---

3   Tom Jones is the roguish title-character of Henry Fielding's *Tom Jones, a Foundling* (1749). This was one of the favourite childhood readings of both Dickens and David (**p. 102**), but as Andrews notes, Fielding would require 'Bowdlerising' (expurgating and rewriting) to be acceptable to middle-class Victorian readers.

From **Mary Poovey, 'The Man-of-Letters Hero: *David Copperfield* and the Professional Writer'**, *Uneven Developments: The Ideological Work of Gender in Mid-Victorian England* (Chicago, Ill.: University of Chicago Press, 1988), pp. 89–125

In *Jane Eyre*, which she also discusses, and *David Copperfield* Mary Poovey finds rich subjects for gender study (the social constructs of both femininity and masculinity) and also for consideration of social class and of the psychology of sexual and emotional desires. These extracts are from her discussion of David's relationships with the numerous women in his life. Her argument bears upon the book's initial question of David's heroism, because so many of the other people who have claims upon him are the mother-, sister-, daughter-, wife-figures he encounters. Overall in these relationships, Poovey thinks David makes a cumulative transfer of his affection 'through the constellation of desire' for these women. Thus for Poovey, David the novelist finally derives 'the terms of his ideological work from an idealized vision of domestic labor epitomized in Agnes'. Seldom does a Victorian novel so fully delineate the nineteenth-century social construct, the angel in the house (see **pp. 10–11**). Many readers and critics have noted the importance of the numerous women in David's life, and of Agnes Wickfield in particular. Poovey, however, sees her as the most important instance of David's (and Dickens's) imaginative effort to subsume various stories of women in the psychology of male development.

The kind of subject described and reproduced by *David Copperfield* is individualized, psychologized, and ahistorical; it is also gendered. In fact, (masculine) gender is the constitutive feature of this subject; identity here takes the form of a physical and emotional development in which the male subject tempers his sexual and emotional desires by the possibilities of the social world. This conceptualization of the subject, then, also entails a specific model of desire. This desire is insatiable and potentially transgressive; it begins in the home as the condition of the individual's individuation and growth; it motivates his quest for self-realization; and, ideally, it is stabilized and its transgressive potential neutralized in the safe harbor of marriage.[1]

[. . .]

The way David's relationship with Emily is narrated—with the fact of sexuality a secret shared by the adult narrator and the reader[2]—effaces any connection

---

1   [Poovey's note.] For a critical essay that complements my discussion of *David Copperfield*, see John O. Jordan, "The Social Sub-Text of *David Copperfield*," *Dickens Studies Annual* 14 (1985), 61–92.
2   The passage Poovey is discussing comes early, when David as a child first meets the beautiful little girl and, speaking also as adult narrator, alludes to her sexual attractiveness to the man who seduces her and, implicitly, to David himself (**pp. 96–9**).

between young David and sexual knowledge. Even though David's maturation is implicit in his responses to Emily, the narrative assigns to woman—in this case, Emily—responsibility for the "stain" of sexual provocation, even though the extent to which Emily is conscious of her sexuality is left unclear. In *David Copperfield*, then, woman is the site at which sexuality becomes visible: not only does her provocation make men conscious of their own sexuality, but her vanity and willfulness show that no man can be sure of securing her affections. In *David Copperfield* [. . .] woman is made to bear the burden of sexuality and to be the site of sexual guilt because the problematic aspects of sexuality can be rhetorically (if not actually) mastered when they are externalized and figured in an other. In Dickens's novel, this mastery entails both the punitive exile whereby Emily's sexuality is "cured" and the symbolic substitutions of less explicitly sexual women for ones who are more closely linked to sexuality.

Even though Emily's sexual transgression can be punished and "cured," however, she also poses another, more indirect threat to the identity of the hero—a threat that will ultimately prove resistant even to such elaborate narrative treatment. Specifically, the possibility that David's childhood infatuation with Emily might mature into love introduces into the rhetoric of affection the specter of class. Class difference exists as a threat in *David Copperfield* because "innocence" in this novel entails not only sexual ignorance, but also the indifference to class distinctions that enables David to befriend and bring together "chuckle-headed" Ham Peggotty and the well-born Steerforth. [. . .S]uch indifference to class is as crucial to David's heroism as is his boyish "freshness," and one important sign of this is precisely David's affection for Emily, the fisherman's daughter. One promise of the liberal rhetoric of Victorian individualism was that every individual had the "right" to follow the heart; according to this logic, class difference should not stand between David and Emily. And yet other incidents in the novel suggest that a sexual relationship between the two could only lead to harm: if he seduced but did not marry her, it would ruin David's honor; if he made Emily his wife, it would exclude David from the social position he "deserves." Both of these possibilities are made explicit in the representation of Steerforth, the character who takes over the infatuation from which David professes to have recovered. Steerforth brings dishonor on himself by seducing Emily, but, as his mother suggests, marriage might have been worse: "Such a marriage," Mrs. Steerforth informs Mr. Peggotty, "would irretrievably blight my son's career, and ruin his prospects" (Ch. 30). Steerforth's presence in the novel enables Dickens to levy this admonitory lesson without contaminating David's "freshness" by an overly self-protective consciousness of class. Through Steerforth, Dickens has it both ways: on the one hand, in carrying out an infatuation initially associated with David, Steerforth acts out the complex of desire and punitive anger of which hostility towards sexuality is the cause and Emily the object; on the other hand, in actually doing what David will not do, Steerforth underscores David's honorable innocence.

[. . .] In *David Copperfield*, the "stain" that seems to be a function simply of sexual knowledge is actually this "blight": the possibility not just that innocence might grow into knowledge but that a desire conceptualized as sexual and irrational might be oblivious to class distinctions. In terms of the ideological operations of the novel, this possibility proves to be even more intractable than the "simple" problem of sexuality, for too much attention to class rather than feeling smacks of callous self-interest just as too little threatens dishonor or ruin. To protect his hero from both of these disastrous fates, Dickens simply effaces this unresolvable dilemma: Ham and Steerforth intercede between David and Emily, and the problem of sexuality is transferred from the arena of class relations on to the figure of woman, where it can be symbolically addressed in the substitutions I have been describing. The symbolic "solution" the novel offers to both the explicit problem of sexual knowledge and the implicit problem of the way in which desire can cross class lines is Agnes.

In repeating the "angelic" qualities David associates with Clara Copperfield, Agnes preserves what is best about David's mother, but, because she is not vain, she "cancels" the faults of the mother [. . .]. Because Agnes's love involves self-discipline rather than self-indulgence, she incarnates fidelity and is therefore proof against the kinds of temptation that drew poor Clara into that disastrous second marriage, [. . .] and Emily to Steerforth. David's turn to Agnes does not "stain" him because he never has to see in her sexuality that exceeds or strays from her relation to him, and his love for her does not "blight" his prospects because she brings to David the dowry of her middle-class virtue and efficient housekeeping skills. Transferring David's affection from his mother to Emily to Dora to Agnes thus works through the constellation of desire, anger, and anxiety structurally associated with but narratively distanced from the mother. By means of these substitutions, Dickens splits off and leaves behind the contradiction written into the mother that threatened to subvert the boy's happiness and to undermine the home. [. . .]

Because the process I have been describing is represented as a series of ever more judicious choices made by a maturing hero, the imaginative work carried out on the various incarnations of woman is subsumed by the effect it creates— that of (male) "psychology" and development. That this effect is literally the work of the (male) novelist and not a mimetic description of either an emotional development or the power of a woman's influence is underscored by the fact that David Copperfield has become a professional writer by the time he chooses Agnes; even at the level of the novel's fictive world, the extraordinary image that inscribes Agnes as both the center and circumference of David's identity is itself contained within the autobiographical narrative that Copperfield has written (which is, in turn, contained within Dickens's autobiographical novel). This narrative division of labor, whereby the (male) novelist's responsibility for his own self-creation is transferred to the woman he also creates but claims to describe, repeats the process by which contaminating sexuality is rhetorically controlled by being projected onto the woman. [. . .]

[. . .]

If Agnes and the home implicitly collude in covering over the hypocrisy and alienation that pervade class society, then so does the literary man. In fact, the literary man derives the terms of his ideological work from the idealized vision of domestic labor epitomized in Agnes. Like a good housekeeper, the good writer works invisibly, quietly, without calling attention to his labor; both master dirt and misery by putting things in their proper places; both create a sphere to which one can retreat—a literal or imaginative hearth where anxiety and competition subside, where one's motives do not appear as something other than what they are because self-interest and self-denial really are the same. But even though they seem to provide an alternative to the alienation endemic to class society, the creation and maintenance of the domestic sphere and the work of the literary man actually reproduce the very society from which they seem to offer escape: in creating the illusion of equality on which the false promises of capitalism depend, both contribute to (and depend on) a rhetoric of individualism and likeness that hides the facts of class difference and alienated labor. Indeed, both produce the illusion that class society *could* end and alienation *could* be overcome through their efforts to make others like themselves and work a selfless act. Because of the middle-class woman's influence, the working-class servant could be encouraged to aspire to bourgeois virtues; by the writer's pen, the English "national character" could be presented as what it should be—domestic and middle class; by the exemplary exception of literary labor, all workers could imagine that some kinds of work lay outside the inexorable logic of market relations, even if they were not so lucky in their own work-a-day lives.

That this ideological work was performed at midcentury upon the two sites of the woman and the literary man points to the critical—and highly problematic— position these two figures occupied in Victorian society. On the one hand, representations of the woman and the literary man could disguise the inequities and hypocrisies of class society because these figures carried the symbolic authority of moral superiority in a society everywhere else visibly permeated by self-interest and exploitation. On the other hand, the extent of symbolic work necessary to deploy these figures as markers of morality revealed that they were not really outside of the market economy or class society. The effort necessary to construct and maintain the separate spheres of the home and literary labor reveals itself in its failure: the reappearance elsewhere of what has had to be displaced—the "stain" of sexuality, the "blight" of class, the "degradation" of work.

From **Juliet John, 'Byronic Baddies, Melodramatic Anxieties'**, *Dickens's Villains: Melodrama, Character, Popular Culture* (Oxford: Oxford University Press, 2001), pp. 171–82

Dickens's villains assume many forms and Juliet John finds Steerforth one of Dickens's most Byronic types. Agnes refers to Steerforth as David's 'bad angel', and he is a friend David remains attracted to even when Steerforth seduces Little Em'ly, to whom David had introduced him. To the extent that Steerforth is heroic in David's eyes, David's opening question of whether he or someone else may be the hero of his life leads to the larger question of whether the Victorian hero epitomizes or flouts, as does Steerforth, the age's conventional morality. In either case, for the young David, Steerforth is a larger-than-life figure. The older David, aware of the evil Steerforth perpetrated, understands both the naturalness and the wrongness of his earlier blind admiration of Steerforth.

The Byronic hero[1] appears to symbolize the kind of Romantic individualism Dickens despised. He is a self-destructive role-player, whose pale, aristocratic features mask a mysterious inner life. His energy is largely internalized, as the external world – excepting, perhaps, the female sex – seems to offer little for which he cares, little in fact which interests him as much as the theatre of his own ego. It is not surprising that this symbol of the involuted, antisocial, often aristocratic individual was demonized in melodrama. [. . .]

[. . .] It is the Byronic hero who is aristocratic: Steerforth plays the part of the Byronic hero for social status and power. His Byronism is not simply an act, however, nor is he a social climber. Steerforth and his Byronism are his mother's creations.

From the first, Mrs Steerforth, with her 'stateliness' of manner and 'lofty' air, has brought her son up to play a regal and heroic role which sits oddly with her choice of a minor public school like Salem House, for example, or with Steerforth's frequent choice of lower-class companions. She tells David that Salem House

> was not a fit school generally for my son, . . . but . . . my son's high spirit made it desirable that he should be placed with some man who felt its superiority, and would be content to bow himself before it; and we found such a man there. (Ch. 20)

Her emphasis on her son's 'high spirit', 'superiority', rebelliousness, and individualism – all qualities admired by the Romantics Byron and Shelley particularly – demonstrates the role she has moulded for her son in life, that of Romantic hero. It is a model of heroism which takes little account of conventional morality. [. . .][2]

Indeed, despite the impression of intense subjectivity often associated with the Byronic pose, Steerforth's moments of experienced, rather than performed, Byronism – as far as we can distinguish between the two – paradoxically reflect the angst he feels at his inability to experience the world subjectively. That Steerforth's problematic relationship with his own subjectivity is rendered through David's first person narrative is easy to forget. David's characteristic inconspicuousness is a product of his external, melodramatic focus (and vice versa), and an

1   The hero based on popular images both of the poet George Gordon Byron (1788–1824) himself and of the sensual, oft-brooding, heroes of his poems and plays. Popular melodrama often characterized villains as Byronically larger than life.
2   Both Byron and Percy Bysshe Shelley (1792–1822) were radically unconventional men from upper-class families. It is possible Dickens had in mind Shelley's drowning while sailing when writing of the end of Steerforth's life in Chapter 55 (pp. 150–5).

impersonality reflexively related to Steerforth's own. Steerforth experiences his own selfhood as dislocated – or even fictional – and consequently finds it difficult to believe in the self-projections of others. His view of the world as a stage is verbalized most explicitly when he describes Doctors' Commons as staffed by 'actors' engaged in 'a very pleasant, profitable little affair of private theatricals, presented to an uncommonly select audience' (Ch. 23).

Steerforth's sophisticated performativity is largely responsible for his power over David. The friendship between the two boys, in fact, can be seen as dramatizing the hierarchical relationship which exists in our culture between the Romantic and the melodramatic mode. The young David (or 'Daisy') needs to believe in fictions in order to make life bearable: we think of him as a boy 'reading as if for life' (Ch. 4). Steerforth, by contrast, associates performativity with power and personal gain, demonstrating a cynical, adult view of the world even in childhood. It is thus not surprising that David's attitude to Steerforth is throughout the infatuation that one has for an actor or screen idol. David has an emotional need for heroes and villains. Indeed, throughout the novel, he casts characters in melodramatic roles, the insufficiency and dangerousness of which is implied by the retrospective narrative voice. [. . .]

[. . .]

The reader's response to Steerforth, like David's, is ultimately bifocal. It combines the moralism of melodrama with an awareness of the incompleteness of a 'moral-conduct' view of either art or identity. The final, ambivalent, verdict on Steerforth's character is pronounced by David, who has not rejected the melodramatic vision but decided to employ it self-consciously:

> In the keen distress of the discovery of his unworthiness, I . . . did more justice to the qualities that might have made him a man of a noble nature . . ., than ever I had done in the height of my devotion to him. . . . What his remembrances of me were, I have never known – they were light enough, perhaps, and easily dismissed – but mine of him were as the remembrances of a cherished friend, who was dead. (Ch. 32)

The double time scheme of the novel, of course, facilitates this double perspective, David the child viewing the world melodramatically and David the adult lamenting the unreality of this vision. Perhaps even more intriguing is the fact, reported by Forster, that Dickens told a girl that he himself cried when he read about Steerforth. [. . .]

[. . .]

What is also at stake in the characterization of Steerforth and Dickens's other Byronic individuals is an analysis of the relationship between fictional and social models of identity. Despite the many critical attempts to categorize Steerforth as either 'villain' or 'hero', a 'theatrical' reading of Steerforth's character illustrates the fabricated nature of absolute moral categories (such as those which underpin melodrama). The novel does not ultimately endorse Byronism, however. 'Sympathy' with the actor of the Byronic role, or an understanding of the social conditions which fostered it, does not make that role socially desirable. The Byronic individual in *David Copperfield* highlights the unreality yet indispensability of melodramatic fictions in a post-Romantic age.

From **Alexander Welsh, 'A Novelist's Novelist'** and **'Women Passing By'**, *From Copyright to Copperfield: The Identity of Dickens* (Cambridge, Mass.: Harvard University Press, 1987), pp. 104–40

Welsh focuses his study of the mid-part of Dickens's career, on relationships among the works he wrote following his 1842 visit to America, where many of his political and social assumptions about that yet-young republic were radically contradicted, and where, on behalf of a number of fellow British authors, he argued most unpopularly for international copyright. These extracts are from two of his several chapters dealing with *David Copperfield*. 'A Novelist's Novelist' notes that Dickens as an active spokesman for his profession not only made this novel's hero a novelist but also, in presenting other characters, portrayed less successful authors. 'Women Passing By' deals with a number of the women characters, but particularly the fallen women, and Little Em'ly and her friend who attempts suicide, Martha Endell. Welsh's full study is one of the most complete late twentieth-century discussions of this novel.

Dickens made sure that alert readers of *David Copperfield*, without any special knowledge, could realize that certain games were being played. Like other great novelists and even at his most serene—as he seems to have been or become in writing *Copperfield*—Dickens could not refrain from providing an ironic context or counterpart for each positive representation he desired to make (so that if Copperfield works hard, for example, a character named Micawber waits for something to turn up). More particularly, in this novel about the "progress" of a writer, every writer but the hero—or his muse—writes wildly or hopelessly. The very refusal of the narrator to tell of his professional writing bespeaks confidence; the confusion and redundancy of nearly every other producer of writing whom he describes—Mr. Micawber, Dr. Strong, and the curiously named Mr. Dick[1]—tell another story. If these other experiences with writing were merely recorded to set off Copperfield's success, that would be one thing—and not disruptive of any reader's credulity. But in fact they seem to comment a little mischievously on Dickens's enterprise in writing this novel and, by extension, any other novel.

---

1 Strong does not appear in any of this Sourcebook's extracts, but he is the kindly old master under whom David studies at Canterbury and husband of the younger Annie, who describes to David how she resisted 'the first mistaken impulses of an undisciplined heart'. David later so regards his own impulsive attraction to his first wife, Dora. Mr Dick is the lodger-companion of David's aunt Betsey Trotwood.

[. . .] Micawber, of course, would almost rather write a letter than speak, and when he speaks, voluminously, he sometimes provides himself in advance with written memoranda. His rhetoric is grandiloquently excessive and compensates for the financial straits in which he constantly finds himself. He uses language [. . .] to overcome realities. "Perhaps, indeed, there is a secret identity between the linguistic enterprise of Micawber and that of Dickens himself, as it is transposed in the attempt by David Copperfield to tell all that he remembers about himself and about his experience."[2] If there is such an identity with Micawber, it would seem to be nearly opposite to the confirming relation with Agnes, whose tending of memories is hieratic[3] but not to be thought of as exaggerated. Micawber, after all, achieves transcendence only from a certain point of view; his actions—or rather words, words, words—are from a material point of view entirely futile and, being endlessly so, are far from constituting a progress. So it is with that other master of words, the lexicographer Dr. Strong. He is innocent and considerate, but his Dictionary will never be completed or read by anyone. At the end of the novel we read that Strong is still laboring "somewhere about the letter D," and it is fair to take the hint that "D" may also stand for Dickens, the novelist having wryly admitted in this fashion the ultimate unlikelihood of transcending the self by writing.[4]

Stanley Tick was the first to argue persuasively that Mr. Dick was "an image of the author himself," and not merely one of the series of characters who assist Copperfield on his way.[5] The name itself, "Mr. Dick," is the giveaway. The history of the name, which has been known for some time from the manuscript of *Copperfield* and is retraced in the textual notes of the Clarendon edition, reveals that Dickens was mischievously poking fun at himself. [. . .]

[. . .]

The sorts of alternative lives of writing I have been tracing, though they may be subversive,[6] are further evidence of the originality of *David Copperfield*. There is finally no secret about them, but rather a partial withholding, as in a guessing game. The game played with the reader in regard to Mr. Dick is deliberate on Dickens's part, as the revisions of his draft of the novel demonstrate. [. . .]

[. . .] With Rosa Dartle and the prostitute Martha, Emily is the focus of a small constellation of fallen women whose fate is also controlled by the two novelists [David and Micawber]. Being neither wives nor mothers, they come closest to what Micawber singles out as "woman" and they suffer what the title of the chapter relating Emily's seduction refers to as "A greater Loss" than death.

---

2   [Welsh's note.] Miller, *Charles Dickens*, p. 151. See also John P. McGowan, "*David Copperfield*: The Trial of Realism," *Nineteenth-Century Fiction* 34 (1979), 1–19.
3   Who treats memories as though they were sacred.
4   [Welsh's note.] Cf. Garrett Stewart, *Death Sentences: Styles of Dying in British Fiction* (Cambridge: Harvard University Press, 1984), p. 80.
5   [Welsh's note.] "The Memorializing of Mr. Dick" *Nineteenth-Century Fiction* 24 (1969), 142–153.
6   Subversive because they are fragmented writings quite different from the wholeness of David's fictional autobiography.

For two years before the commencement of the novel, Dickens had been engaged with Angela Burdett Coutts in the establishment of a shelter, or "Home," for ex-prostitutes at Shepherd's Bush. This was not, as some writers on Dickens have implied, a daring innovation but rather a modest version of a kind of charity common in London since the eighteenth century. Dickens was acting as almoner for Coutts, an extremely wealthy woman who was providing for the education of his eldest son at the time. His involvement was businesslike, imaginative, and—as Victorian philanthropy went—kindly. The work did bring him into contact with women who had been prostitutes, but the only direct transfer to *David Copperfield* of the novelist's experience would seem to be Martha Endell, who is instrumental in locating the lost Emily. In the words of Mr. Peggotty (words that filter most of what we learn of Emily at the end), Martha "walked among 'em with my child," stole her from among the unreformed prostitutes of London, "and brought her safe out, in the dead of the night, from that black pit of ruin!" (Ch. 51). By contrast with Emily, in fact, the good bad girl Martha is quite a real person, a version of what Dickens and his associates hoped to accomplish at Shepherd's Bush. Like some few of the reformed women from the home, Martha is destined to reach Australia and to marry there. Martha, whom Mr. Peggotty once regarded as "dirt underneath my Em'ly's feet," earns his respect (Ch. 46).

The relatively forthright treatment of Martha Endell in the novel contrasts sharply with the narrator's treatment of her friend. [. . .] Emily is a contradiction of motives from beginning to end. Her remorse begins well before she elopes with Steerforth and grips her so consistently that it is impossible to believe she could have run away. It is she, not Martha, who suffers the proverbial fate worse than death, and for whom it might "have been better . . . to have had the waters close above her head that morning in my sight," when she and the narrator were children (Ch. 3). Unlike Martha, she refuses decent proposals of marriage in Australia—an affront to the best hopes of Shepherd's Bush. Little Emily, one judges, is a projection of Copperfield's guilt and desire and is doomed from the start. Among his women, she is the one in whom he has glimpsed sexual desire, chiefly because she is aroused by his account of Steerforth. When he first meets her, they are both children; when they meet again, only he is a child, and "when she drew nearer, and I saw . . . her whole self prettier and gayer, a curious feeling came over me that made me pretend not to know her, and pass by as if I were looking at something a long way off" (Ch. 10). When it comes to positioning himself toward this woman, the narrator is most nearly relentless. The image is always that of a woman passing by and the male trying not to look.

[. . .]

[. . .] When a character glides calmly in this novel, the reader knows well enough that it *is* Agnes, the same Agnes who became intimate with the hero's child-wife in her last illness. Both relations are confirmed later, when Agnes "spoke to me of Emily, whom she had visited, in secret, many times; spoke to me tenderly of Dora's grave" (Ch. 60). Thus Agnes would seem immune to the baleful sight of a fallen woman and positively wants to know these earlier friends of her Trotwood, quite possibly to gain by the acquaintance. The ministration of that parting kiss is not only from angelic purity to fallen sexuality but usefully the other way around as well. Agnes contacts thereby a sexuality that the hero dares not look upon, so much does he desire it. These partially hidden relations among women are fancied by Dickens on behalf of his young man Copperfield. [. . .]

[. . .] Memory, of both misery and tenderness, is what the early chapters of *Copperfield* are all about. From the writing of *A Christmas Carol* on, Dickens had been urging the case for "what you might have been, and what you are . . . what you may be yet" with respect to male figures, from Scrooge to the personification of himself as novelist; and once the five Christmas books were behind him, he continued to address the subject in his Christmas stories for *Household Words* and *All the Year Round*. Dickens insisted especially on the value of *un*pleasant memories in securing a present sense of identity. [. . .] The tendency of such fictions, typical of fairy tales and prior to psychoanalysis, is to posit a fall that takes place in childhood: but this fall could also be displaced sideways upon women whose pasts so much more obviously needed managing in the present, and whose concealed shame and remembrance had something in common with the situation of Dickens, involved in his partial revelation to Forster, his autobiographical fiction, and his fictional autobiography.

A fallen woman is a mythical figure of a self that is discontinuous; and a reformed prostitute, an image of the necessity of concealing the past while privately remembering. These are my grounds for suggesting that Dickens could partially identify with such figures, real and imagined. Though he only briefly supervised the lives of former prostitutes, he is one of our prominent creators of fallen women in fiction.

From **Stephen Lutman, 'Reading Illustrations: Pictures in *David Copperfield'*** in Ian Gregor, ed., *Reading the Victorian Novel: Detail Into Form* (London: Vision Press, 1980), pp. 196–225

Lutman's title reminds us of the importance of the illustrations which accompanied each monthly number of *David Copperfield* and which the better modern editions include. These are not just images extracted from the written words, but are inherent visual text by Dickens's collaborating illustrator, Hablot K. Browne ('Phiz'). Browne worked under Dickens's supervision, but the illustrations do provide his 'reading' of the novel. Therefore, we need to recognize similarities and differences between written words and etched pictures and also to regard illustrations as 'picturing', interpretative acts. For both writer and illustrator, 'to see' is to picture and therefore 'to know'. My comments concerning selected illustrations (**pp. 87, 93, 111, 118, 148** and **158**, etc.) suggest ways of understanding the narrative and characterization within the illustrations and their relationship to the written story.

To the modern reader the central paradox of the illustrated novel is the combination of a static picture with a dynamic narrative form. In terms of reading experience the reader must stop and consider an illustration, even for a moment, before the page is flicked on and the flow of reading continued. There are moments like this in any prose narrative—the pause at the end of the chapter or book, the end of an episode, or a passage where the prose itself slows down and reflects on what has passed before. The illustrated novel is different because the mixture of visual and verbal forms suggests that the reader pauses to pursue a different kind of reading in the illustration from that of the text. This in turn raises questions of how the reader 'visualises' a novel and 'reads' an illustration, and of the relationship between these processes in a single work. [. . .]

[. . .]

To discuss the 'interaction' of the two forms in Dickens's novels is not necessarily to make the assumption that they are really discrete elements. [. . .] The illustrations were developed during the course of writing the novels, and having grown with the text can be described as having an organic relationship to it, rather than the more mechanical relationship of illustrations added to a finished work.[1] [. . .] The question of how accessible the illustrations are in terms of their aesthetic to the modern reader is a more open question. But the survival of melodrama in film and television, the development of the picture sequence in comics, and the continuing popular interest in Victorian art, suggest that the ordinary modern reader is not completely cut off from his Victorian predecessors.

[. . .]

Visual awareness is a learnt skill, and it is clear that Browne's illustrations require a sensitivity to both detail and composition in the reader, and an informed aesthetic eye. One assumption made in the illustrations is that the viewer is familiar with melodramatic conventions. In more specific terms this is communicated by a shared language of gesture which both Browne and Dickens use, and which is related to dramatically conventional ways of expressing emotion. [. . .]

The illustrations operate sequentially and therefore create visual repetitions and cues which can become significant for the reader in both the development of character and in giving direction to the novel. They can also suggest parallels and complementary comparisons which may only be latent, or even suppressed in the text. In terms of the developing plot of *David Copperfield* it is important that some characters are kept apart. Dora and Emily never meet, nor Heep and Steerforth. The connecting links must be developed through David of course, but there

---

1 [Lutman's note.] The details of the collaboration between Dickens and Browne are too complex to examine here. Dickens would give Browne the subject and suggest its treatment often checking the preliminary sketches, while Browne had considerable autonomy in the treatment of detail and of course the execution of the plates. See M. Steig, 'Dickens, Hablot Browne and the Tradition of English Caricature', *Criticism* 11 (1969), pp. 219–33.

are reasons why some characters must be kept apart in the text, but can be relevantly, if tactfully compared in the illustrations. [. . .]

The novel works through parallels and comparisons of characters who are separated, and these pairings and comparisons act as a kind of grading of personalities within which the reader locates the character of David. Browne can add to and develop these hints through the illustrations and in so doing suggest longer term patterns in the novel.

The Novel in Performance

Introduction

Dickens had a life-long interest in theatre, and his third novel, *Nicholas Nickleby*, devotes many hilarious pages to an itinerant theatrical family. Dickens wrote, produced and acted in numerous amateur theatricals, witnessed the unauthorized stage adaptation of many of his works, including *David Copperfield*, and over the last twenty years of his life brought one-man readings from his writing to the stage. Thus it should be no surprise to find that from the beginnings of motion pictures Dickens's works were frequently made into movies, and in recent years a considerable number of commentators have discussed Dickens and film, Dickens on film. For the reader coming from film to novel, there is much to discover about the dramatic visuality and vocality of Dickens's writings, especially in his descriptions and characterizations. Stage versions, unauthorized by Dickens, appeared almost instantly with the serial publication of *David Copperfield*. Although Dickens objected to such piracy of his work, he did not profit from theatrical presentations of his work until beginning public readings of his works a few years after writing *Copperfield*, and, as Philip Collins notes, the reading from that novel was one he produced much later. His version was a reworking for performance, and it reflects his sense of what a two-hour reading might provide from the original. In its entirety, edited by Collins, the published reading includes Dickens's cues for his one-man show, and we can readily see what Dickens found most dramatic in the novel. Among numerous film versions, two that remain generally available stand out: the 1934 MGM production featuring W. C. Fields as Mr Micawber, and the 1999 BBC production.

From **Philip Collins**, **'*David Copperfield*'**, *Charles Dickens: The Public Readings* (Oxford: Clarendon Press, 1975), pp. 213–48

Before having the prompt-copy printed, Dickens had effected a great deal of condensation and rearrangement, conflating into one episode passages from various chapters, raiding various chapters for happy phrases or speeches (by the Micawbers, for instance), and drastically reducing the length of the narrative retained. The printed text of the prompt-copy contains almost 26,500 words; the corresponding parts of the novel total about 35,500 words, though the total would be much larger if one counted the full wordage of the chapters from which various snippets were taken. Then, in manuscript, Dickens deleted over 10,000 words; only nine of the 120 pages of the text are left unemended. [. . .] When *Copperfield* was first performed, it was a two-hour Reading, as the *Carol* and other Christmas Books, and *Little Dombey*, had originally been. In January 1862, however, he began giving a shortened version, at first in his 'morning' readings (at 2.30 p.m. or 3 p.m., sometimes advertised to take 'about an hour and a half', sometimes 'within two hours'), and then in the evenings (still two hours) together with a shorter item. [. . .]

[. . .]

Like the novel from which it was taken, this Reading was Dickens's favourite. 'It is far more interesting to me than any of the other Readings,' he told Mrs. Monckton Milnes, 'and I am half-ashamed to confess, even to you, what a tenderness I have for it' (T. Wemyss Reid, *Life of Richard Monckton Milnes* (1890), ii. 80). [. . .]

[. . .]

Forty-odd years after Dickens's death, the *Copperfield* Reading was remembered by two people who had seen it, and both stressed the same moment. 'Never shall I forget', wrote Lord Redesdale, 'the effect produced by his reading of the death of Steerforth; it was tragedy itself, and when he closed the book and his voice ceased, the audience for a moment seemed paralysed, and one could almost hear a sigh of relief'. Thackeray's daughter Annie (Lady Ritchie) also recalled the storm scene as more thrilling than anything she had ever seen in a theatre. She was present at Dickens's last performance of *Copperfield* (1 March 1870), and was impressed by the power of this 'slight figure (so he appeared to me)' to hold a huge audience 'in some mysterious way [. . .] It was not acting, it was not music, nor harmony of sound and colour, and yet I still have an impression of all these things as I think of that occasion'.[1] This finale was, for most people who heard it, the great moment in the Reading, indeed the most sublime moment in all the Readings: and, for many critics, this storm scene had seemed, anyway, the finest thing Dickens ever wrote. Charles Kent was expressing a common opinion when he wrote:

> In all fiction there is no grander description than that of one of the sublimest spectacles in nature. The merest fragments of it conjured up the entire scene aided as those fragments were by the look, the tones, the whole manner of the Reader. . . . There, in truth, the success achieved

---

1   [Collins's note.] See *Dickensian* 33 (1937), p. 68.

was more than an elocutionary triumph—it was the realisation to his hearers, by one who had the soul of a poet, and the gifts of an orator, and the genius of a great and imaginative author, of a convulsion of nature when nature bears an aspect the grandest and the most astounding.[2]

The only criticism that was made of his rendering was that, to 'the most hyper-critical, . . . there seemed a lack of something which, for want of a better term, may be denominated "physical energy".' Kate Field made the same point, though thrilled by the tragic power Dickens here displayed: the passage was, nevertheless, 'capable of even greater effect. The scene admits of wonderful scope for a mighty voice and mighty action'.[3]

The Reading as a whole was, however, as Kate Field continued, 'an extraordin-ary performance . . . and no one actor living can embody the twelve characters of this reading with the individuality given them by Dickens, unaided, too, as he is, by theatrical illusion.'

From **James R. Kincaid, 'Viewing and Blurring in Dickens: The Misrepresentation of Representation'**, *Dickens Studies Annual* 16 (1987), pp. 95–111

Later twentieth-century cinematography and cinema studies provide us with new perspectives about Dickens's writing, which is so visual and visualizing. Kincaid challenges film-makers to 'construct, not represent or reflect a Dickens novel', and in doing so Kincaid reminds us of the 'slippery and uncertain nature of perspective and representation in Dickens', especially in *David Copperfield*.

[T]he most fascinating films playing off of Dickens, it seems to me, have been those that approach the novels with the most bizarre of squints. [. . .] A film-maker, like a Dickens reader, has to be prepared for a good many jolts, no matter what our own conventional expectations may be. Dickens does not merely re-form our eyes and ears; he confuses them by asking them to be turned in too many directions at once, by giving a clear signal that then vanishes, by offering a con-founding variety of interpretive possibilities. Films, like readers, can only pretend that they have "got it," then, since there is no "it" to get.

My subject is the slippery and uncertain nature of perspective and of represen-tation in Dickens. Such a thesis rests solidly on one grand cliché: that nineteenth-century novelists loved to fool around with both physical and moral perspective. There is, however, another cliché lurking behind my thesis [. . .] namely, that Dickens is a "cinematic novelist." What can that mean? In its naive form, this

---

2   [Collins's note.] *Charles Dickens as a Reader* (1872) Photographic reprint, intro. Philip Collins (1971).
3   [Collins's note.] *Pen Photographs of Charles Dickens's Readings* (1871).

"cinematic" notion suggests that there is a movie right there in the novel: all one has to do is slip a camera into the book, follow the directions in the pages, and let the movie emerge. I do not mean to attack what I am sure everyone will agree is a ludicrous notion (held by no one making films); but, instead, to examine some of the ways in which the whole question of representation is made both difficult and problematic in the novels, how what at first seems clear becomes blurred. Most of all, I want to argue that a film-maker must construct, not represent or reflect, a Dickens novel.

[. . .]

To start with the simplest matter, perspective, is to start with something not very simple. How close does a camera want to get to David Copperfield's eyes and his troubled heart? David admits that he invents histories for some people, histories that "hang like a mist of fancy over well-remembered facts," and adds the startlingly self-enclosed and self-limited statement: "When I tread the old ground, I do not wonder that I seem to see and pity, going on before me, an innocent romantic boy, making his imaginative world out of such strange experiences and sordid things" (Ch. 11). Where do the "experiences" and "things" end and the romantic and imaginative inventions take over? Further, what are we to do with a self-pitying mode? How can a camera turn in on itself and weep for the injustice it has suffered?

[. . .]

As David matures (a pretty loaded term in this context), he develops a habit of removing people he knows from social, class, and economic contexts in order to explain them and deal with them in isolated, psychological terms. He is a relentless individualizer. All this is understandable, of course, since he would like to present himself as the hero the first sentence of the novel coyly announces, a figure uninfluenced by his surroundings and youth, a self-sufficient, industrious fellow, made by himself. Thus, he is remarkably blind to the class-induced snobbery of Steerforth, refusing to acknowledge it even when Steerforth tells him of it, abducts Em'ly, and is drowned. In fact, the drowning represents a great psychological bonanza for David, since it allows him to maintain the notion that one—or David at least—is captain of his own fate. Similarly, when Uriah Heep presents to David a scorching indictment of the hierarchical social and educational system that instills hypocritical 'umbleness, David ignores altogether the wider implications and remarks only that Uriah's remarks provide him with a fuller insight into Uriah's personality, his "detestable cant," his "base, unrelenting, and revengeful spirit" (Ch. 39).

David's curious personalizing and individualizing habit raises questions about how he sees his own life, what form or structure he is attempting to impose on it—and to what extent a film-maker might be guided by it. The problem is made severe by David's confused and contradictory efforts to provide a clear framework himself. What kind of causal connections can he draw between events and his own developing self? Well, the problem turns out to be that David both needs and abhors the whole notion of causality. He both is and is not the product of what he has encountered. [. . .]

[. . .] David is, in other words, undertaking a novelistic task that is self-contradictory. [. . .] He would, on one hand, like to formulate his narrative as a causal and clear line of self-development: a series of events and reactions to those events that will explain his maturation, his notorious ability to discipline his heart and so forth. In part, David is striving to write a straight-line Horatio Alger story,[1] describing the ability of a strong character to mold the shape of his own destiny.

We recognize, however, that this clear developmental model for understanding is countered by a contradictory one that the Victorians would have understood as "catastrophic." David's many new beginnings depend on a cancellation of what came before, not a smooth progression from it. Notice how many times he speaks of himself starting anew: most extensively when he gets to Dover, but also when his mother marries, when he is sent to school, when he lands in London, when he becomes a "new boy" at Dr. Strong's, when he marries Dora, when she dies, when he ascends to Agnes. The straight-line form is thus shadowed by a radically disconnected one, the disconnections being attached to David's need both to explore and to forget parts of his life. This great novel of memory also doubles back on the very function of memory, attempting to erase its uncomfortable disclosures. It would be wrong to say that this is a self-consuming novel—it is far too complex for that—but David (or a part of him) would very much like for it to be so. "The remembrance of that life is fraught with so much pain to me, with so much mental suffering and want of hope" (Ch. 14): all that suffering wars against the coherent narrative the adult author is trying to fashion.

Joining in this war against a coherent single plot is a backcurrent that perversely refuses to run uphill in the direction David wants, but keeps circling back to home, to David's infancy, refusing to advance very far for very long. All this is rather familiar material, and I will not repeat the evidence that would link Dora or Agnes to David's mother and his nurse. The perception, however, that he is trapped trying to tell a progressive narrative with materials that refuse, finally, to budge from a stasis, an idealized infancy and young childhood, haunts the novel. I think most readers have a sense, concurrent with other possibilities, that David's story is over after a few chapters, that he can engage only in a series of sad repetitions, retracing a cyclic, non-progressive pattern.

Adding more murk is the argument advanced by some critics that David has a straight-line story to tell, all right, but that the line leads downward, not upward. According to this reading, David travels on a road that leads away from beauty, youth, playfulness (figured either in his mother or in Dora) to a dreary, account-book, pinched-in life. His report of what it is to be a novelist, one might say, sounds very much like the latest business school graduate. [. . .] This surely is a

---

1 Simplistic rags-to-riches tale of materialistic success, taking the form of the popular late nine-teenth-century stories by Alger (1832–99).

portrait of the artist as an organization man. [. . .] The question is how we are to
understand this development in David, this subtle and pathetic acceptance of the
Murdstonian ethic of firmness, energy, and self-control. [. . .]

To get back to our hypothetical film or film-maker: what does one do with these
four patterns: linear and progressive, discontinuous and catastrophic, cyclic and
static, linear and regressive? One can choose among them; one can, doubtless,
represent somehow the possibility of all four.

Making a film that embodies four diverse and often contradictory narrative
structures would surely be a tough assignment, leaving all but the most ingenious
floored. But there is an even more difficult problem for a film-maker lurking just
around the corner. The four patterns mentioned above all leave undisturbed the
notion of the individual, the self. However disturbed or discoordinated, the self is
at the center. We still tend to take for granted the notion of the individualized self
and are likely to imagine that Dickens did also. That self, as with David, is
contained and marked off, its boundaries as distinct as the sharp black lines
delineating a cartoon character. That self is formed (as in a mold), develops clearly
from that core, and goes through life, as it happens, with largely tenuous connections with other selves so formed. Defined in isolation, the self tends to live in
isolation. David's narrative and his life depend on such notions, which is why, I
suggest, he feels so uncomfortable with the self-less Micawbers.

It is not just that the Micawbers seem impecunious, wildly able to teeter-totter
gaily in defiance of the commercial and economic reality about them. They seem
to be a different order of beings (or being). They live in an amorphous, largely
undifferentiated state, with a variety of children, willing to share happily the
nourishment which runs without stint from Mrs. Micawber's ever-ready founts.
The Micawbers embody, I am suggesting, a notion of being that is without clear
boundaries, that is out-flowing, accepting, absorbing. As such, they exist in a
more radical non-pattern that subverts all four of the models we have proposed.
The Micawbers neither advance nor decline; they refuse to acknowledge the pres-
sures of time, of linear or discontinuous narratives, of cyclic movement or of
stasis. David is, to them, both an equal, a child, and, later, "Friend of my youth!
Companion of my earlier days!" Their language always wipes away boundaries;
their characteristic gesture is an embrace or—one is tempted to say but
shouldn't—an erasure. David is not happy to meet Mr. Micawber in Canterbury,
uneasily tries to explain him in terms that have nothing to do with Micawber's
state of being, is churlish and grumpy during his grand and illogical unmasking of
Uriah Heep, and finally ships the Micawbers off to Australia, where, in the last
words we hear from him, he is writing a narrative of his own. Justly so, since
David's cannot contain him and his antagonistic notion of what "being" amounts
to.

[. . .]

To return again to our filming, how do you represent "characters" who do not
conform to post-Enlightenment notions of individualism? Put a figure on the
screen, even with gauze in front of the camera, and one risks eliciting con-

ventional mimetic assumptions about what constitutes a "character." My contention is that Dickens pushes on us possibilities that should make all of us, not just screenwriters and directors, scratch our heads and squirm a little.

I do not, of course, mean to suggest that Dickens is unfilmable. Obviously, films, and brilliant ones, can be made and have been made. But what is it that is being filmed? Dickens, we might say, puts up astonishingly sophisticated resistances to interpretation, offering us his own blank stare just when we most need help and playing with the very process of interpretation. A film, then, is necessarily an interpretation of an interpretation (or a non-interpretation), not a reflection. But, then, so is interpretive commentary. Both, finally, are constructions, not reconstructions. There is a story that W. C. Fields,[2] on being asked why he added juggling to Mr. Micawber's repertoire when there was nothing about juggling in the text, said, "Dickens forgot it." That's the right idea. Dickens, with his various obfuscating squiggles going all over hell and gone, would have loved juggling. He was, after all, the most consummate juggler of them all.

From **Glenn K. S. Mann, 'Cukor's and Selznick's *David Copperfield*: Dickens in Hollywood'**, *Reading David Copperfield: Resource Handbook for Teaching and Study* (University of California: The Dickens Project, 1990), pp. 235–40

> From the mid-1930s through to the late 1940s, film-makers in both America and England produced a number of classic black and white films of nineteenth-century English novels. These popular films, in turn, stimulated strong sales for new editions of novels by Charles Dickens, Jane Austen, and particularly the Brontë sisters. James Kincaid, as we have seen, later challenged film-makers, and implicitly readers and viewers, 'to construct, not represent or reflect' *David Copperfield*. Mann here discusses the 1934 adaptation as a successful presentation of the essence of the original.

When producer David O. Selznick and director George Cukor collaborated on the 1934 Hollywood version of *David Copperfield*, they were both concerned about recreating the "Dickens' feeling" and "brilliant characters" on the screen over and above the sheer melodrama of the novel. In an interview, Cukor said that by the time he directed the movie,

> I'd discovered my own rule in doing adaptations, which I've told you about: you must get the essence of the original, which may involve accepting some of the weaknesses. When you read *David Copperfield* you know why it's lasted. There's too much melodrama and the second

---

2   Fields was a memorable Mr Micawber in the Selznick film of the novel; see the following extract for Glenn K. S. Mann's discussion of that film.

half is unsatisfactory, but there's this underlying vitality and invention. For me that determined the style of the picture. In the same way there was the problem of re-creating Dickens' characters, making them slightly grotesque, at times caricature, yet completely human—as Dickens did himself.[1]

And in a memo concerning translating *A Tale of Two Cities* to the screen (the year after *David Copperfield* was released), Selznick wrote:

> . . . minus Dickens's brilliant narrative passages, the mechanics of melo-dramatic construction are inclined to be more than apparent, and, in fact, to creak. . . . I am simply trying to point out to you the difficulties of getting the Dickens feeling, within our limitations of being able to put on screen only action and dialogue scenes, without Dickens's comments as a narrator.[2]

Cukor and Selznick were highly successful in fulfilling one of their twin goals—that of cinematically recreating the Dickensian characters (more on this later). However, it is uncertain whether they were equally successful in recreating the "essence of the original," "the underlying vitality and invention," and "Dickens's brilliant narrative passages" beyond the melodramatic, the mere action and dia-logue. One reason for the uncertainty is the vagueness of their terms, but the overriding reason is that, ironically, it is precisely the melodrama which domin-ates the film. That "something" the two men saw as more essentially Dickensian than melodrama, one can only guess at. It is clear from the novel, that *its* "essence" consists of both the role of the narrator in the telling of the tale as well as the tale itself. The film shows only half of the narrative by concentrating on the latter. This is no surprise since Cukor's and Selznick's careers spanned the heyday of the Hollywood Studio years from the early 1930s to the later 1940s. *David Copperfield* was made at MGM in 1934 and bears all the hallmarks of the clas-sical style of the studio system: a movie strong in story, star, and production values, its editing and visual style primarily functional, rarely detracting from the story and the characters in action.

[. . .]

If the movie eschews the novel's internal mode of narration, its own external mode of telling is conducive to creating equivalents to the novel's story elements, especially its comic-melodramatic episodes and its Dickensian caricatures. The movie distributes the novel's episodes over two parts. The first part features Dav-id's childhood from his birth to his schooling in Canterbury; the second part covers his young adulthood from his graduation to his impending marriage to

---

1   [Mann's note.] Gavin Lambert, *On Cukor* (New York, 1972): 83.
2   [Mann's note.] David O. Selznick, *Memo from David O. Selznick*, ed. Rudy Behlmer (New York, 1972): 119.

Agnes. The early part contains four episodes: the first, involving Aunt Betsey and her disappointment over David's gender after his birth, is a kind of prologue which prepares for her reappearance in the third episode; the second episode concerns Clara Copperfield's marriage to Murdstone and the conflict between David and his stepfather; the third David's indenture in a London blacking [sic] factory, his boarding with the Micawbers, his escape to Dover and Aunt Betsey, and her rescue of him from the clutches of Murdstone and his sister. The fourth episode is a transition to the second part. David goes to school in Canterbury where he lives with Mr. Wickfield and meets Agnes and Uriah Heep. The second part of the film consists of four stories which intertwine, the omniscient camera shifting from one story to the other: the Steerforth-Emily-Ham episode, David's and Dora's courtship and marriage, the Heep-Wickfield-Micawber intrigue, and the Agnes-David relationship.

It is clear that Selznick and Cukor were intent on including as many as possible of the novel's story patterns and characters in the film. The episodes in the movie touch on most of the novel's events, with the exception of David's experiences at Mr. Creakle's and Dr. Strong's schools and his career as a legal apprentice and parliamentary reporter. The number of characters excluded is minimal compared with those retained. Of the major characters, only Dr. and Annie Strong, Rosa Dartle, Mrs. Steerforth, and Tommy Traddles and his Sophy are left out. Both the characterizations and episodes stress their melodramatic nature. Each part has a clear villain and hero. In part one, villain Murdstone is routed by Aunt Betsey; in part two, villain Heep is trounced by Micawber. These two dominant conflicts and resolutions mirror the basic pattern of the episodes, conforming to the proven box office formula of the classical cinema in which strong conflicts have definite resolutions and good triumphs over evil. David's conflict with Murdstone climaxes in Aunt Betsey's triumph over the latter, the Steerforth-Emily-Ham conflict climaxes in the tragic irony of the tempest scene, and the David-Dora-Agnes conflict climaxes in Dora's death which makes possible the film's final resolution, David's proposal to Agnes.

[. . .]

Beyond successfully presenting the melodrama of the novel's events, the movie is also successful in bringing the Dickensian characters to cinematic life. Dickens created many of his memorable characters through the art of caricature, isolating one or two dominant traits and conveying them through gestures and mannerisms. In *David Copperfield*, Dickens does this through David's eye, which is especially acute in picking out the essential qualities of the persons who make up his world and vividly depicting them through their external manifestations. The film doesn't observe the characters from David's point of view, but its third person omniscient point of view, its camera's eye and external mode of telling, is highly conducive to the formation of Dickensian caricature. In addition, the film boasts fine actresses and actors, each of whom invests his role with the appropriate eccentricity and the telling gesture. [. . .]

Cukor and Selznick solved "the problem of re-creating Dickens' characters, making them slightly grotesque, at times caricature, yet completely human—as Dickens did himself." [. . .] But the complete *Copperfield* has yet to be realized cinematically; to do so, such a film must integrate the narrator's depiction of the characters and the events of his life with his retrospective attitude; it must mesh the tale with the telling of it.

From **Robert Giddings, '*David Copperfield* on BBC I (1999)'**, Dickensian 96 (2000): 69–73

Among numerous television and film adaptations of *David Copperfield* over the second half of the twentieth century, the 1999 BBC version, which aired also in America, remains one of the most readily available and most often viewed. It avoids the temptation to transplant the story line to the present or near-present, as have numerous film and television versions of *A Christmas Carol*. Giddings acknowledges film's problem of employing limited time for representing a lengthy novel, and also realizes how hard it can be to film a book's reflective first-person narration. What is one to do with the narrator who often speaks of time past from a 'present' perspective?

[. . .] *David Copperfield* has a vastly [. . .] constructed plot, but an elusive tone which is very hard to translate to screen. BBC-1's Christmas *Copperfield* was a joint effort by BBC Drama and Light Entertainment departments and lost the work's sombre dimension. The original title was: *The Personal History, Adventures, Experiences, and Observations of David Copperfield the Younger, of Blunderstone Rookery (which he never meant to be published on any account).* There are some interesting clues here. In the *life-and-adventures-and-opinions* there is a distinct echo of *Tristram Shandy*.[1] Dickens seemed to be reverting to his beloved eighteenth-century models, but additionally there is the interesting reference to autobiographical elements which were to be kept secret – as of course they were to most of his readers. [. . .]

The autobiographical tone is established by the celebrated opening words: 'Whether I shall turn out to be the hero of my own life, or whether that station will be held by anybody else, these pages must show . . .' This is indeed the nub of the problem, for [. . .] the eponymous hero is a bland, often empty central figure, surrounded by raving grotesques and eccentrics. [. . .] This production had good moments of brutality and melodrama – young David's thrashing at the hands of Murdstone (the magnificent Trevor Eve) convincingly filmed from a young David's viewpoint, the bottle factory in all its grimness, the hideous Creakle (Ian McKellen) and the mortal storm which drowns Ham (James Thornton) and Steerforth (Oliver Milburn) – and achieved much of the novel's grotesque comicality. [. . .]

1   Laurence Sterne's novel of 1759–64, another of Dickens's favourites.

Because this production conflated the novel, the tone was altered. *David Copperfield* is deceptive. Beneath the blissful innocence of its finale, and the rooks cawing round the old cathedral at Canterbury, there is a deep, disturbing psychological quality which lingers in the imagination. The scenes of Murdstone's barbarities are haunting, and his insanely reasonable arithmetic problems have a startling surreal quality. Equally dreamlike are the sunny innocent moments of retreat, the love and comfort of Peggotty, the stay in the boat at Yarmouth. But the hero has to grow up and face the world. He makes some catastrophic errors of judgement (Steerforth, Dora) and has to endure the pain of maturing, but after the storm he drifts serenely into harbour. With its deployment of the several threads of time, memory, chance and fortune, the past, the present and the future, this is a very revealing novel of middle-period Dickens. He described *David Copperfield* as 'written memory'. Here he is a successful and established writer, looking back into his past: 'I think the memory of most of us can go further back into such times than many of us suppose . . .' (Ch. 2) Later he writes: '. . . The man who reviews his own life, as I do mine . . . had need to have been a good man indeed, if he would be spared the opportunities wasted . . .' (Ch. 42)

One of the significant qualities of *David Copperfield* is in the perspective of its narrative, that sense of looking back over a past life which seems to have brought personal success, yet with the vision tinged with sorrow. Some of this might well result from the fact that the basic narrative tense of television is present continuous, whereas in narrative prose fiction we have the omnipresent authorial voice dwelling simultaneously in the present and the past. [. . .] Memory in *Copperfield* is not to be tamed. It is a wild and wilful agent which delights and disturbs as it waywardly decides. Like Scrooge, David does not recall the past, but sees it done, it happens again before him. He is in the scene with his former self. There is also a pervading sense of what might have been, a searing awareness of chance in life – the friend not met, the street not turned up, the decision not made – that tormenting if-only, subjunctive past.

Many of these qualities are lacking in this new version directed by Simon Curtis. There is some use of the narrative voice-over (by the admirable Tom Wilkinson) but much of the melancholy, that sense of aspects of life unfulfilled, has gone. BBC1's *David Copperfield* had a consistently bright surface quality. The sun was always shining, the flowers were out, the trees were leafy, skies were blue, joy was just around the corner and events crowded past one another as the narrative unfolded. There was ne'er a backward glance. Odd really, for New Year and Millennium would have been such a good time to look back, as well as forward.

3

Key Passages

Introduction

David Copperfield is one of Dickens's most expansive works, surrounding David with many memorable characters, each with stories of their own. As in A. A. Milne's *Winnie the Pooh*, where along comes Rabbit with all his friends and relations, so in *David Copperfield* we meet one family group after another. A number of these – the Murdstones, Peggottys, Micawbers, Heeps, Wickfields and Steerforths – figure in the following extracts, but a few others – the Mells, Traddles and the Strongs do not. Mell is a much-abused teacher at David's first school, Traddles a boy he meets there, and Strong is David's elderly schoolteacher in Canterbury. Strong's young wife attracts but resists the attention of a younger man and thus provides for David an example of the 'disciplined heart'.

These extracts from *Copperfield* provide neither complete summary nor abridgement but best serve as incentive and introduction for those who have not read the book, as review for those who have, and resource for the novel's contexts and critical reception, especially for the significant attention it has received over the past quarter of a century. Extracts vary in length, sometimes consisting of parts of single chapters, sometimes of parts from separate chapters, dealing with a continuing issue or event related to the novel's principal subject matter: David's passage to adulthood, questions he directly raises about himself and others, his representation of Victorian heroism, and of gender and class stratification. The extracts also well reflect the novel's form and style: fictional autobiography, the overlay of present retrospect on past experience, characterization, narrative that 'pictures' and illustrations that characterize and narrate. In five instances, extracts include illustrations which accompany the written text. Twenty-first-century viewers may be used to 'reading' film, photography and painting but may not be aware of the inherent relationship of illustration and written text in *David Copperfield*. The cross-references give some pointers, and headnotes invite readers to think further about the illustrations. The passages are excerpted from the Charles Dickens Edition (1867), the last Dickens himself authorized.

Key Passages

1 The Monthly Parts Cover

The *David Copperfield* serial-part cover page, like those of all his larger books, was designed for the first number and would reappear with each yet-unwritten forthcoming part (see Figure 1). The distinctive green wrapper Dickens had used since his first major work, *The Pickwick Papers*, provided instant familiarity to readers eagerly awaiting his new book. The monthly part cover for *David Copperfield* prefigures a full story-world, even though neither Dickens nor Hablot K. Browne, his illustrator, had the full story yet in mind. The whole of the cover design frames the extended title. The globe is surrounded by the lengthy first full title, *The Personal History, Adventures, Experience, & Observation of David Copperfield* [sketch of a baby sitting between the first and last names] *The Younger. Of Blunderstone Rookery. (Which He never meant to be Published on any Account.)* That this is truly Dickens's and not some unknown David's work is evident from the title-page declaration, 'By Charles Dickens. With Illustrations by H. K. Browne'. Ascending clockwise from the bottom, the framing scenes trace the passage of time through a life story. David is 'the younger', a post-humous child, so at six-o'clock bottom left centre stands a pruned tree trunk and an image of the babe on his mother's lap, while to the right, seemingly at the other end of the story, is the tombstone with the word 'SACRED' and another child playfully turning head and foot stones into an imaginary horse and wagon. Otherwise the sequence of illustrations remains vague, moving clockwise from childhood through adulthood and old age (farther than the story will actually go), and, other than the bottom left representation of David's mother and his nursemaid Clara Peggotty with him at an early age, there are no close parallels between other cover-page characters and those so well individualized in both the story and in Browne's subsequent forty illustrations.

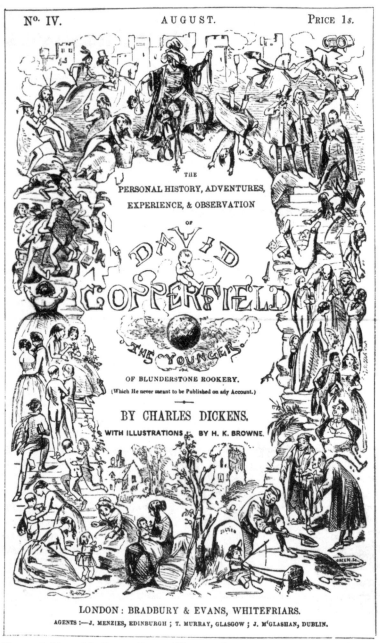

Figure 1 **Monthly Parts Cover Illustrations.**

2 1867 Preface

To those who knew him, the closeness of Dickens to his creations was evident throughout his career, and it became very obvious in the public readings he gave in later years. In this preface, which in shortened form accompanied the final monthly number and then appeared at the front of the first complete edition, Dickens acknowledged a particular intimacy with *David Copperfield*. Only after his death in 1870 did biographers and critics discover and begin to debate the mixture of mirth and melancholy, sunshine and shadow in Dickens's private life which figures prominently in *David Copperfield* (see **p. 202**). It is noteworthy that in both the 1850 and 1867 prefaces Dickens remarked that when finishing it, he felt that he had sent a part of himself out into the world; to his last preface, reprinted here, he added the point that among his books this was his 'favourite child' (1867).

I REMARKED in the original Preface to this Book, that I did not find it easy to get sufficiently far away from it, in the first sensations of having finished it, to refer to it with the composure which this formal heading would seem to require. My interest in it was so recent and strong, and my mind was so divided between pleasure and regret—pleasure in the achievement of a long design, regret in the separation from many companions—that I was in danger of wearying the reader with personal confidences and private emotions.

Besides which, all that I could say of the Story to any purpose, I have endeavoured to say in it.

It would concern the reader little, perhaps, to know how sorrowfully the pen is laid down at the close of a two-years' imaginative task; or how an Author feels as if he were dismissing some portion of himself into the shadowy world, when a crowd of the creatures of his brain are going from him for ever. Yet, I had nothing else to tell; unless, indeed, I were to confess (which might be of less moment still), that no one can ever believe this Narrative, in the reading, more than I believed it in the writing.

So true are these avowals at the present day, that I can now only take the reader into one confidence more. Of all my books, I like this the best. It will be easily believed that I am a fond parent to every child of my fancy, and that no one can ever love that family as dearly as I love them. But, like many fond parents, I have in my heart of hearts a favourite child. And his name is DAVID COPPERFIELD.

3 The Opening Chapters

Obviously an autobiographer cannot record either his death or birth from memory, so the fictional autobiographer David tells of his birth by piecing together what he had heard about it and by incorporating folk wisdom about being a Friday child and having been born with a caul. But this information comes after the famous first line which frames one of the novel's most important issues, that of just who and what David becomes as the result of his experience and observation. Whether he or someone else in his history proves to be the hero of his own life is the question of the future of the character David; that the story to come must show that future is the task facing the novelist David, here speaking from an undefined date. For readers in 1849 and 1850, the question of David's future remained open from month to month during the nineteen months of serial part publication. Many critical commentaries cite the opening chapters as wonderful examples of Dickens's fusion of memory and imagination and of his ability to portray the character and experience of a child (see especially Andrews, pp. 55–8).

CHAPTER 1
I AM BORN

WHETHER I shall turn out to be the hero of my own life, or whether that station will be held by anybody else, these pages must show. To begin my life with the beginning of my life, I record that I was born (as I have been informed and believe) on a Friday, at twelve o'clock at night. It was remarked that the clock began to strike, and I began to cry, simultaneously.

In consideration of the day and hour of my birth, it was declared by the nurse, and by some sage women in the neighbourhood who had taken a lively interest in me several months before there was any possibility of our becoming personally acquainted, first, that I was destined to be unlucky in life; and secondly, that I was privileged to see ghosts and spirits; both these gifts inevitably attaching, as they believed, to all unlucky infants of either gender, born towards the small hours on a Friday night.

[. . .]

I was born with a caul, which was advertised for sale, in the newspapers, at the low price of fifteen guineas. Whether sea-going people were short of money about that time, or were short of faith and preferred cork jackets, I don't know; all I know is, that there was but one solitary bidding, and that was from an attorney connected with the bill-broking business, who offered two pounds in cash, and the balance in sherry, but declined to be guaranteed from drowning on any higher bargain. Consequently the advertisement was withdrawn at a dead loss—for as to sherry, my poor dear mother's own sherry was in the market then—and ten years afterwards the caul was put up in a raffle down in our part of the country, to fifty members at half-a-crown a head, the winner to spend five shillings. I was present myself, and I remember to have felt quite uncomfortable and confused, at a part of myself being disposed of in that way.[1]

[. . .]

I was born at Blunderstone, in Suffolk, or "thereby," as they say in Scotland. I was a posthumous child.[2] My father's eyes had closed upon the light of this world six months, when mine opened on it. There is something strange to me, even now, in the reflection that he never saw me; and something stranger yet in the shadowy remembrance that I have of my first childish associations with his white grave-stone in the churchyard, and of the indefinable compassion I used to feel for it lying out alone there in the dark night, when our little parlour was warm and bright with fire and candle, and the doors of our house were—almost cruelly, it seemed to me sometimes—bolted and locked against it.[3]

CHAPTER 2
I OBSERVE

THE first objects that assume a distinct presence before me, as I look far back, into the blank of my infancy, are my mother with her pretty hair and youthful shape, and Peggotty, with no shape at all, and eyes so dark that they seemed to darken their whole neighbourhood in her face, and cheeks and arms so hard and red that I wondered the birds didn't peck her in preference to apples.

I believe I can remember these two at a little distance apart, dwarfed to my sight by stooping down or kneeling on the floor, and I going unsteadily from the one to the other. I have an impression on my mind which I cannot distinguish from actual remembrance, of the touch of Peggotty's fore-finger as she used to hold it out to me, and of its being roughened by needlework, like a pocket nutmeg-grater.

This may be fancy, though I think the memory of most of us can go farther back into such times than many of us suppose; just as I believe the power of observation in numbers of very young children to be quite wonderful for its closeness and accuracy. Indeed, I think that most grown men who are remarkable in this

---

1 There is no evidence that Dickens had been so born, but it was not uncommon to so regard and preserve the protective foetal covering (caul), sometimes dried and flattened to resemble a parchment or kept in a small container. Here the superstition of birth with a caul as a protection against drowning is pertinent to a novel that later will deal so much with shipwreck; see critical extract by William Palmer, pp. 52–5. This is the first of several key moments in the story when David remembers having felt a strange detachment from himself, a sensation which at the time presented him with discomfort and which complicates the task of remaking his life through memory.
2 Dickens, born at Portsmouth and with his father living, here seems deliberately to separate David's from his own life.
3 These details carry out the prediction that David was destined to see spirits; the association with this graveyard comes when he hears the story of Lazarus in the second chapter; see also the extract from Chapter 31 (pp. 128–31).

respect, may with greater propriety be said not to have lost the faculty, than to have acquired it; the rather, as I generally observe such men to retain a certain freshness, and gentleness, and capacity of being pleased, which are also an inheritance they have preserved from their childhood.

I might have a misgiving that I am "meandering" in stopping to say this, but that it brings me to remark that I build these conclusions, in part upon my own experience of myself; and if it should appear from anything I may set down in this narrative that I was a child of close observation, or that as a man I have a strong memory of my childhood, I undoubtedly lay claim to both of these characteristics.[4]

Looking back, as I was saying, into the blank of my infancy, the first objects I can remember as standing out by themselves from a confusion of things, are my mother and Peggotty. What else do I remember? Let me see.

There comes out of the cloud, our house—not new to me, but quite familiar, in its earliest remembrance. On the ground-floor is Peggotty's kitchen, opening into a back yard; with a pigeon-house on a pole, in the centre, without any pigeons in it; a great dog-kennel in a corner, without any dog; and a quantity of fowls that look terribly tall to me, walking about, in a menacing and ferocious manner. There is one cock who gets upon a post to crow, and seems to take particular notice of me as I look at him through the kitchen-window, who makes me shiver, he is so fierce. Of the geese outside the side-gate who come waddling after me with their long necks stretched out when I go that way, I dream at night: as a man environed by wild beasts might dream of lions.

Here is a long passage[5]—what an enormous perspective I make of it!—leading from Peggotty's kitchen to the front-door. A dark storeroom opens out of it, and that is a place to be run past at night; for I don't know what may be among those tubs and jars and old tea-chests, when there is nobody in there with a dimly-burning light, letting a mouldy air come out at the door, in which there is the smell of soap, pickles, pepper, candles, and coffee, all at one whiff. Then there are the two parlours: the parlour in which we sit of an evening, my mother and I and Peggotty—for Peggotty is quite our companion, when her work is done and we are alone—and the best parlour where we sit on a Sunday; grandly, but not so comfortably. There is something of a doleful air about that room to me, for Peggotty has told me—I don't know when, but apparently ages ago—about my father's funeral, and the company having their black cloaks put on. One Sunday night my

---

4   The autobiographical fragment (**pp. 20–2**) demonstrates how fully the adult Dickens visualized details of his early experience. His eye for fullness as well as precision of telling details provided abundant fuel for both his journalistic and imaginative writing. Here and often in David Copperfield Dickens has his fictional narrator presenting impressions which he 'cannot distinguish from actual remembrance'. So acknowledging the importance of close observation cultivated in childhood as a valuable adult 'inheritance', David moves into present-tense picturing of remembered scenes and events. Later, he writes whole chapters of such 'retrospect', stylistically capturing his point about how imagination and memory come together and 'retain a certain freshness, and gentleness'.

5   Literally the passage is the house hallway, but with the present-tense 'Here is', Dickens also demonstrates how in recollection the past is newly passing before the adult David, a technique he will use more fully in the later 'Retrospect' chapters (**pp. 129–31, 141–3 and 157–62**).

mother reads to Peggotty and me in there, how Lazarus was raised up from the dead. And I am so frightened that they are afterwards obliged to take me out of bed, and show me the quiet churchyard out of the bedroom window, with the dead all lying in their graves at rest, below the solemn moon.

There is nothing half so green that I know anywhere, as the grass of that churchyard; nothing half so shady as its trees; nothing half so quiet as its tombstones. The sheep are feeding there, when I kneel up, early in the morning, in my little bed in a closet within my mother's room, to look out at it; and I see the red light shining on the sundial, and think within myself, 'Is the sun-dial glad, I wonder, that it can tell the time again?'[6]

Here is our pew in the church. What a high-backed pew! With a window near it, out of which our house can be seen, and *is* seen many times during the morning's service, by Peggotty, who likes to make herself as sure as she can that it's not being robbed, or is not in flames. But though Peggotty's eye wanders, she is much offended if mine does, and frowns to me, as I stand upon the seat, that I am to look at the clergyman. But I can't always look at him—I know him without that white thing on, and I am afraid of his wondering why I stare so, and perhaps stopping the service to inquire—and what am I to do? It's a dreadful thing to gape, but I must do something. I look at my mother, but *she* pretends not to see me. I look at a boy in the aisle, and *he* makes faces at me. I look at the sunlight coming in at the open door through the porch, and there I see a stray sheep—I don't mean a sinner, but mutton—half making up his mind to come into the church. I feel that if I looked at him any longer, I might be tempted to say something out loud; and what would become of me then! I look up at the monumental tablets on the wall, and try to think of Mr. Bodgers late of this parish, and what the feelings of Mrs. Bodgers must have been, when affliction sore, long time Mr. Bodgers bore, and physicians were in vain. I wonder whether they called in Mr. Chillip,[7] and he was in vain; and if so, how he likes to be reminded of it once a week. I look from Mr. Chillip, in his Sunday neckcloth, to the pulpit; and think what a good place it would be to play in, and what a castle it would make, with another boy coming up the stairs to attack it, and having the velvet cushion with the tassels thrown down on his head. In time my eyes gradually shut up; and, from seeming to hear the clergyman singing a drowsy song in the heat, I hear nothing, until I fall off the seat with a crash, and am taken out, more dead than alive, by Peggotty.

6 Later in the second chapter, David recalls a day at church, and at this point Dickens and his illustrator effectively combine their efforts to visualize and dramatize the moment (see Figure 2).
  To 'read' and recognize the mutual reinforcement of illustration and descriptive prose, our eye needs to move from left to right over the picture, just as across a page of print, and it is essential to note characters observing one another within the illustration. In this case at the bottom left there is the intent Mr Murdstone gazing across the aisle at David's mother. She sits directly below the memorialized bust whose face is more animated than her own which is clear but featureless with eyes turned away, while young David and the bonneted Peggotty look towards the window. In the lower right foreground stands a figure behind the pew-box. Unmentioned in the written text, he is an outsider; he watches the whole of the church scene, just as do narrator, novelist, illustrator and reader. As we shall see in other illustrations (**pp. 113, 119, 149** and **162**) the friendly onlooker is frequently present, whether or not noticed by the central figures.
7 Chillip was the attendant physician at David's birth.

Figure 2 **Our Pew at Church.**

4 Little Em'ly and the Peggottys

In Chapter 3, sent away to Yarmouth to visit the Peggotty family, David experiences the first of a series of dislocations which acquaint him with a variety of places and different classes of people. Here he meets Little Em'ly, niece of Peggotty and an orphan. David forms strong feelings for her, for her cousin Ham Peggotty and her cheerful uncle, Daniel Peggotty. In these passages, Dickens, working as usual with only a tentative plan for the whole, lays the foundation for the important plot line developing from Em'ly's desire to be a lady and from her fear of the sea, and he characterizes the Peggottys as vulnerable exemplars of generosity and good cheer. The extended family David meets are the widowed and orphaned victims of shipwrecks (see **pp. 52–5**), and in the course of the story, they will be hurt by the seduction of their beloved Little Em'ly. But as Q. D. Leavis notes (**pp. 46–9**), Daniel Peggotty's faithful love for Em'ly is one of Dickens's most impressive psychological studies.

CHAPTER 3
I HAVE A CHANGE

I LOOKED in all directions, as far as I could stare over the wilderness, and away at the sea, and away at the river, but no house could *I* make out. There was a black barge, or some other kind of superannuated boat, not far off, high and dry on the ground, with an iron funnel sticking out of it for a chimney and smoking very cosily; but nothing else in the way of a habitation that was visible to *me*.

"That's not it?" said I. "That ship-looking thing?"

"That's it, Mas'r Davy," returned Ham.

If it had been Aladdin's palace, roc's egg[1] and all, I suppose I could not have been more charmed with the romantic idea of living in it. There was a delightful door cut in the side, and it was roofed in, and there were little windows in it; but the wonderful charm of it was, that it was a real boat which had no doubt been upon the water hundreds of times, and which had never been intended to be lived in, on dry land. That was the captivation of it to me. If it had ever been meant to be lived in, I might have thought it small, or inconvenient, or lonely; but never having been designed for any such use, it became a perfect abode.

It was beautifully clean inside, and as tidy as possible. There was a table, and a Dutch clock, and a chest of drawers, and on the chest of drawers there was a tea-tray with a painting on it of a lady with a parasol, taking a walk with a military-looking child who was trundling a hoop. The tray was kept from tumbling down, by a bible; and the tray, if it had tumbled down, would have smashed a quantity of cups and saucers and a teapot that were grouped around the book. On the walls there were some common coloured pictures, framed and glazed, of Scripture

---

1   In the *Arabian Nights* (1815 English translation) there is mention of the roc, a species of condor, as a mythical bird of enormous size.

subjects; such as I have never seen since in the hands of pedlars, without seeing the whole interior of Peggotty's brother's house again, at one view. Abraham in red going to sacrifice Isaac in blue,[2] and Daniel in yellow cast into a den of green lions, were the most prominent of these. Over the little mantel-shelf, was a picture of the *Sarah Jane* lugger, built at Sunderland, with a real little wooden stern stuck on to it;[3] a work of art, combining composition with carpentry, which I considered to be one of the most enviable possessions that the world could afford. There were some hooks in the beams of the ceiling, the use of which I did not divine then; and some lockers and boxes and conveniences of that sort, which served for seats and eked out the chairs.

All this, I saw in the first glance after I crossed the threshold—child-like, according to my theory[4]—and then Peggotty opened a little door and showed me my bedroom. It was the completest and most desirable bedroom ever seen—in the stern of the vessel; with a little window, where the rudder used to go through; a little looking-glass, just the right height for me, nailed against the wall, and framed with oyster-shells; a little bed, which there was just room enough to get into; and a nosegay of seaweed in a blue mug on the table. The walls were whitewashed as white as milk, and the patchwork counterpane made my eyes quite ache with its brightness. One thing I particularly noticed in this delightful house, was the smell of fish; which was so searching, that when I took out my pocket-handkerchief to wipe my nose, I found it smelt exactly as if it had wrapped up a lobster. On my imparting this discovery in confidence to Peggotty, she informed me that her brother dealt in lobsters, crabs, and crawfish; and I afterwards found that a heap of these creatures, in a state of wonderful conglomeration with one another, and never leaving off pinching whatever they laid hold of, were usually to be found in a little wooden outhouse where the pots and kettles were kept.

[. . .]

As slumber gradually stole upon me, I heard the wind howling out at sea and coming on across the flat so fiercely, that I had a lazy apprehension of the great deep rising in the night. But I bethought myself that I was in a boat, after all; and that a man like Mr. Peggotty was not a bad person to have on board if anything did happen.

Nothing happened, however, worse than morning. Almost as soon as it shone upon the oyster-shell frame of my mirror I was out of bed, and out with little Em'ly, picking up stones upon the beach.

---

2 Here in prose description Dickens provides the sort of picture-within-picture that Browne often built into the novel's illustrations. In both cases, the subject matter of the pictures on the wall of a fictional room relate thematically to larger points in Dickens's story. Here, mention of the Biblical patriarch Abraham's willingness to sacrifice his son Isaac should God require it (Genesis 22) underscores Dickens's characterization of Mr Peggotty as a dutiful man; that the other picture concerns Daniel's survival in the lion's den (Daniel 6) both underscores Peggotty's courage and suggests a source for his first name, which is Daniel.

3 A small vessel.

4 The ideas he stated concerning the closeness of childhood observation in the second chapter.

"You're quite a sailor, I suppose?" I said to Em'ly. I don't know that I supposed anything of the kind, but I felt it an act of gallantry to say something; and a shining sail close to us made such a pretty little image of itself, at the moment, in her bright eye, that it came into my head to say this.

"No," replied Em'ly, shaking her head, "I'm afraid of the sea."

"Afraid!" I said, with a becoming air of boldness, and looking very big at the mighty ocean. "*I* an't!"

"Ah! but it's cruel," said Em'ly. "I have seen it very cruel to some of our men. I have seen it tear a boat as big as our house all to pieces."

"I hope it wasn't the boat that——"

"That father was drownded in?" said Em'ly. "No. Not that one. I never see that boat."

"Nor him?" I asked her.

Little Em'ly shook her head. "Not to remember!"

Here was a coincidence! I immediately went into an explanation how I had never seen my own father; and how my mother and I had always lived by ourselves in the happiest state imaginable, and lived so then, and always meant to live so; and how my father's grave was in the church-yard near our house, and shaded by a tree, beneath the boughs of which I had walked and heard the birds sing many a pleasant morning. But there were some differences between Em'ly's orphanhood and mine, it appeared. She had lost her mother before her father; and where her father's grave was no one knew, except that it was somewhere in the depths of the sea.

"Besides," said Em'ly, as she looked about for shells and pebbles, "your father was a gentleman and your mother is a lady; and my father was a fisherman and my mother was a fisherman's daughter, and my uncle Dan is a fisherman."

"Dan is Mr. Peggotty, is he?" said I.

"Uncle Dan—yonder," answered Em'ly, nodding at the boat-house.

"Yes. I mean him. He must be very good, I should think?"

"Good?" said Em'ly. "If I was ever to be a lady, I'd give him a sky-blue coat with diamond buttons, nankeen trousers, a red velvet waistcoat, a cocked hat, a large gold watch, a silver pipe, and a box of money."

I said I had no doubt that Mr. Peggotty well deserved these treasures. I must acknowledge that I felt it difficult to picture him quite at his ease in the raiment proposed for him by his grateful little niece, and that I was particularly doubtful of the policy of the cocked hat; but I kept these sentiments to myself.

Little Em'ly had stopped and looked up at the sky in her enumeration of these articles, as if they were a glorious vision. We went on again, picking up shells and pebbles.

"You would like to be a lady?" I said.

Em'ly looked at me, and laughed and nodded "yes."

"I should like it very much. We would all be gentle-folks together, then. Me, and uncle, and Ham, and Mrs. Gummidge.[5] We wouldn't mind then, when there

---

5 Mrs Gummidge, pining widow of a drowned sailor, regards herself as a 'lorn creetur'.

come stormy weather.—Not for our own sakes, I mean. We would for the poor fishermen's, to be sure, and we'd help 'em with money when they come to any hurt."

This seemed to me to be a very satisfactory, and therefore not at all improbable picture. I expressed my pleasure in the contemplation of it, and little Em'ly was emboldened to say, shyly,

"Don't you think you are afraid the sea, now?"

It was quiet enough to reassure me, but I have no doubt if I had seen a moderately large wave come tumbling in, I should have taken to my heels, with an awful recollection of her drowned relations. However, I said "No," and I added, "You don't seem to be, either, though you say you are;"—for she was walking much too near the brink of a sort of old jetty or wooden causeway we had strolled upon, and I was afraid of her falling over.

"I'm not afraid in this way," said little Em'ly. "But I wake when it blows, and tremble to think of Uncle Dan and Ham, and believe I hear 'em crying out for help. That's why I should like so much to be a lady. But I'm not afraid in this way. Not a bit. Look here!"

She started from my side, and ran along a jagged timber which protruded from the place we stood upon, and overhung the deep water at some height, without the least defence. The incident is so impressed on my remembrance, that if I were a draughtsman I could draw its form here, I dare say, accurately as it was that day, and little Em'ly springing forward to her destruction (as it appeared to me), with a look that I have never forgotten, directed far out to sea.[6]

The light, bold, fluttering little figure turned and came back safe to me, and I soon laughed at my fears, and at the cry I had uttered; fruitlessly in any case, for there was no one near. But there have been times since, in my manhood, many times there have been, when I have thought, Is it possible, among the possibilities of hidden things, that in the sudden rashness of the child and her wild look so far off, there was any merciful attraction of her into danger, any tempting her towards him permitted on the part of her dead father, that her life might have a chance of ending that day. There has been a time since when I have wondered whether, if the life before her could have been revealed to me at a glance, and so revealed as that a child could fully comprehend it, and if her preservation could have depended on a motion of my hand, I ought to have held it up to save her. There has been a time since—I do not say it lasted long, but it has been—when I have asked myself the question, would it have been better for little Em'ly to have had the waters close above her head that morning in my sight; and when I have answered Yes, it would have been.[7]

This may be premature. I have set it down too soon, perhaps. But let it stand.

---

6   The language here suggests that Dickens might have considered an illustration for this passage, but there was no such illustration, and it stands as an example of his highly pictorial writing. Several of the modern film versions of the novel do much with this scene.

7   The foreshadowing here is more overt than is often the case in Dickens's writing. Morbid though the sentiment may be regarding an early death for Em'ly, and clichéd as the suggestion that before her lies 'a fate worse than death', later in the novel she will be disgraced, and a fallen-woman friend of hers nearly drowns herself.

We strolled a long way, and loaded ourselves with things that we thought curious, and put some stranded starfish carefully back into the water—I hardly know enough of the race at this moment to be quite certain whether they had reason to feel obliged to us for doing so, or the reverse—and then made our way home to Mr. Peggotty's dwelling. We stopped under the lee of the lobster-outhouse to exchange an innocent kiss, and went in to breakfast glowing with health and pleasure.

"Like two young mavishes," Mr. Peggotty said. I knew this meant, in our local dialect, like two young thrushes, and received it as a compliment.

Of course I was in love with little Em'ly. I am sure I loved that baby quite as truly, quite as tenderly, with greater purity and more disinterestedness, than can enter into the best love of a later time of life, high and ennobling as it is. I am sure my fancy raised up something round that blue-eyed mite of a child, which etherealised, and made a very angel of her. If, any sunny forenoon, she had spread a little pair of wings, and flown away before my eyes, I don't think I should have regarded it as much more than I had had reason to expect.

We used to walk about that dim old flat at Yarmouth in a loving manner, hours and hours. The day sported by us, as if Time had not grown up himself yet, but were a child too, and always at play. I told Em'ly I adored her, and that unless she confessed she adored me I should be reduced to the necessity of killing myself with a sword. She said she did, and I have no doubt she did.

As to any sense of inequality, or youthfulness, or other difficulty in our way, little Em'ly and I had no such trouble, because we had no future. We made no more provision for growing older, than we did for growing younger.

5 The Murdstones

The first monthly part concludes when David ends his visit at Yarmouth and, just as he reaches home, Clara Peggotty informs him that he has a father. Not knowing what to make of this, he first thinks of the graveyard 'and the raising of the dead'. Peggotty then tells him that he has a stepfather, the stern Mr Murdstone. Accompanied by his stern sister, Mr Murdstone epitomizes sombre firmness, a quality often associated with evangelical religion in nineteenth-century writing. Dickens thus points to 'a gloomy taint [. . .] in the Murdstone blood darkening the Murdstone religion, which was austere and wrathful'. They are the radical opposite of the cheerful Peggottys in carrying to an extreme the Victorian idea of earnestness, orderliness, self-discipline. As Kincaid points out (pp. 49–52), Dickens's portrayal of the Murdstones is not mere satire and comic exaggeration but representation of Victorian earnestness gone awry yet to some extent persisting in the adult David.

CHAPTER 4
I FALL INTO DISGRACE

IT was Miss Murdstone who was arrived, and a gloomy-looking lady she was; dark, like her brother, whom she greatly resembled in face and voice; and with very heavy eyebrows, nearly meeting over her large nose, as if, being disabled by the wrongs of her sex from wearing whiskers, she had carried them to that account. She brought with her two uncompromising hard black boxes, with her initials on the lids in hard brass nails. When she paid the coachman she took her money out of a hard steel purse, and she kept the purse in a very jail of a bag which hung upon her arm by a heavy chain, and shut up like a bite. I had never, at that time, seen such a metallic lady altogether as Miss Murdstone was.

She was brought into the parlour with many tokens of welcome, and there formally recognized my mother as a new and near relation. Then she looked at me, and said:

"Is that your boy, sister-in-law?"

My mother acknowledged me.

"Generally speaking," said Miss Murdstone, "I don't like boys. How d'ye do, boy?"

Under these encouraging circumstances, I replied that I was very well, and that I hoped she was the same; with such an indifferent grace, that Miss Murdstone disposed of me in two words:

"Wants manner!"

Having uttered which, with great distinctness, she begged the favour of being shown to her room, which became to me from that time forth a place of awe and dread, wherein the two black boxes were never seen open or known to be left unlocked, and where (for I peeped in once or twice when she was out) numerous little steel fetters and rivets, with which Miss Murdstone embellished herself when she was dressed, generally hung upon the looking-glass in formidable array.

As well as I could make out, she had come for good, and had no intention of ever going again. She began to "help" my mother next morning, and was in and out of the store-closet all day, putting things to rights, and making havoc in the old arrangements. Almost the first remarkable thing I observed in Miss Murdstone was, her being constantly haunted by a suspicion that the servants had a man secreted somewhere on the premises. Under the influence of this delusion, she dived into the coal-cellar at the most untimely hours, and scarcely ever opened the door of a dark cupboard without clapping it to again, in the belief that she had got him.

Though there was nothing very airy about Miss Murdstone, she was a perfect Lark in point of getting up. She was up (and, as I believe to this hour, looking for that man) before anybody in the house was stirring. Peggotty gave it as her opinion that she even slept with one eye open; but I could not concur in this idea; for I tried it myself after hearing the suggestion thrown out, and found it couldn't be done.

[. . .]

The gloomy taint that was in the Murdstone blood, darkened the Murdstone religion, which was austere and wrathful. I have thought, since, that its assuming that character was a necessary consequence of Mr. Murdstone's firmness, which wouldn't allow him to let anybody off from the utmost weight of the severest penalties he could find any excuse for. Be this as it may, I well remember the tremendous visages with which we used to go to church, and the changed air of the place. Again the dreaded Sunday comes round, and I file into the old pew first, like a guarded captive brought to a condemned service. Again, Miss Murdstone, in a black velvet gown, that looks as if it had been made out of a pall, follows close upon me; then my mother; then her husband. There is no Peggotty now, as in the old time. Again, I listen to Miss Murdstone mumbling the responses, and emphasising all the dread words with a cruel relish. Again, I see her dark eyes roll round the church when she says "miserable sinners," as if she were calling all the congregation names. Again, I catch rare glimpses of my mother, moving her lips timidly between the two, with one of them muttering at each ear like low thunder. Again, I wonder with a sudden fear whether it is likely that our good old clergy-man can be wrong, and Mr. and Miss Murdstone right, and that all the angels in heaven can be destroying angels. Again, if I move a finger or relax a muscle of my face, Miss Murdstone pokes me with her prayer-book, and makes my side ache.

[. . .]

Even when the lessons are done, the worst is yet to happen, in the shape of an appalling sum. This is invented for me, and delivered to me orally by Mr. Murdstone, and begins, "If I go into a cheese-monger's shop, and buy five thousand double-Gloucester cheeses at fourpence-halfpenny each, present payment"—at which I see Miss Murdstone secretly overjoyed. I pore over these cheeses without any result or enlightenment until dinner-time, when, having made a mulatto of myself by getting the dirt of the slate into the pores of my skin, I have a slice of bread to help me out with the cheeses, and am considered in disgrace for the rest of the evening.

It seems to me, at this distance of time, as if my unfortunate studies generally took this course. I could have done very well if I had been without the Murd-stones; but the influence of the Murdstones upon me was like the fascination of two snakes on a wretched young bird. Even when I did get through the morning with tolerable credit, there was not much gained but dinner; for Miss Murdstone never could endure to see me untasked, and if I rashly made any show of being unemployed, called her brother's attention to me by saying, "Clara, my dear, there's nothing like work—give your boy an exercise;" which caused me to be clapped down to some new labour there and then. As to any recreation with other children of my age, I had very little of that; for the gloomy theology of the Murdstones made all children out to be a swarm of little vipers (though there *was* a child once set in the midst of the Disciples), and held that they contaminated one another.

The natural result of this treatment, continued, I suppose, for some six months or more, was to make me sullen, dull, and dogged. I was not made the less so, by my sense of being daily more and more shut out and alienated from my mother. I believe I should have been almost stupefied but for one circumstance.

It was this. My father had left a small collection of books in a little room up-stairs, to which I had access (for it adjoined my own) and which nobody else in our house ever troubled. From that blessed little room, Roderick Random, Peregrine Pickle, Humphrey Clinker, Tom Jones, the Vicar of Wakefield, Don Quixote, Gil Blas, and Robinson Crusoe, came out, a glorious host, to keep me company. They kept alive my fancy, and my hope of something beyond that place and time,—they, and the Arabian Nights, and the Tales of the Genii,—and did me no harm; for whatever harm was in some of them was not there for me; *I* knew nothing of it. It is astonishing to me now, how I found time, in the midst of my porings and blunderings over heavier themes, to read those books as I did. It is curious to me how I could ever have consoled myself under my small troubles (which were great troubles to me), by impersonating my favourite characters in them—as I did—and by putting Mr. and Miss Murdstone into all the bad ones—which I did too. I have been Tom Jones (a child's Tom Jones, a harmless creature) for a week together. I have sustained my own idea of Roderick Random for a month at a stretch, I verily believe.[1]

[. . .]

This was my only and my constant comfort. When I think of it, the picture always rises in my mind, of a summer evening, the boys at play in the churchyard, and I sitting on my bed, reading as if for life. Every barn in the neighbourhood, every stone in the church, and every foot of the churchyard, had some association of its own, in my mind, connected with these books, and stood for some locality made famous in them.

[. . .]

[Mr. Murdstone] walked me up to my room slowly and gravely—I am certain he had a delight in that formal parade of executing justice—and when we got there, suddenly twisted my head under his arm.

"Mr. Murdstone! Sir!" I cried to him. "Don't! Pray don't beat me! I have tried to learn, Sir, but I can't learn while you and Miss Murdstone are by. I can't indeed!"

"Can't you, indeed, David?" he said. "We'll try that."

He had my head as in a vice, but I twined round him somehow, and stopped him for a moment, entreating him not to beat me. It was only for a moment that I

---

1   These books are ones Dickens mentions in his autobiographical fragment as ones he enjoyed in his early years. 'Tales of the Genii' were versions of *The Arabian Nights. Roderick Random, Peregrine Pickle* and *Humphrey Clinker* are novels by Tobias Smollett (1721–71); *Tom Jones* a novel by Henry Fielding (1707–54); *The Vicar of Wakefield* a sentimental novel by Oliver Goldsmith (1730?–74); *Don Quixote* a picaresque adventure tale by Miguel Cervantes (1547–1616); *Gil Blas* a picaresque romance by Alain Le Sage (1668–1747); and *Robinson Crusoe* a novel by Daniel Defoe (1660?–1731).

stopped him, for he cut me heavily an instant afterwards, and in the same instant I caught the hand with which he held me in my mouth, between my teeth, and bit it through. It sets my teeth on edge to think of it.

He beat me then, as if he would have beaten me to death. Above all the noise we made, I heard them running up the stairs, and crying out—I heard my mother crying out—and Peggotty. Then he was gone; and the door was locked outside; and I was lying, fevered and hot, and torn, and sore, and raging in my puny way, upon the floor.

How well I recollect, when I became quiet, what an unnatural stillness seemed to reign through the whole house! How well I remember, when my smart and passion began to cool, how wicked I began to feel!

I sat listening for a long while, but there was not a sound. I crawled up from the floor, and saw my face in the glass, so swollen, red, and ugly, that it almost frightened me. My stripes were sore and stiff, and made me cry afresh, when I moved; but they were nothing to the guilt I felt. It lay heavier on my breast than if I had been a most atrocious criminal, I dare say.

6 Salem House

To put him out of the way, Murdstone sends David to boarding school, where, like Dickens, he receives limited formal schooling, cut short by events beyond his control. This account of Salem House school, with the sadist Creakle as master and the boys under such tyranny, ranks with the criticism of nineteenth-century schools in Dickens's *Nicholas Nickleby* (1838–9) and Charlotte Brontë's *Jane Eyre* (1847). Thomas Hughes's vastly popular *Tom Brown's Schooldays* (1857) presents a more positive view for educational development of muscular young Christians. While David is at school a half-brother is born, and his schooling ends when both his mother and half-brother die. In an end-of-monthly-number climax, David in retrospect declares this a death of himself as he visualizes the dead half-brother as another version of his own infant being: 'The mother who lay in the grave, was the mother of my infancy; the little creature in her arms, was myself, as I had once been, hushed for ever on her bosom.' This recognition is important to both the issue of David's self-sufficiency and heroism and to the importance of his relationship with a number of women in his life (see **pp. 10–11, 45–6, 59–62** and **66–8**). Murdstone then sends David to work at Murdstone and Grinby, wine merchants. Home life, formal schooling and first employment scar the young David. Readers need to remember, however, that in each situation David encounters people who have more sympathy than power, but from whom he receives comfort and support. At this point of the story these include Clara Peggotty, schoolmate James Steerforth and the Micawbers.

CHAPTER 5
I AM SENT AWAY FROM HOME

SALEM HOUSE was a square brick building with wings; of a bare and unfurnished appearance. All about it was so very quiet, that I said to Mr. Mell[1] I supposed the boys were out; but he seemed surprised at my not knowing that it was holiday-time. That all the boys were at their several homes. That Mr. Creakle, the proprietor, was down by the sea-side with Mrs. and Miss Creakle; and that I was sent in holiday-time as a punishment for my misdoing, all of which he explained to me as we went along.

I gazed upon the schoolroom into which he took me, as the most forlorn and desolate place I had ever seen. I see it now. A long room, with three long rows of desks, and six of forms, and bristling all round with pegs for hats and slates. Scraps of old copybooks and exercises litter the dirty floor. Some silkworms' houses, made of the same materials, are scattered over the desks. Two miserable little white mice, left behind by their owner, are running up and down in a fusty castle made of pasteboard and wire, looking in all the corners with their red eyes for anything to eat. A bird, in a cage very little bigger than himself, makes a mournful rattle now and then in hopping on his perch, two inches high, or dropping from it; but neither sings nor chirps. There is a strange unwholesome smell upon the room, like mildewed corduroys, sweet apples wanting air, and rotten books. There could not well be more ink splashed about it, if it had been roofless from its first construction, and the skies had rained, snowed, hailed, and blown ink through the varying seasons of the year.

Mr. Mell having left me while he took his irreparable boots up-stairs, I went softly to the upper end of the room, observing all this as I crept along. Suddenly I came upon a pasteboard placard, beautifully written, which was lying on the desk, and bore these words—*"Take care of him. He bites."*[2]

I got upon the desk immediately, apprehensive of at least a great dog underneath. But, though I looked all round with anxious eyes, I could see nothing of him. I was still engaged in peering about, when Mr. Mell came back, and asked me what I did up there.

"I beg your pardon, Sir," says I, "if you please, I'm looking for the dog."

"Dog?" says he. "What dog?"

"Isn't it a dog, Sir?"

"Isn't what a dog?"

"That's to be taken care of, Sir; that bites."

"No, Copperfield," says he gravely, "that's not a dog. That's a boy. My instructions are, Copperfield, to put this placard on your back. I am sorry to make such a beginning with you, but I must do it."

With that, he took me down, and tied the placard, which was neatly con-

---

1   The kindly and much abused Salem House teacher.
2   This recalls the experience of Jane Eyre, a recent (1847) female fictional autobiographer, who, when sent to school, was forced to wear a placard labelled 'Liar'.

structed for the purpose, on my shoulders like a knapsack; and wherever I went, afterwards, I had the consolation of carrying it.

What I suffered from that placard nobody can imagine. Whether it was possible for people to see me or not, I always fancied that somebody was reading it. It was no relief to turn round and find nobody; for wherever my back was, there I imagined somebody always to be. That cruel man with the wooden leg,[3] aggravated my sufferings. He was in authority; and if he ever saw me leaning against a tree, or a wall, or the house, he roared out from his lodge-door in a stupendous voice, "Hallo, you Sir! You Copperfield! Show that badge conspicuous, or I'll report you!" The playground was a bare gravelled yard, open to all the back of the house and the offices; and I knew that the servants read it, and the butcher read it, and the baker read it; that everybody, in a word, who came backwards and forwards to the house, of a morning when I was ordered to walk there, read that I was to be taken care of, for I bit. I recollect that I positively began to have a dread of myself, as a kind of wild boy who did bite.

CHAPTER 6
I ENLARGE MY CIRCLE OF ACQUAINTANCE

MR. CREAKLE's part of the house was a good deal more comfortable than ours, and he had a snug bit of garden that looked pleasant after the dusty playground, which was such a desert in miniature, that I thought no one but a camel, or a dromedary, could have felt at home in it. It seemed to me a bold thing even to take notice that the passage looked comfortable, as I went on my way, trembling, to Mr. Creakle's presence: which so abashed me, when I was ushered into it, that I hardly saw Mrs. Creakle or Miss Creakle (who were both there, in the parlour), or anything but Mr. Creakle, a stout gentleman with a bunch of watch-chain and seals, in an arm-chair, with a tumbler and bottle beside him.

"So!" said Mr. Creakle. "This is the young gentleman whose teeth are to be filed! Turn him round."

The wooden-legged man turned me about so as to exhibit the placard; and having afforded time for a full survey of it, turned me about again, with my face to Mr. Creakle, and posted himself at Mr. Creakle's side. Mr. Creakle's face was fiery, and his eyes were small, and deep in his head; he had thick veins in his forehead, a little nose, and a large chin. He was bald on the top of his head; and had some thin wet-looking hair that was just turning grey, brushed across each temple, so that the two sides interlaced on his forehead. But the circumstance about him which impressed me most, was, that he had no voice, but spoke in a whisper. The exertion this cost him, or the consciousness of talking in that feeble way, made his angry face so much more angry, and his thick veins so much thicker, when he spoke, that I am not surprised, on looking back, at this peculiarity striking me as his chief one.

3   Tungay, schoolmaster Creakle's assistant.

"Now," said Mr. Creakle. "What's the report of this boy?"

"There's nothing against him yet," returned the man with the wooden leg. "There has been no opportunity."

I thought Mr. Creakle was disappointed. I thought Mrs. and Miss Creakle (at whom I now glanced for the first time, and who were, both, thin and quiet) were not disappointed.

"Come here, Sir!" said Mr. Creakle, beckoning to me.

"Come here!" said the man with the wooden leg, repeating the gesture.

"I have the happiness of knowing your father-in-law," whispered Mr. Creakle, taking me by the ear; "and a worthy man he is, and a man of a strong character. He knows me, and I know him. Do *you* know me? Hey?" said Mr. Creakle, pinching my ear with ferocious playfulness.

"Not yet, Sir," I said, flinching with the pain.

"Not yet? Hey?" repeated Mr. Creakle. "But you will soon. Hey?"

"You will soon. Hey?" repeated the man with the wooden leg. I afterwards found that he generally acted, with his strong voice, as Mr. Creakle's interpreter to the boys.

I was very much frightened, and said, I hoped so, if he pleased. I felt, all this while, as if my ear were blazing; he pinched it so hard.

"I'll tell you what I am," whispered Mr. Creakle, letting it go at last, with a screw at parting that brought the water into my eyes, "I'm a Tartar."

"A Tartar," said the man with the wooden leg.

"When I say I'll do a thing, I do it," said Mr. Creakle; "and when I say I will have a thing done, I will have it done."

"—Will have a thing done, I will have it done," repeated the man with the wooden leg.

"I am a determined character," said Mr. Creakle. "That's what I am. I do my duty. That's what *I* do. My flesh and blood—" he looked at Mrs. Creakle as he said this—"when it rises against me, is not my flesh and blood. I discard it."

[. . .]

I was not considered as being formally received into the school, however, until J. Steerforth arrived. Before this boy, who was reputed to be a great scholar, and was very good-looking, and at least half-a-dozen years my senior, I was carried as before a magistrate. He enquired, under a shed in the playground, into the particulars of my punishment, and was pleased to express his opinion that it was 'a jolly shame,' for which I became bound to him ever afterwards.

CHAPTER 7
MY FIRST HALF AT SALEM HOUSE

STEERFORTH continued his protection of me, and proved a very useful friend; since nobody dared to annoy one whom he honoured with his countenance. He couldn't—or at all events, he didn't defend me from Mr. Creakle, who was very severe with me; but whenever I had been treated worse than usual, he always told me that I wanted a little of his pluck, and that he wouldn't have stood it himself; which I felt he intended for encouragement, and considered to be very kind of him.

7 Murdstone and Grinby's

For about six months in 1824 twelve-year-old Dickens was sent to work pasting labels on bottles of shoe blacking, and for a good part of this period lodged on his own because his father had been imprisoned for debt. The impact of this experience was life-long, a source both of shame that caused him to keep it secret and of fierce self-sufficiency in his later life (see **pp. 57–8**). The description of David's workplace, Murdstone and Grinby's, closely parallels Dickens's impressions of the blacking factory he worked in as a child (**pp. 20–2**).

CHAPTER 11
I BEGIN LIFE ON MY OWN ACCOUNT, AND DON'T LIKE IT

I KNOW enough of the world now, to have almost lost the capacity of being much surprised by anything; but it is matter of some surprise to me, even now, that I can have been so easily thrown away at such an age. A child of excellent abilities, and with strong powers of observation, quick, eager, delicate, and soon hurt bodily or mentally, it seems wonderful to me that nobody should have made any sign in my behalf. But none was made; and I became, at ten years old, a little labouring hind in the service of Murdstone and Grinby.

Murdstone and Grinby's warehouse was at the water-side. It was down in Blackfriars. Modern improvements have altered the place; but it was the last house at the bottom of a narrow street, curving down hill to the river, with some stairs at the end, where people took boat. It was a crazy old house with a wharf of its own, abutting on the water when the tide was in, and on the mud when the tide was out, and literally overrun with rats. Its panelled rooms, discoloured with the dirt and smoke of a hundred years, I dare say; its decaying floors and staircase; the squeaking and scuffling of the old grey rats down in the cellars; and the dirt and rottenness of the place; are things, not of many years ago, in my mind, but of the present instant. They are all before me, just as they were in the evil hour when I went among them for the first time, with my trembling hand in Mr. Quinion's.

Murdstone and Grinby's trade was among a good many kinds of people, but an important branch of it was the supply of wines and spirits to certain packet-ships. I forget now where they chiefly went, but I think there were some among them that made voyages both to the East and West Indies. I know that a great many empty bottles were one of the consequences of this traffic, and that certain men and boys were employed to examine them against the light, and reject those that were flawed, and to rinse and wash them. When the empty bottles ran short, there were labels to be pasted on full ones, or corks to be fitted to them, or seals to be put upon the corks, or finished bottles to be packed in casks. All this work was my work, and of the boys employed upon it I was one.

[. . .]

No words can express the secret agony of my soul as I sank into this companionship; compared these henceforth every-day associates with those of my happier childhood—not to say with Steerforth, Traddles, and the rest of those boys;[1] and felt my hopes of growing up to be a learned and distinguished man crushed in my bosom. The deep remembrance of the sense I had, of being utterly without hope now; of the shame I felt in my position; of the misery it was to my young heart to believe that day by day what I had learned, and thought, and delighted in, and raised my fancy and my emulation up by, would pass away from me, little by little, never to be brought back any more; cannot be written[2] [. . .].

The counting-house clock was at half-past twelve, and there was general preparation for going to dinner, when Mr. Quinion tapped at the counting-house window, and beckoned to me to go in. I went in, and found there a stoutish, middle-aged person, in a brown surtout and black tights and shoes, with no more hair upon his head (which was a large one, and very shining) than there is upon an egg, and with a very extensive face, which he turned full upon me. His clothes were shabby, but he had an imposing shirt-collar on. He carried a jaunty sort of a stick, with a large pair of rusty tassels to it; and a quizzing-glass hung outside his coat,—for ornament, I afterwards found, as he very seldom looked through it, and couldn't see anything when he did.

"This," said Mr. Quinion, in allusion to myself, "is he."

"This," said the stranger, with a certain condescending roll in his voice, and a certain indescribable air of doing something genteel, which impressed me very much, "is Master Copperfield. I hope I see you well, Sir?"

I said I was very well, and hoped he was. I was sufficiently ill at ease, Heaven knows; but it was not in my nature to complain much at that time of my life, so I said I was very well, and hoped he was.

"I am," said the stranger, "thank Heaven, quite well. I have received a letter from Mr. Murdstone, in which he mentions that he would desire me to receive into an apartment in the rear of my house, which is at present unoccupied—and is, in short, to be let as a—in short," said the stranger, with a smile and in a burst of confidence, "as a bedroom—the young beginner whom I have now the pleasure to——" and the stranger waved his hand, and settled his chin in his shirt-collar.

"This is Mr. Micawber," said Mr. Quinion to me.

"Ahem!" said the stranger, "that is my name."

---

1   David's schoolmates at Salem House.
2   Some of that experience had in fact already been rewritten. Dickens took the name of one boy, Bob Fagin, who had befriended him, and used it for the villain in *Oliver Twist*, but Dickens's demeaning time in the factory remained a life-long secret, even to his own family.

"Mr. Micawber," said Mr. Quinion, "is known to Mr. Murdstone. He takes orders for us on commission, when he can get any. He has been written to by Mr. Murdstone, on the subject of your lodgings, and he will receive you as a lodger."

"My address," said Mr. Micawber, "is Windsor Terrace, City Road. I—in short," said Mr. Micawber, with the same genteel air, and in another burst of confidence—"I live there."

I made him a bow.

"Under the impression," said Mr. Micawber, "that your peregrinations in this metropolis have not as yet been extensive, and that you might have some difficulty in penetrating the arcana of the Modern Babylon in the direction of the City Road—in short," said Mr. Micawber, in another burst of confidence, "that you might lose yourself—I shall be happy to call this evening, and instal you in the knowledge of the nearest way."[3]

I thanked him with all my heart, for it was friendly in him to offer to take that trouble.

[. . .]

At last Mr. Micawber's difficulties came to a crisis, and he was arrested early one morning, and carried over to the King's Bench Prison in the Borough. He told me, as he went out of the house, that the God of day had now gone down upon him—and I really thought his heart was broken and mine too. But I heard, afterwards, that he was seen to play a lively game at skittles, before noon.

On the first Sunday after he was taken there, I was to go and see him, and have dinner with him. I was to ask my way to such a place, and just short of that place I should see such another place, and just short of that I should see a yard, which I was to cross, and keep straight on until I saw a turnkey. All this I did; and when at last I did see a turnkey (poor little fellow that I was!), and thought how, when Roderick Random[4] was in a debtors' prison, there was a man there with nothing on him but an old rug, the turnkey swam before my dimmed eyes and my beating heart.

Mr. Micawber was waiting for me within the gate, and we went up to his room (top story but one), and cried very much. He solemnly conjured me, I remember, to take warning by his fate; and to observe that if a man had twenty pounds a year for his income, and spent nineteen pounds nineteen shillings and sixpence, he would be happy, but that if he spent twenty pounds one he would be miserable. After which he borrowed a shilling of me for porter, gave me a written order on Mrs. Micawber for the amount, and put away his pocket-handkerchief, and cheered up.

[. . .]

3 One of Dickens's most memorable comic creations, Micawber is based upon Dickens's father, John, who was arrested for debt, and was convivial and loquacious.
4 Title character of novel by Tobias Smollett.

All this time I was working at Murdstone and Grinby's in the same common way, and with the same common companions, and with the same sense of unmerited degradation as at first. But I never, happily for me no doubt, made a single acquaintance, or spoke to any of the many boys whom I saw daily in going to the warehouse, in coming from it, and in prowling about the streets at meal-times. I led the same secretly unhappy life; but I led it in the same lonely, self-reliant manner. The only changes I am conscious of are, firstly, that I had grown more shabby, and secondly, that I was now relieved of much of the weight of Mr. and Mrs. Micawber's cares; for some relatives or friends had engaged to help them at their present pass, and they lived more comfortably in the prison than they had lived for a long while out of it. I used to breakfast with them now, in virtue of some arrangement, of which I have forgotten the details. I forget, too, at what hour the gates were opened in the morning, admitting of my going in; but I know that I was often up at six o'clock, and that my favourite lounging-place in the interval was old London Bridge, where I was wont to sit in one of the stone recesses, watching the people going by, or to look over the balustrades at the sun shining in the water, and lighting up the golden flame on the top of the Monument. The Orfling[5] met me here sometimes, to be told some astonishing fictions respecting the wharves and the Tower; of which I can say no more than that I hope I believed them myself. In the evening I used to go back to the prison, and walk up and down the parade with Mr. Micawber; or play casino with Mrs. Micawber, and hear reminiscences of her papa and mama. Whether Mr. Murdstone knew where I was, I am unable to say. I never told them at Murdstone and Grinby's.

[. . .]

[. . .] When my thoughts go back now, to that slow agony of my youth, I wonder how much of the histories I invented for such people hangs like a mist of fancy over well-remembered facts! When I tread the old ground, I do not wonder that I seem to see and pity, going on before me, an innocent romantic boy, making his imaginative world out of such strange experiences and sordid things![6]

CHAPTER 12
LIKING LIFE ON MY OWN ACCOUNT NO BETTER,
I FORM A GREAT RESOLUTION

[. . .] I had resolved to run away.—To go, by some means or other, down into the country, to the only relation I had in the world, and tell my story to my aunt, Miss Betsey.

---

5 An orphan who was a loyal, but certainly unpaid, servant of the Micawbers.
6 David's idea interestingly recurs in Dickens's preface to *Bleak House*, his next novel, where he stated that he had purposely dealt with the romantic side of familiar things. But David's fond recollection of his earlier imaginings contrasts with his determination later to draw the curtain on his time working for Murdstone and Grinby (**p. 116**).

I have already observed that I don't know how this desperate idea came into my brain. But, once there, it remained there; and hardened into a purpose than which I have never entertained a more determined purpose in my life. I am far from sure that I believed there was anything hopeful in it, but my mind was thoroughly made up that it must be carried into execution.

Again, and again, and a hundred times again, since the night when the thought had first occurred to me and banished sleep, I had gone over that old story of my poor mother's about my birth, which it had been one of my great delights in the old time to hear her tell, and which I knew by heart. My aunt walked into that story,[7] and walked out of it, a dread and awful personage; but there was one little trait in her behaviour which I liked to dwell on, and which gave me some faint shadow of encouragement. I could not forget how my mother had thought that she felt her touch her pretty hair with no ungentle hand; and though it might have been altogether my mother's fancy, and might have had no foundation whatever in fact, I made a little picture, out of it, of my terrible aunt relenting towards the girlish beauty that I recollected so well and loved so much, which softened the whole narrative. It is very possible that it had been in my mind a long time, and had gradually engendered my determination.

8 Betsey Trotwood

Betsey Trotwood is a rare instance in Dickens's writing of an independent woman, separated from a brutal husband, who, before David's birth, had been reported dead in India. Living in Dover, she tends to her seaside cottage, determined that donkeys (her term for fools as well as animals) not trespass on the green lawn beyond her garden gate, and seeing David, she at once declares, 'No boys here!' Figure 3 registers her shock when the ragged boy turns out to be her great-nephew. The picture signals promise of new life for David. The world outside the garden fence is sketchy, and just beyond the garden lurks a man on a donkey, bemusedly wondering what will come of David's incursion. Tumbling backward in surprise, Betsey is open armed. Although neither character at this point realizes it, this is a critical turning point in David's life, for she will be his most constant mother-figure and he the sometimes heedless recipient of her good counsel.

Towards the end of this extract David the narrator notes that once he was established at Dover, a curtain fell between his new life and his earlier time at Murdstone and Grinby. Certainly, with a new home, family and friends, this was

---

7 Betsey Trotwood is David's great-aunt, and, as this passage recalls, she had marched in and out of his life on the day of his birth. Having suddenly appeared and frightened David's timid mother into labour, she awaited the birth, certain the child would be female and named after her. The moment she learned from the doctor that the baby was a boy, she left the house and was not heard from until David finds her.

a fresh start for young David, and the adult David now tells us that he had produced the earlier parts of his story 'with a reluctant hand', but, after noting that at the time young David thought little about either himself or his 'curious couple of guardians', he moves forward confidently with his narration. Like Dickens when putting away his autobiographical fragment (**pp. 20–2**), David's novel has written out and seemingly closed the book on humiliating childhood experiences. As the extracts from modern critics J. Hillis Miller and Malcolm Andrews show (**pp. 44–6** and **55–8**), the part of David's history dealing with his deliverance from the humiliating labour never completely frees him from some painful recollection or any new worries.

CHAPTER 13
THE SEQUEL OF MY RESOLUTION

MY SHOES were by this time in a woeful condition. The soles had shed themselves bit by bit, and the upper leathers had broken and burst until the very shape and form of shoes had departed from them. My hat (which had served me for a night-cap, too) was so crushed and bent, that no old battered handleless saucepan on a dunghill need have been ashamed to vie with it. My shirt and trousers, stained with heat, dew, grass, and the Kentish soil on which I had slept—and torn besides—might have frightened the birds from my aunt's garden, as I stood at the gate. My hair had known no comb or brush since I left London. My face, neck, and hands, from unaccustomed exposure to the air and sun, were burnt to a berry-brown. From head to foot I was powdered almost as white with chalk and dust, as if I had come out of a lime-kiln. In this plight, and with a strong con-sciousness of it, I waited to introduce myself to, and make my first impression on, my formidable aunt.

The unbroken stillness of the parlour-window leading me to infer, after a while, that she was not there, I lifted up my eyes to the window above it, where I saw a florid, pleasant-looking gentleman, with a grey head, who shut up one eye in a grotesque manner, nodded his head at me several times, shook it at me as often, laughed, and went away.

I had been discomposed enough before; but I was so much the more dis-composed by this unexpected behaviour, that I was on the point of slinking off, to think how I had best proceed, when there came out of the house a lady with a handkerchief tied over her cap, and a pair of gardening gloves on her hands, wearing a gardening-pocket like a tollman's apron, and carrying a great knife. I knew her immediately to be Miss Betsey, for she came stalking out of the house exactly as my poor mother had so often described her stalking up our garden at Blunderstone Rookery.

"Go away!" said Miss Betsey, shaking her head, and making a distant chop in the air with her knife. "Go along! No boys here!"

I watched her, with my heart at my lips, as she marched to a corner of her garden, and stooped to dig up some little root there. Then, without a scrap of

Figure 3 I Make Myself Known to my Aunt.

courage, but with a great deal of desperation, I went softly in and stood beside her, touching her with my finger.

"If you please, ma'am," I began.

She started, and looked up.

"If you please, aunt."

"EH?" exclaimed Miss Betsey, in a tone of amazement I have never heard approached.

"If you please, aunt, I am your nephew."

"Oh, Lord!" said my aunt. And sat flat down in the garden-path.

"I am David Copperfield, of Blunderstone, in Suffolk—where you came, on the night when I was born, and saw my dear mama. I have been very unhappy since she died. I have been slighted, and taught nothing, and thrown upon myself, and put to work not fit for me. It made me run away to you. I was robbed at first setting out, and have walked all the way, and have never slept in a bed since I began the journey." Here my self-support gave way all at once; and with a movement of my hands, intended to show her my ragged state, and call it to witness that I had suffered something, I broke into a passion of crying, which I suppose had been pent up within me all the week.

My aunt, with every sort of expression but wonder discharged from her countenance, sat on the gravel, staring at me, until I began to cry; when she got up in a great hurry, collared me, and took me into the parlour. Her first proceeding there was to unlock a tall press, bring out several bottles, and pour some of the contents of each into my mouth. I think they must have been taken out at random, for I am sure I tasted aniseed water, anchovy sauce, and salad dressing. When she had administered these restoratives, as I was still quite hysterical, and unable to control my sobs, she put me on the sofa, with a shawl under my head, and the handkerchief from her own head under my feet, lest I should sully the cover; and then, sitting herself down behind the green fan or screen I have already mentioned, so that I could not see her face, ejaculated at intervals, "Mercy on us!" letting those exclamations off like minute-guns.

After a time she rang the bell. "Janet," said my aunt, when her servant came in. "Go up stairs, give my compliments to Mr. Dick, and say I wish to speak to him."

Janet looked a little surprised to see me lying stiffly on the sofa (I was afraid to move lest it should be displeasing to my aunt) but went on her errand. My aunt, with her hands behind her, walked up and down the room, until the gentleman who had squinted at me from the upper window came in laughing.

"Mr. Dick," said my aunt, "don't be a fool, because nobody can be more discreet than you can, when you choose. We all know that. So don't be a fool, whatever you are."

The gentleman was serious immediately, and looked at me, I thought, as if he would entreat me to say nothing about the window.

"Mr. Dick," said my aunt, "you have heard me mention David Copperfield? Now don't pretend not to have a memory, because you and I know better."

"David Copperfield?" said Mr. Dick, who did not appear to me to remember much about it. "*David* Copperfield? Oh yes, to be sure. David, certainly."

"Well," said my aunt, "this is his boy—his son. He would be as like his father as it's possible to be, if he was not so like his mother, too."

"His son?" said Mr. Dick. "David's son? Indeed!"

"Yes," pursued my aunt, "and he has done a pretty piece of business. He has run away. Ah! His sister, Betsey Trotwood,[1] never would have run away." My aunt shook her head firmly, confident in the character and behaviour of the girl who never was born.

"Oh! you think she wouldn't have run away?" said Mr. Dick.

"Bless and save the man," exclaimed my aunt, sharply, "how he talks! Don't I know she wouldn't? She would have lived with her godmother, and we should have been devoted to one another. Where, in the name of wonder, should his sister, Betsey Trotwood, have run from, or to?"

"Nowhere," said Mr. Dick.

"Well then," returned my aunt, softened by the reply, "how can you pretend to be wool-gathering, Dick, when you are as sharp as a surgeon's lancet? Now, here you see young David Copperfield, and the question I put to you is, what shall I do with him?"

"What shall you do with him?" said Mr. Dick, feebly, scratching his head. "Oh! do with him?"

"Yes," said my aunt, with a grave look, and her forefinger held up. "Come! I want some very sound advice."

"Why, if I was you," said Mr. Dick, considering, and looking vacantly at me, "I should——" The contemplation of me seemed to inspire him with a sudden idea, and he added, briskly, "I should wash him!"

"Janet," said my aunt, turning round with a quiet triumph, which I did not then understand, "Mr. Dick sets us all right. Heat the bath!"

Although I was deeply interested in this dialogue, I could not help observing my aunt, Mr. Dick, and Janet, while it was in progress, and completing a survey I had already been engaged in making of the room.

My aunt was a tall, hard-featured lady, but by no means ill-looking. There was an inflexibility in her face, in her voice, in her gait and carriage, amply sufficient to account for the effect she had made upon a gentle creature like my mother; but her features were rather handsome than otherwise, though unbending and austere. I particularly noticed that she had a very quick, bright eye. Her hair, which was grey, was arranged in two plain divisions, under what I believe would be called a mob-cap: I mean a cap, much more common then than now, with side-pieces fastening under the chin. Her dress was of a lavender colour, and perfectly neat; but scantily made, as if she desired to be as little encumbered as possible. I remember that I thought it, in form, more like a riding-habit with the superfluous skirt cut off, than anything else. She wore at her side a gentleman's gold watch, if I might judge from its size and make, with an appropriate chain and seals; she had some linen at her throat not unlike a shirt-collar, and things at her wrists like little shirt-wristbands.

Mr. Dick, as I have already said, was grey-headed and florid: I should have said

---

1 The point here is that there never had been a Betsey Trotwood Copperfield, although Betsey will insistently call David 'Trotwood Copperfield'.

all about him, in saying so, had not his head been curiously bowed—not by age; it reminded me of one of Mr. Creakle's boys' heads after a beating—and his grey eyes prominent and large, with a strange kind of watery brightness in them that made me, in combination with his vacant manner, his submission to my aunt, and his childish delight when she praised him, suspect him of being a little mad; though, if he were mad, how he came to be there puzzled me extremely. He was dressed like any other ordinary gentleman, in a loose grey morning coat and waistcoat, and white trousers; and had his watch in his fob, and his money in his pockets: which he rattled as if he were very proud of it.[2]

[. . .]

"You'll consider yourself guardian, jointly with me, of this child, Mr. Dick," said my aunt.

"I shall be delighted," said Mr. Dick, "to be the guardian of David's son."

"Very good," returned my aunt, "*that's* settled. I have been thinking, do you know, Mr. Dick, that I might call him Trotwood?"

"Certainly, certainly. Call him Trotwood, certainly," said Mr. Dick. "David's son's Trotwood."

"Trotwood Copperfield, you mean," returned my aunt.

"Yes, to be sure. Yes. Trotwood Copperfield," said Mr Dick, a little abashed.

My aunt took so kindly to the notion, that some ready-made clothes, which were purchased for me that afternoon, were marked "Trotwood Copperfield," in her own handwriting, and in indelible marking-ink, before I put them on; and it was settled that all the other clothes which were ordered to be made for me (a complete outfit was bespoke that afternoon) should be marked in the same way.

Thus I began my new life, in a new name, and with everything new about me. Now that the state of doubt was over, I felt, for many days, like one in a dream. I never thought that I had a curious couple of guardians, in my aunt and Mr. Dick. I never thought of anything about myself, distinctly. The two things clearest in my mind were, that a remoteness had come upon the old Blunderstone life—which seemed to lie in the haze of an immeasurable distance; and that a curtain had for ever fallen on my life at Murdstone and Grinby's. No one has ever raised that curtain since. I have lifted it for a moment, even in this narrative, with a reluctant hand, and dropped it gladly. The remembrance of that life is fraught with so much pain to me, with so much mental suffering and want of hope, that I have never had the courage even to examine how long I was doomed to lead it. Whether it lasted for a year, or more, or less, I do not know. I only know that it was, and ceased to be; and that I have written, and there I leave it.[3]

---

2   Space prevents including sections concerning Mr Dick's principal activity, the writing of a massive memorial that keeps getting blocked by his obsession with the beheading of King Charles; to attempt to overcome this, Mr Dick pastes together manuscript and flies it as a kite. Modern commentators have noted that Mr Dick is but one of several writers in this novel (pp. 65–8).

3   Although the phrasing might suggest this was the final line of a monthly part, it was not. David's stating that he has written what 'was, and ceased to be' first raises a point that recurs in Chapter 31 when, looking forward, he realizes that he must write what is to come, much as he would prefer not to (p. 128).

9 Agnes Wickfield and Uriah Heep

In Chapter 15 David makes 'another beginning', a beginning in schooling far better than he had received at Salem House, when his Aunt Betsey sends him off to Canterbury to study with Dr Strong and to lodge with Mr Wickfield, who handles Betsey's business affairs. Betsey intends David to have an education that will make him happy and useful. At Canterbury he encounters another set of interesting characters surrounding Wickfield, a brooding widower who is subject to drink and to the wiles of his scheming clerk, Uriah Heep. As he had earlier at Yarmouth with Little Em'ly, David forms a friendship with a beautiful young girl, Agnes, daughter and 'little housekeeper' for Mr Wickfield. David, Em'ly, Agnes and Dora Spenlow with whom he later falls in love, are all motherless; and soon after meeting Agnes, he notes her likeness to the portrait of her dead mother: 'On her face, I saw immediately the placid and sweet expression of the lady whose picture had looked at me down-stairs. It seemed to my imagination as if the portrait had grown womanly, and the original remained a child. Although her face was quite bright and happy, there was a tranquillity about it, and about her—a quiet, good, calm spirit—that I never have forgotten; that I never shall forget' (Chapter 15).

Modern critics question how realistically and complexly Dickens characterizes Agnes and situates her among the young women in David's life (see **pp. 10–11, 45–6, 61–2** and **67–8**). To some, Agnes seems an ineffectual angel, an ideal rather than realistic representation of a woman subjected from childhood to loving service to various male characters. It is important to regard her and also Em'ly and Dora as products of David's imagination; his blindness to realities in each of their lives is a key part of his own story. In the case of Agnes, he long fails to recognize her love for him or to see her apart from his own needs. At Canterbury he meets the odious Uriah Heep. Uriah, like David, is fatherless and is trying (with many self-congratulatory protestations of humbleness) to make a better life for himself. Heep lusts both for Wickfield's business and daughter. Small wonder, then, that the initial attraction/repulsion David feels when first meeting Uriah later culminates in his assistance in exposing Heep's schemes (**pp. 144–7**).

CHAPTER 15
I MAKE ANOTHER BEGINNING

When the pony-chaise stopped at the door, and my eyes were intent upon the house, I saw a cadaverous face appear at a small window on the ground floor (in a little round tower that formed one side of the house), and quickly disappear. The low arched door then opened, and the face came out. It was quite as cadaverous as it had looked in the window, though in the grain of it there was that tinge of red which is sometimes to be observed in the skins of red-haired people. It belonged to a red-haired person—a youth of fifteen, as I take it now, but looking much older—

whose hair was cropped as close as the closest stubble; who had hardly any eyebrows, and no eyelashes, and eyes of a red-brown, so unsheltered and unshaded, that I remember wondering how he went to sleep. He was high-shouldered and bony; dressed in decent black, with a white wisp of a neckcloth; buttoned up to the throat; and had a long, lank, skeleton hand, which particularly attracted my attention, as he stood at the pony's head, rubbing his chin with it, and looking up at us in the chaise.

"Is Mr. Wickfield at home, Uriah Heep?" said my aunt.

"Mr. Wickfield's at home, ma'am," said Uriah Heep, "if you'll please to walk in there—" pointing with his long hand to the room he meant.

We got out; and leaving him to hold the pony, went into a long low parlour looking towards the street, from the window of which I caught a glimpse, as I went in, of Uriah Heep breathing into the pony's nostrils, and immediately covering them with his hand, as if he were putting some spell upon him.

10 Somebody Turns Up

Figure 4, 'Somebody Turns Up' from Chapter 17, is rich with detail and action. Modestly furnished, in accord with the lowly Heeps' circumstances, the room contains objects and pictures pertaining to Uriah's study in law. On the Heeps' side of the illustration are live and also figurine cats (adding to the various animal images characterizing Uriah), and above the mantel a stuffed owl under glass gazes on the scene with interest. The composition divides the forces of Heep and Copperfield, Uriah served by his mother, David not yet aware that his old ally, Micawber, has 'turned up' in the Heeps' doorway. At the very centre, David, still about the same size he was in the illustration of his arrival at Dover, sits upright on the edge of his chair as Uriah, with grasping skeletal hands and sickly smile, leans forward to address him. All on the left of the picture is enclosed and cluttered, the supposedly humble hearth over which the gaunt Heeps preside. To the right in the light of the open door is the substantial body of Micawber, who, as the story goes on, seems to fall under the power of Heep, but ultimately prevails over him.

CHAPTER 17
SOMEBODY TURNS UP

[. . .] "Here is my umble dwelling, Master Copperfield!"

We entered a low, old-fashioned room, walked straight into from the street, and found there Mrs. Heep, who was the dead image of Uriah, only short. She received me with the utmost humility, and apologized to me for giving her son a kiss, observing that, lowly as they were, they had their natural affections, which they

Figure 4 **Somebody Turns Up.**

hoped would give no offence to any one. It was a perfectly decent room, half
parlour and half kitchen, but not at all a snug room. The tea-things were set upon
the table, and the kettle was boiling on the hob. There was a chest of drawers
with an escritoire top, for Uriah to read or write at of an evening; there was
Uriah's blue bag lying down and vomiting papers; there was a company of
Uriah's books commanded by Mr. Tidd;[1] there was a corner cupboard; and
there were the usual articles of furniture. I don't remember that any individual
object had a bare, pinched, spare look; but I do remember that the whole
place had.

It was perhaps a part of Mrs. Heep's humility, that she still wore weeds. Notwithstanding the lapse of time that had occurred since Mr. Heep's decease, she still
wore weeds. I think there was some compromise in the cap; but otherwise she was
as weedy as in the early days of her mourning.[2]

---

1   Given Heep's later success in ruining Mr Wickfield, he evidently benefits from this knowledge of
    William Tidd's *The practice of the Court of King's Bench in personal actions*, which was published
    in 1790.
2   Often in his fiction and journalism Dickens was critical of ostentatious and protracted mourning,
    and in his will stated his desire that 'those who attend my funeral wear no scarf, cloak, black bow,
    long hat-band, or any other such revolting absurdity'. Fred Kaplan, *Charles Dickens* (New York:
    William Morrow, 1988), p. 543.

"This is a day to be remembered, my Uriah, I am sure," said Mrs. Heep, making the tea, "when Master Copperfield pays us a visit."

"I said you'd think so, mother," said Uriah.

"If I could have wished father to remain among us for any reason," said Mrs. Heep, "it would have been, that he might have known his company this afternoon."

I felt embarrassed by these compliments; but I was sensible, too, of being entertained as an honoured guest, and I thought Mrs. Heep an agreeable woman.

"My Uriah," said Mrs. Heep, "has looked forward to this, Sir, a long while. He had his fears that our umbleness stood in the way, and I joined in them myself. Umble we are, umble we have been, umble we shall ever be," said Mrs. Heep.

"I am sure you have no occasion to be so, ma'am," I said, "unless you like."

"Thank you, Sir," retorted Mrs. Heep. "We know our station and are thankful in it."

I found that Mrs. Heep gradually got nearer to me, and that Uriah gradually got opposite to me, and that they respectfully plied me with the choicest of the eatables on the table. There was nothing particularly choice there, to be sure; but I took the will for the deed, and felt that they were very attentive. Presently they began to talk about aunts, and then I told them about mine; and about fathers and mothers, and then I told them about mine; and then Mrs. Heep began to talk about fathers-in-law, and then I began to tell her about mine; but stopped, because my aunt had advised me to observe a silence on that subject. A tender young cork, however, would have had no more chance against a pair of corkscrews, or a tender young tooth against a pair of dentists, or a little shuttlecock against two battledores, than I had against Uriah and Mrs. Heep. They did just what they liked with me; and wormed things out of me that I had no desire to tell, with a certainty I blush to think of: the more especially as, in my juvenile frankness, I took some credit to myself for being so confidential, and felt that I was quite the patron of my two respectful entertainers.

They were very fond of one another: that was certain. I take it, that had its effect upon me, as a touch of nature; but the skill with which the one followed up whatever the other said, was a touch of art which I was still less proof against. [...]

[...]

I had begun to be a little uncomfortable, and to wish myself well out of the visit, when a figure coming down the street passed the door—it stood open to air the room, which was warm, the weather being close for the time of year—came back again, looked in, and walked in, exclaiming loudly, "Copperfield! Is it possible?"

It was Mr. Micawber! Mr. Micawber, with his eye-glass, and his walking-stick, [...] and the condescending roll in his voice, all complete!

"My dear Copperfield," said Mr. Micawber, putting out his hand, "this is indeed a meeting which is calculated to impress the mind with a sense of the instability and uncertainty of all human—in short, it is a most extraordinary meeting. Walking along the street, reflecting upon the probability of something turning up (of which I am at present rather sanguine), I find a young but valued friend turn up, who is connected with the most eventful period of my life; I must say, with the turning-point of my existence. Copperfield, my dear fellow, how do you do?"

11 Steerforth

As David's schooldays end, he finds Heep gaining more power over the declining Mr Wickfield, and, when he moves to London, David by chance meets his old Salem House school friend, Steerforth, now an Oxford man. Given Betsey's recent reminder to David that she wants him to be a morally 'firm fellow, with a will of [his] own, [. . .] with strength of character that is not to be influenced, except on good reason, by anybody, or by anything' (Chapter 19), this reunion with the young man he so idolized and who soon proves to be the antithesis of Betsey's manly model does not augur well. When he visits the Steerforth home (in Chapter 20) he finds, as he had at the Heeps' humble residence, a mother doting on an only son, but this time there is also a strange young woman, Rosa Dartle, sharp-tongued (her speech comes in dart-like pitches) and bearing a scar from a blow young Steerforth had inflicted years earlier. Steerforth's is the social status to which David aspires, and David's own aspirations are ones Heep both emulates and does his best to undermine. Ultimately the unchecked desires of both Steerforth and Heep harm or threaten women close to David. The gender and class issues inherent in both the Heep–Agnes Wickfield–David and the Steerforth–Em'ly–David triangles are focal points for modern *David Copperfield* criticism (**pp. 44–6** and **59–62**).

Steerforth (in Chapter 22) accompanies David on a fortnight's visit to the Peggottys in Yarmouth, and one evening David finds his friend brooding before the fire, stripped of class pride and also of the swashbuckling but kindly manner he had displayed when first meeting the Peggottys. Here Steerforth voices the self-torment of a Byronic hero (see Juliet John, **pp. 62–4**). Interestingly, when he contrasts David's life with his own, Steerforth discounts the fact that David, too, had had no father's guidance. Thus when Steerforth feels that David comes upon him like 'a reproachful ghost', he unknowingly echoes David's earlier observation that as a posthumous child he may have been 'privileged to see ghosts and spirits' (**p. 90**).

CHAPTER 20
STEERFORTH'S HOME

THERE was a second lady in the dining-room, of a slight short figure, dark, and not agreeable to look at, but with some appearance of good looks too, who attracted my attention: perhaps because I had not expected to see her; perhaps because I found myself sitting opposite to her; perhaps because of something really remarkable in her. She had black hair and eager black eyes, and was thin, and had a scar upon her lip. It was an old scar—I should rather call it, seam, for it was not discoloured, and had healed years ago—which had once cut through her mouth, downward towards the chin, but was now barely visible across the table, except above and on her upper lip, the shape of which it had altered. I concluded in my own mind that she was about thirty years of age, and that she wished to be married. She was a little dilapidated—like a house—with having been so long to let; yet had, as I have said, an appearance of good looks. Her thinness seemed to be the effect of some wasting fire within her, which found a vent in her gaunt eyes.

She was introduced as Miss Dartle and both Steerforth and his mother called her Rosa. I found that she lived there, and had been for a long time Mrs. Steerforth's companion. It appeared to me that she never said anything she wanted to say, outright; but hinted it, and made a great deal more of it by this practice. [. . .]

[. . .]

Her own views of every question, and her correction of everything that was said to which she was opposed, Miss Dartle insinuated in the same way: sometimes, I could not conceal from myself, with great power, though in contradiction even of Steerforth. An instance happened before dinner was done. Mrs. Steerforth speaking to me about my intention of going down into Suffolk, I said at hazard how glad I should be, if Steerforth would only go there with me; and explaining to him that I was going to see my old nurse, and Mr. Peggotty's family, I reminded him of the boatman whom he had seen at school.

"Oh! That bluff fellow!" said Steerforth. "He had a son with him, hadn't he?"

"No. That was his nephew," I replied; "whom he adopted, though, as a son. He has a very pretty little niece too, whom he adopted as a daughter. In short, his house (or rather his boat, for he lives in one, on dry land) is full of people who are objects of his generosity and kindness. You would be delighted to see that household."

"Should I?" said Steerforth. "Well, I think I should. I must see what can be done. It would be worth a journey—not to mention the pleasure of a journey with you, Daisy[1]—to see that sort of people together, and to make one of 'em."

My heart leaped with a new hope of pleasure. But it was in reference to the tone in which he had spoken of "that sort of people," that Miss Dartle, whose sparkling eyes had been watchful of us, now broke in again.

"Oh, but, really? Do tell me. Are they, though?" she said.

"Are they what? And are who what?" said Steerforth.

"That sort of people.—Are they really animals and clods, and beings of another order? I want to know so much."

"Why, there's a pretty wide separation between them and us," said Steerforth, with indifference. "They are not to be expected to be as sensitive as we are. Their delicacy is not to be shocked, or hurt very easily. They are wonderfully virtuous, I

---

1   David has accepted this pet, feminizing name from Steerforth. David, to the jaded Steerforth, seems
    fresh as a daisy. This is but one of many names bestowed upon David.

dare say—some people contend for that, at least; and I am sure I don't want to contradict them—but they have not very fine natures, and they may be thankful that, like their coarse rough skins, they are not easily wounded."

"Really!" said Miss Dartle. "Well, I don't know, now, when I have been better pleased than to hear that. It's so consoling! It's such a delight to know that, when they suffer, they don't feel! Sometimes I have been quite uneasy for that sort of people; but now I shall just dismiss the idea of them, altogether. Live and learn. I had my doubts, I confess, but now they're cleared up. I didn't know, and now I do know; and that shows the advantage of asking—don't it?"

I believed that Steerforth had said what he had, in jest, or to draw Miss Dartle out; and I expected him to say as much when she was gone, and we two were sitting before the fire. But he merely asked me what I thought of her.

"She is very clever, is she not?" I asked.

"Clever! She brings everything to a grindstone," said Steerforth, "and sharpens it, as she has sharpened her own face and figure these years past. She has worn herself away by constant sharpening. She is all edge."

"What a remarkable scar that is upon her lip!" I said.

Steerforth's face fell, and he paused a moment.

"Why, the fact is," he returned, "—I did that."

"By an unfortunate accident!"

"No. I was a young boy, and she exasperated me, and I threw a hammer at her. A promising young angel I must have been!"

I was deeply sorry to have touched on such a painful theme, but that was useless now.

"She has borne the mark ever since, as you see," said Steerforth; "and she'll bear it to her grave, if she ever rests in one; though I can hardly believe she will ever rest anywhere. She was the motherless child of a sort of cousin of my father's. He died one day. My mother, who was then a widow, brought her here to be company to her. She has a couple of thousand pounds of her own, and saves the interest of it every year, to add to the principal. There's the history of Miss Rosa Dartle for you."

"And I have no doubt she loves you like a brother?" said I.

"Humph!" retorted Steerforth, looking at the fire. "Some brothers are not loved over much; and some love—but help yourself, Copperfield! We'll drink the daisies of the field, in compliment to you; and the lilies of the valley that toil not, neither do they spin, in compliment to me—the more shame for me!" A moody smile that had overspread his features cleared off as he said this merrily, and he was his own frank, winning self again.

I could not help glancing at the scar with a painful interest when we went in to tea. It was not long before I observed that it was the most susceptible part of her face, and that, when she turned pale, that mark altered first, and became a dull, lead-coloured streak, lengthening out to its full extent, like a mark in invisible ink brought to the fire. There was a little altercation between her and Steerforth about a cast of the dice at backgammon—when I thought her, for one moment, in a storm of rage; and then I saw it start forth like the old writing on the wall.

CHAPTER 22
SOME OLD SCENES, AND SOME NEW PEOPLE

IT was with a singular jumble of sadness and pleasure that I used to linger about my native place, until the reddening winter sun admonished me that it was time to start on my returning walk. But, when the place was left behind, and especially when Steerforth and I were happily seated over our dinner by a blazing fire, it was delicious to think of having been there. So it was, though in a softened degree, when I went to my neat room at night; and, turning over the leaves of the crocodile-book (which was always there, upon a little table),[2] remembered with a grateful heart how blest I was in having such a friend as Steerforth, such a friend as Peggotty, and such a substitute for what I had lost as my excellent and generous aunt.

My nearest way to Yarmouth, in coming back from these long walks, was by a ferry. It landed me on the flat between the town and the sea, which I could make straight across, and so save myself a considerable circuit by the high road. Mr. Peggotty's house being on that waste-place, and not a hundred yards out of my tract, I always looked in as I went by. Steerforth was pretty sure to be there expecting me, and we went on together through the frosty air and gathering fog towards the twinkling lights of the town.

One dark evening, when I was later than usual—for I had, that day, been making my parting visit to Blunderstone, as we were now about to return home— I found him alone in Mr. Peggotty's house, sitting thoughtfully before the fire. He was so intent upon his own reflections that he was quite unconscious of my approach. This, indeed, he might easily have been if he had been less absorbed, for footsteps fell noiselessly on the sandy ground outside; but even my entrance failed to rouse him. I was standing close to him, looking at him; and still, with a heavy brow, he was lost in his meditations.

He gave such a start when I put my hand upon his shoulder, that he made me start too.

"You come upon me," he said, almost angrily, "like a reproachful ghost!"

"I was obliged to announce myself somehow," I replied. "Have I called you down from the stars?"

"No," he answered. "No."

"Up from anywhere, then?" said I, taking my seat near him.

"I was looking at the pictures in the fire," he returned.

"But you are spoiling them for me," said I, as he stirred it quickly with a piece of burning wood, striking out of it a train of red-hot sparks that went careering up the little chimney, and roaring out into the air.

"You would not have seen them," he returned. "I detest this mongrel time, neither day nor night. How late you are! Where have you been?"

"I have been taking leave of my usual walk," said I.

---

2   This was the book Clara Peggotty read to him when he was a child. Mention of it here and also at the end of the novel serves to link past and present, a comforting text-within-the-text of *David Copperfield*.

"And I have been sitting here," said Steerforth, glancing round the room, "thinking that all the people we found so glad on the night of our coming down, might—to judge from the present wasted air of the place—be dispersed, or dead, or come to I don't know what harm. David, I wish to God I had had a judicious father these last twenty years!"

"My dear Steerforth, what is the matter?"

"I wish with all my soul I had been better guided!" he exclaimed. "I wish with all my soul I could guide myself better!"

There was a passionate dejection in his manner that quite amazed me. He was more unlike himself than I could have supposed possible.

"It would be better to be this poor Peggotty, or his lout of a nephew," he said, getting up and leaning moodily against the chimney-piece, with his face towards the fire, "than to be myself, twenty times richer and twenty times wiser, and be the torment to myself that I have been, in this Devil's bark of a boat, within the last half-hour!"

I was so confounded by the alteration in him, that at first I could only observe him in silence, as he stood leaning his head upon his hand, and looking gloomily down at the fire. At length I begged him, with all the earnestness I felt, to tell me what had occurred to cross him so unusually, and to let me sympathise with him, if I could not hope to advise him. Before I had well concluded, he began to laugh—fretfully at first, but soon with returning gaiety.

"Tut, it's nothing, Daisy! nothing!" he replied. "I told you, at the inn in London, I am heavy company for myself, sometimes. I have been a nightmare to myself, just now—must have had one, I think. At odd dull times, nursery tales come up into the memory, unrecognised for what they are. I believe I have been confounding myself with the bad boy who 'didn't care,' and became food for lions—a grander kind of going to the dogs, I suppose. What old women call the horrors, have been creeping over me from head to foot. I have been afraid of myself."

"You are afraid of nothing else, I think," said I.

"Perhaps not, and yet may have enough to be afraid of too," he answered. "Well! So it goes by! I am not about to be hipped again, David; but I tell you, my good fellow, once more, that it would have been well for me (and for more than me) if I had had a steadfast and judicious father!"

His face was always full of expression, but I never saw it express such a dark kind of earnestness as when he said these words, with his glance bent on the fire.

12 Dora

As preparation for David's law career, Betsey provides funds for him to be articled to Mr Spenlow in London's Doctors' Commons. The 'captivity' he speaks of is his love at first sight of Spenlow's daughter Dora. The novel's opening sentences had raised the question of whether David would be the hero of his own life, or whether someone else might hold that position, and we have seen already that, to contrasting extremes, both Heep and Steerforth hold strong influence over David. By terming his attraction to Dora 'captivity', he jokingly admits his vulnerability to other people. Readers may too readily dismiss the characterization of Dora as Victorian male relegation of women to separate and lesser spheres of life, or merely as satire of silly girlhood persisting into womanhood. Considered more closely, however, the characterization of Dora mixes satire and sentimentality, and in retrospect David both criticizes his earlier treatment of her and also recognizes that Dora herself better understood why, through lack of education and guidance, she would never be more than his 'child-wife'. (For more discussion of Dora, see **pp. 10–11, 45** and **61**.)

CHAPTER 26
I FALL INTO CAPTIVITY

WE turned into a room near at hand, [. . .] and I heard a voice say, "Mr. Copperfield, my daughter Dora, and my daughter Dora's confidential friend!" It was, no doubt, Mr. Spenlow's voice, but I didn't know it, and I didn't care whose it was. All was over in a moment. I had fulfilled my destiny. I was a captive and a slave. I loved Dora Spenlow to distraction!

She was more than human to me. She was a Fairy, a Sylph, I don't know what she was—anything that no one ever saw, and everything that everybody ever wanted. I was swallowed up in an abyss of love in an instant. There was no pausing on the brink; no looking down, or looking back; I was gone, headlong, before I had sense to say a word to her.

"I," observed a well-remembered voice, when I had bowed and murmured something, "have seen Mr. Copperfield before."

The speaker was not Dora. No; the confidential friend, Miss Murdstone!

I don't think I was much astonished. To the best of my judgement, no capacity of astonishment was left in me. There was nothing worth mentioning in the material world, but Dora Spenlow, to be astonished about. I said, "How do you do, Miss Murdstone? I hope you are well." She answered, "Very well." I said, "How is Mr. Murdstone?" She replied, "My brother is robust, I am obliged to you."

Mr. Spenlow, who, I suppose, had been surprised to see us recognise each other, then put in his word.

"I am glad to find," he said, "Copperfield, that you and Miss Murdstone are already acquainted."

"Mr. Copperfield and myself," said Miss Murdstone, with severe composure, "are connexions. We were once slightly acquainted. It was in his childish days. Circumstances have separated us since. I should not have known him."

I replied that I should have known her, anywhere. Which was true enough.

"Miss Murdstone has had the goodness," said Mr. Spenlow to me, "to accept the office—if I may so describe it—of my daughter Dora's confidential friend. My daughter Dora having, unhappily, no mother, Miss Murdstone is obliging enough to become her companion and protector."

A passing thought occurred to me that Miss Murdstone, like the pocket-instrument called a life-preserver,[1] was not so much designed for purposes of protection as of assault. But as I had none but passing thoughts for any subject save Dora, I glanced at her, directly afterwards, and was thinking that I saw, in her prettily pettish manner, that she was not very much inclined to be particularly confidential to her companion and protector, when a bell rang, which Mr. Spenlow said was the first dinner-bell, and so carried me off to dress.

The idea of dressing one's self, or doing anything in the way of action, in that state of love, was a little too ridiculous. I could only sit down before my fire, biting the key of my carpet-bag, and think of the captivating, girlish, bright-eyed, lovely Dora. What a form she had, what a face she had, what a graceful, variable, enchanting manner!

The bell rang again so soon that I made a mere scramble of my dressing, instead of the careful operation I could have wished under the circumstances, and went downstairs. There was some company. Dora was talking to an old gentleman with a grey head. Grey as he was—and a great-grandfather into the bargain, for he said so—I was madly jealous of him.

What a state of mind I was in! I was jealous of everybody. I couldn't bear the idea of anybody knowing Mr. Spenlow better than I did. It was torturing to me to hear them talk of occurrences in which I had had no share. When a most amiable person, with a highly polished bald head, asked me across the dinner-table, if that were the first occasion of my seeing the grounds, I could have done anything to him that was savage and revengeful.

I don't remember who was there, except Dora. I have not the least idea what we had for dinner, besides Dora. My impression is, that I dined off Dora entirely, and sent away half-a-dozen plates untouched. I sat next to her. I talked to her. She had the most delightful little voice, the gayest little laugh, the pleasantest and most fascinating little ways, that ever led a lost youth into hopeless slavery. She was rather diminutive altogether. So much the more precious, I thought.

13 Em'ly and Steerforth

Chapter 30, 'A Loss', concerns David's return to Yarmouth to witness the death of Barkis, Clara Peggotty's husband. Chapter 31, nearly half-way through the novel, is one of the most important, because it concerns the Peggottys' and David's loss of Little Em'ly to Steerforth, whom Ham Peggotty at once labels

---

1 What we today call a 'blackjack', a life-preserver is a stick loaded with heavier material used as a cudgel by criminals. The *OED* notes that in the Illustrated Catalogue of the Great Exhibition (1851) such a life-preserver was listed.

'damned villain'. Not simply a key moment in the plot, this event and what follows challenge David both as character and later narrator. It was he who had introduced Steerforth to the Yarmouth people, and he who had trusted him. Thus David deeply feels 'my own unconscious part in his pollution of an honest home'. Here Dickens draws upon his own experiences in management of a shelter for fallen women (**pp. 22–3**). 'A Greater Loss' is framed by an uncanny moment after Barkis's funeral. As a boy David had looked down from his room window on his father's grave. Now back in that graveyard, he looks up to the window of his former home to see a madman leering out. The displacement is not simply that of madman for imaginative boy in the window. Rather it is the larger disorientation of David the autobiographer suddenly finding himself in an uncanny moment which recasts both past and present in ways he, as storyteller, finds hard to control. Thus when he says 'A dread falls on me here', the 'here' is the place and time of the disoriented David in the churchyard psychologically coincident with the present time of writing. Chapter 32 begins with a confessional moment clearly set in the present time of the writing, but David's point is that his immediate feelings about Steerforth when the ties that bound them were broken have remained 'the remembrances of a cherished friend'. The chapter concludes with Mr Peggotty's resolution to seek Emily and bring her home, and the focus shifts from the melodramatic event of her departure to its effect, psychologically, on Daniel (see **pp. 46–9**).

CHAPTER 31
A GREATER LOSS

[. . .]

I did not attend the funeral in character, if I may venture to say so. I mean I was not dressed up in a black cloak and a streamer, to frighten the birds;[1] but I walked over to Blunderstone early in the morning, and was in the churchyard when it came, attended only by Peggotty and her brother. The mad gentleman looked on, out of my little window; Mr. Chillip's baby wagged its heavy head, and rolled its goggle eyes, at the clergyman, over its nurse's shoulder; Mr. Omer breathed short in the background; no one else was there; and it was very quiet. We walked about the churchyard for an hour, after all was over; and pulled some young leaves from the tree above my mother's grave.

A dread falls on me here. A cloud is lowering on the distant town, towards which I retraced my solitary steps. I fear to approach it. I cannot bear to think of what did come, upon that memorable night; of what must come again, if I go on.

It is no worse, because I write of it. It would be no better, if I stopped my most

---

1   Often in his journalism and fiction Dickens opposed the theatrical extravagance of funerals.

unwilling hand. It is done. Nothing can undo it; nothing can make it otherwise than as it was.

Leaving the churchyard, David makes his way through the rainy night to Mr Peggotty's, where Ham, the cousin to whom Em'ly had been engaged, tells David she is gone.

"Em'ly's run away! Oh, Mas'r Davy, think *how* she's run away, when I pray my good and gracious God to kill her (her that is so dear above all things) sooner than let her come to ruin and disgrace!"[2]

The face he turned up to the troubled sky, the quivering of his clasped hands, the agony of his figure, remain associated with that lonely waste, in my remembrance, to this hour. It is always night there, and he is the only object in the scene.

"You're a scholar," he said, hurriedly, "and know what's right and best. What am I to say, indoors? How am I ever to break it to him, Mas'r Davy?"

I saw the door move, and instinctively tried to hold the latch on the outside, to gain a moment's time. It was too late. Mr. Peggotty thrust forth his face; and never could I forget the change that came upon it when he saw us, if I were to live five hundred years.

I remember a great wail and cry, and the women hanging about him, and we all standing in the room; I with a paper in my hand, which Ham had given me; Mr. Peggotty, with his vest torn open, his hair wild, his face and lips quite white, and blood trickling down his bosom (it had sprung from his mouth, I think), looking fixedly at me.

"Read it, Sir," he said, in a low shivering voice. "Slow, please. I doen't know as I can understand."

In the midst of this silence of death, I read thus, from a blotted letter:—

" 'When you, who love me so much better than I ever have deserved, even when my mind was innocent, see this, I shall be far away.' "

"I shall be fur away," he repeated slowly. "Stop! Em'ly fur away. Well!"

" 'When I leave my dear home—my dear home—oh, my dear home!—in the morning,'

the letter bore date on the previous night:

'—It will be never to come back, unless he brings me back a lady. This will be found at night, many hours after, instead of me. Oh, if you knew how my heart is torn. If even you, that I have wronged so much, that never can forgive me, could only know what I suffer! I am too wicked to

2 Ham's words here recall those David the narrator had used earlier when mentioning Em'ly's wish to become a lady (**p. 97**).

write about myself. Oh, take comfort in thinking that I am so bad. Oh, for mercy's sake, tell uncle that I never loved him half so dear as now. Oh, don't remember how affectionate and kind you have all been to me—don't remember we were ever to be married—but try to think as if I died when I was little, and was buried somewhere. Pray Heaven that I am going away from, have compassion on my uncle! Tell him that I never loved him half so dear. Be his comfort. Love some good girl, that will be what I was once to uncle, and be true to you, and worthy of you, and know no shame but me. God bless all! I'll pray for all, often, on my knees. If he don't bring me back a lady, and I don't pray for my own self, I'll pray for all. My parting love to uncle. My last tears, and my last thanks, for uncle!' "

That was all.

He stood, long after I had ceased to read, still looking at me. At length I ventured to take his hand, and to entreat him, as well as I could, to endeavour to get some command of himself. He replied, "I thank'ee, Sir, I thank'ee!" without moving.

Ham spoke to him. Mr. Peggotty was so far sensible of *his* affliction, that he wrung his hand; but, otherwise, he remained in the same state, and no one dared to disturb him.

Slowly, at last, he moved his eyes from my face, as if he were waking from a vision, and cast them round the room. Then he said, in a low voice:

"Who's the man? I want to know his name."

Ham glanced at me, and suddenly I felt a shock that struck me back.

"There's a man suspected," said Mr. Peggotty. "Who is it?"

"Mas'r Davy!" implored Ham. "Go out a bit, and let me tell him what I must. You doen't ought to hear it, Sir."

I felt the shock again. I sank down in a chair, and tried to utter some reply; but my tongue was fettered, and my sight was weak.

"I want to know his name!" I heard said, once more.

[. . .]

"For the Lord's love," said Mr. Peggotty, falling back, and putting out his hand, as if to keep off what he dreaded. "Doen't tell me his name's Steerforth."

"Mas'r Davy," exclaimed Ham, in a broken voice, "it ain't no fault of yourn—and I am far from laying of it to you—but his name is Steerforth, and he's a damned villain!"

Mr. Peggotty uttered no cry, and shed no tear, and moved no more, until he seemed to wake again, all at once, and pulled down his rough coat from its peg in a corner.

"Bear a hand with this! I'm struck of a heap, and can't do it," he said, impatiently. "Bear a hand, and help me. Well!" when somebody had done so. "Now give me that theer hat!"

Ham asked him whither he was going.

"I'm a going to seek my niece. I'm a going to seek my Em'ly. I'm a going, first, to stave in that theer boat, and sink it where I would have drownded *him*, as I'm a livin' soul, if I had had one thought of what was in him! As he sat afore me," he said, wildly, holding out his clenched right hand, "as he sat afore me, face to face, strike me down dead, but I'd have drownded him, and thought it right!—I'm a going to seek my niece."

"Where?" cried Ham, interposing himself before the door.

"Anywhere! I'm a going to seek my niece through the wureld. I'm a going to find my poor niece in her shame, and bring her back. No one stop me! I tell you I'm a going to seek my niece!"

CHAPTER 32
THE BEGINNING OF A LONG JOURNEY

WHAT is natural in me, is natural in many other men, I infer, and so I am not afraid to write that I never had loved Steerforth better than when the ties that bound me to him were broken.[3] In the keen distress of the discovery of his unworthiness, I thought more of all that was brilliant in him, I softened more towards all that was good in him, I did more justice to the qualities that might have made him a man of a noble nature and a great name, than ever I had done in the height of my devotion to him. Deeply as I felt my own unconscious part in his pollution of an honest home, I believed that if I had been brought face to face with him, I could not have uttered one reproach. I should have loved him so well still— though he fascinated me no longer—I should have held in so much tenderness the memory of my affection for him, that I think I should have been as weak as a spirit-wounded child, in all but the entertainment of a thought that we could ever be reunited. That thought I never had. I felt, as he had felt, that all was at an end between us. What his remembrances of me were, I have never known—they were light enough, perhaps, and easily dismissed—but mine of him were as the remembrances of a cherished friend, who was dead.

Yes, Steerforth, long removed from the scenes of this poor history! My sorrow may bear involuntary witness against you at the Judgement Throne; but my angry thoughts or my reproaches never will, I know!

---

3 Coincidentally in 1850, Tennyson's *In Memoriam* explored at length such feelings as David here describes, although the subject of grief in the poem was not a fictional character with severe flaws, but Tennyson's close friend, Arthur Henry Hallam. Interestingly, just as in this novel, loss of loved ones tests the will and power to write, so too in the poem does Tennyson acknowledge the inadequacy of efforts to write and yet find consolation in it (pp. 30–1).

14 Work

In Chapter 36 Betsey Trotwood has suffered the 'late misfortune' of losing the investments that fund her living, and she and Mr Dick move to London. Now David knows he must work to assist Betsey and Mr Dick. His recent life had been preoccupied blissfully with courtship of Dora: 'What an idle time! What an unsubstantial, happy, foolish time! Of all the times of mine that Time has in his grip, there is none that in one retrospection I can smile at half so much, and think of half so tenderly' (Chapter 33, 'Blissful'). His first 'What I had to do' statement is a classic instance of the morally earnest Victorian male, turning to what he has been disciplined and trained to do – earn money. The second 'What I had to do' yet reflects his romantic quest of his lady, and in the phrasing, resolute work takes metaphoric flight as axe in woodman's hand. The understated retrospective self-criticism could come only after discovering that once he had won Dora, full happiness did not follow. See Poovey (**pp. 59–62**) for commentary on the moral and social assumptions David here asserts about the nature and spheres of his labours.

In Chapter 42, the mischief of the chapter title is mainly that being worked by Uriah Heep, whose increasing hold over the Wickfields has hurt both them and Betsey, because Wickfield had been the agent responsible for managing her invested funds. This extract contains one of David's few references to himself as a writer, putting forward what is obviously the credo of earnest authorship and hard work enforced by Dickens. David is determined to make these statements, even though the monthly part cover title for this chapter still announced that this was a story 'Which He never meant to be Published on any Account'. On the one hand, David's comments about himself here are timely and in character: he is at the critical point where he must make his own way in life, both in his work and in his courtship, and the values he espouses are those Betsey has long urged for him. On the other hand, David as an adult may express such earnestness but in fact he remains uncertain, passive, sometimes doubt-ridden. Miller points out the contrast between the novel's assertion of a buoyant era's faith in labour and love rewarded and its mention of David's restlessness even when seeming most successful (**pp. 44–6**), and Welsh discusses the counter-pointing of David the novelist with the number of 'writers' in this story (**pp. 65–6**).

CHAPTER 36
ENTHUSIASM

[. . .] I was not dispirited now. I was not afraid of the shabby coat, and had no yearnings after gallant greys. My whole manner of thinking of our late misfortune was changed. What I had to do, was, to show my aunt that her past goodness to me had not been thrown away on an insensible, ungrateful object. What I had to do, was, to turn the painful discipline of my younger days to account, by going to work with a resolute and steady heart. What I had to do, was, to take my woodman's axe in my hand, and clear my own way through the forest of difficulty, by cutting down the trees until I came to Dora. And I went on at a mighty rate, as if it could be done by walking.[1]

CHAPTER 42
MISCHIEF

I FEEL as if it were not for me to record, even though this manuscript is intended for no eyes but mine, how hard I worked at that tremendous shorthand, and all improvement appertaining to it, in my sense of responsibility to Dora and her aunts. I will only add, to what I have already written of my perseverance at this time of my life, and of a patient and continuous energy which then began to be matured within me, and which I know to be the strong part of my character, if it have any strength at all, that there, on looking back, I find the source of my success. I have been very fortunate in worldly matters; many men have worked much harder, and not succeeded half so well; but I never could have done what I have done, without the habits of punctuality, order, and diligence, without the determination to concentrate myself on one object at a time, no matter how quickly its successor should come upon its heels, which I then formed. Heaven knows I write this, in no spirit of self-laudation. The man who reviews his own life, as I do mine, in going on here, from page to page, had need to have been a good man indeed, if he would be spared the sharp consciousness of many talents neglected, many opportunities wasted, many erratic and perverted feelings constantly at war within his breast, and defeating him. I do not hold one natural gift, I daresay, that I have not abused. My meaning simply is, that whatever I have tried to do in life, I have tried with all my heart to do well; that whatever I have devoted myself to, I have devoted myself to completely; that, in great aims and in small, I have always been thoroughly in earnest. I have never believed it possible that any natural or improved ability can claim immunity from the companionship of the steady, plain, hard-working qualities, and hope to gain its end. There is no such thing as such fulfilment on this earth. Some happy talent, and some fortunate opportunity, may form the two sides of the ladder on which some men mount, but the rounds of that ladder must be made of stuff to stand wear and tear; and there is no substitute for thorough-going, ardent, and sincere earnestness. Never to put one hand to anything, on which I could throw my whole self; and never to affect depreciation of my work, whatever it was; I find, now, to have been my golden rules.

---

1 Dickens was an avid walker, engaging friends in walking matches, but often walking great numbers of miles at a fast pace.

15 Child-Wife

The lyrical, active present tense that Dickens used occasionally earlier in the novel appears more frequently in the second half of the book. The manner with which David writes about both Dora and himself – a mix of sweet sentiment and satire, sometimes unrelenting and sometimes forgiving – complicates his retrospective characterization of the young lovers. Although Dickens projected much of the impulsiveness of his own early loves and probably some of his current impatience with his wife's ineptitude in characterizing Dora as infatuating, childish and teasing, modern readers need to focus on what this characterization, in the context of the book's other females, shows about Victorian gender roles. It is too easy to pass over Dora with a smile, a smirk or a sigh as an instance of exaggerated Dickensian humour, sentimentality and pathos more entertaining (or annoying) than instructive to both David and his readers. At the beginning of Chapter 43 David halts the progress of his narrative and steps outside himself (a timely effort, appropriate to his narrative effort to determine whether he is turning out to be the hero of his own life) not just to remember Dora, but to acknowledge that phantoms of his joyful and often exasperating days with Dora remain with him. This lets us see how his love possessed/ possesses him, however misdirected he finally regarded it. Later, in what seems but another childish moment, Dora asks David to remember and to forgive her as his child-wife. The question for readers is how well David, writing in retrospect, recognizes Dora's awareness of her limitations, as well as his own. He never calls himself 'child-husband', but he does reveal much about his earlier self as 'silly boy' partner of Dora. The David–Dora relationship is an important subject in modern criticism of *David Copperfield* (**pp. 10–11, 45–6** and **55–8**).

CHAPTER 43
ANOTHER RETROSPECT

ONCE again, let me pause upon a memorable period of my life. Let me stand aside, to see the phantoms of those days go by me, accompanying the shadow of myself, in dim procession.

Weeks, months, seasons, pass along. They seem little more than a summer day and a winter evening. Now, the Common where I walk with Dora is all in bloom, a field of bright gold; and now the unseen heather lies in mounds and bunches underneath a covering of snow. In a breath, the river that flows through our Sunday walks is sparkling in the summer sun, is ruffled by the winter wind, or thickened with drifting heaps of ice. Faster than ever river ran towards the sea, it flashes, darkens, and rolls away.

Not a thread changes, in the house of the two little bird-like ladies.[1] The clock

---

1   The ladies are the aunts with whom Dora is living.

ticks over the fireplace, the weather-glass hangs in the hall. Neither clock nor weather-glass is ever right; but we believe in both, devoutly.

I have come legally to man's estate. I have attained the dignity of twenty-one. But this is a sort of dignity that may be thrust upon one. Let me think what I have achieved.

I have tamed that savage stenographic mystery.[2] I make a respectable income by it. I am in high repute for my accomplishment in all pertaining to the art, and am joined with eleven others in reporting the debates in Parliament for a Morning Newspaper. Night after night, I record predictions that never come to pass, professions that are never fulfilled, explanations that are only meant to mystify. I wallow in words. Britannia, that unfortunate female, is always before me, like a trussed fowl: skewered through and through with office-pens, and bound hand and foot with red tape.[3] I am sufficiently behind the scenes to know the worth of political life. I am quite an Infidel about it, and shall never be converted.

[. . .]

I have come out in another way. I have taken with fear and trembling to authorship. I wrote a little something, in secret, and sent it to a magazine, and it was published in the magazine. Since then, I have taken heart to write a good many trifling pieces. Now, I am regularly paid for them. Altogether, I am well off; when I tell my income on the fingers of my left hand, I pass the third finger and take in the fourth to the middle joint.

We have removed from Buckingham Street, to a pleasant little cottage very near the one I looked at, when my enthusiasm first came on. My aunt, however (who has sold the house at Dover, to good advantage), is not going to remain here, but intends removing herself to a still more tiny cottage close at hand. What does this portend? My marriage? Yes!

Yes! I am going to be married to Dora! [. . .]

CHAPTER 44
OUR HOUSEKEEPING

IT was a strange condition of things, the honeymoon being over, and the bridesmaids gone home, when I found myself sitting down in my own small house with Dora; quite thrown out of employment, as I may say, in respect of the delicious old occupation of making love.

It seemed such an extraordinary thing to have Dora always there. It was so unaccountable not to be obliged to go out to see her, not to have any occasion to be tormenting myself about her, not to have to write to her, not to be scheming

---

2 Just as young Dickens learned shorthand quickly to become a reporter.
3 Throughout his writing Dickens expresses his exasperation with governmental and bureaucratic bumbling and stalling, and a few months later he wrote a satirical article titled 'Red Tape' (*Household Words*, 15 February 1851).

and devising opportunities of being alone with her. Sometimes of an evening, when I looked up from my writing, and saw her seated opposite, I would lean back in my chair, and think how queer it was that there we were, alone together as a matter of course—nobody's business any more—all the romance of our engagement put away upon a shelf, to rust—no one to please but one another— one another to please, for life.

When there was a debate,[4] and I was kept out very late, it seemed so strange to me, as I was walking home, to think that Dora was at home! It was such a wonderful thing, at first, to have her coming softly down to talk to me as I ate my supper. It was such a stupendous thing to know for certain that she put her hair in papers. It was altogether such an astonishing event to see her do it!

I doubt whether two young birds could have known less about keeping house, than I and my pretty Dora did. We had a servant, of course. She kept house for us. I have still a latent belief that she must have been Mrs. Crupp's[5] daughter in disguise, we had such an awful time of it with Mary Anne.

Her name was Paragon. Her nature was represented to us, when we engaged her, as being feebly expressed in her name. She had a written character, as large as a Proclamation; and, according to this document, could do everything of a domestic nature that ever I heard of, and a great many things that I never did hear of. She was a woman in the prime of life; of a severe countenance; and subject (particularly in the arms) to a sort of perpetual measles or fiery rash.

[. . .]

But she preyed upon our minds dreadfully. We felt our inexperience, and were unable to help ourselves. We should have been at her mercy, if she had had any; but she was a remorseless woman, and had none. She was the cause of our first little quarrel.

"My dearest life," I said one day to Dora, "do you think Mary Anne has any idea of time?"

"Why, Doady?" inquired Dora, looking up, innocently, from her drawing.

"My love, because it's five, and we were to have dined at four."

Dora glanced wistfully at the clock, and hinted that she thought it was too fast.

"On the contrary, my love," said I, referring to my watch, "it's a few minutes too slow."

My little wife came and sat upon my knee, to coax me to be quiet, and drew a line with her pencil down the middle of my nose; but I couldn't dine off that, though it was very agreeable.

"Don't you think, my dear," said I, "it would be better for you to remonstrate with Mary Anne?"

"Oh no, please! I couldn't, Doady!" said Dora.

"Why not, my love?" I gently asked.

"Oh, because I am such a little goose," said Dora, "and she knows I am!"

---

4   Parliamentary debate that, like the younger Dickens, he was covering as a reporter.
5   Mrs Crupp is their landlady.

I thought this sentiment so incompatible with the establishment of any system of check on Mary Anne, that I frowned a little.

"Oh, what ugly wrinkles in my bad boy's forehead!" said Dora, and still being on my knee, she traced them with her pencil; putting it to her rosy lips to make it mark blacker, and working at my forehead with a quaint little mockery of being industrious, that quite delighted me in spite of myself.

"There's a good child," said Dora, "it makes its face so much prettier to laugh."

"But, my love," said I.

"No, no! please!" cried Dora, with a kiss, "don't be a naughty Blue Beard! Don't be serious!"

"My precious wife," said I, "we must be serious sometimes. Come! Sit down on this chair, close beside me! Give me the pencil! There! Now let us talk sensibly. You know, dear;" what a little hand it was to hold, and what a tiny wedding-ring it was to see! "You know, my love, it is not exactly comfortable to have to go out without one's dinner. Now, is it?"

"N—n—no!" replied Dora, faintly.

"My love, how you tremble!"

"Because I KNOW you're going to scold me," exclaimed Dora, in a piteous voice.

"My sweet, I am only going to reason."

"Oh, but reasoning is worse than scolding!" exclaimed Dora, in despair. "I didn't marry to be reasoned with. If you meant to reason with such a poor little thing as I am, you ought to have told me so, you cruel boy!"

I tried to pacify Dora, but she turned away her face, and shook her curls from side to side, and said "You cruel, cruel boy!" so many times, that I really did not exactly know what to do: so I took a few turns up and down the room in my uncertainty, and came back again.

"Dora, my darling!"

"No, I am not your darling. Because you *must* be sorry that you married me, or else you wouldn't reason with me!" returned Dora.

I felt so injured by the inconsequential nature of this charge, that it gave me courage to be grave.

"Now, my own Dora," said I, "you are very childish, and are talking nonsense. You must remember, I am sure, that I was obliged to go out yesterday when dinner was half over; and that, the day before, I was made quite unwell by being obliged to eat underdone veal in a hurry; today, I don't dine at all—and I am afraid to say how long we waited for breakfast—and *then* the water didn't boil. I don't mean to reproach you, my dear, but this is not comfortable."

"Oh, you cruel, cruel boy, to say I am a disagreeable wife!" cried Dora.

"Now, my dear Dora, you must know that I never said that!"

"You said I wasn't comfortable!" said Dora.

"I said the housekeeping was not comfortable."

"It's exactly the same thing!" cried Dora. And she evidently thought so, for she wept most grievously.

I took another turn across the room, full of love for my pretty wife, and distracted by self-accusatory inclinations to knock my head against the door. I sat down again, and said:

"I am not blaming you, Dora. We have both a great deal to learn. I am only trying to show you, my dear, that you must—you really must" (I was resolved not to give this up) "accustom yourself to look after Mary Anne. Likewise to act a little for yourself, and me."

"I wonder, I do, at your making such ungrateful speeches," sobbed Dora. "When you know that the other day, when you said you would like a little bit of fish, I went out myself, miles and miles, and ordered it, to surprise you."

"And it was very kind of you, my own darling," said I. "I felt it so much that I wouldn't on any account have even mentioned that you bought a Salmon—which was too much for two. Or that it cost one pound six—which was more than we can afford."

"You enjoyed it very much," sobbed Dora. "And you said I was a Mouse."

"And I'll say it again, my love," I returned, "a thousand times!"

But I had wounded Dora's soft little heart, and she was not to be comforted. She was so pathetic in her sobbing and bewailing, that I felt as if I had said I don't know what to hurt her. I was obliged to hurry away; I was miserable. I had the conscience of an assassin, and was haunted by a vague sense of enormous wickedness.

[. . .]

"Will you call me a name I want you to call me?" enquired Dora, without moving.

"What is it?" I asked with a smile.

"It's a stupid name," she said, shaking her curls for a moment. "Child-wife."

I laughingly asked my child-wife what her fancy was in desiring to be so called? She answered without moving, otherwise than as the arm I twined about her may have brought her blue eyes nearer to me:

"I don't mean, you silly fellow, that you should use the name, instead of Dora. I only mean that you should think of me that way. When you are going to be angry with me, say to yourself, 'it's only my child-wife!' When I am very disappointing, say 'I knew, a long time ago, that she would make but a child-wife!' When you miss what I should like to be, and I think can never be, say, 'still my foolish child-wife loves me!' For indeed I do."

[. . .]

This appeal of Dora's made a strong impression on me. I look back on the time I write of; I invoke the innocent figure that I dearly loved, to come out from the mists and shadows of the past, and turn its gentle head towards me once again; and I can still declare that this one little speech was constantly in my memory. I may not have used it to the best account; I was young and inexperienced; but I never turned a deaf ear to its artless pleading.

[. . .]

I was a boyish husband as to years. I had known the softening influence of no other sorrows or experiences than those recorded in these leaves. If I did any wrong, as I may have done much, I did it in mistaken love, and in my want of wisdom. I write the exact truth. It would avail me nothing to extenuate it now.

Thus it was that I took upon myself the toils and cares of our life, and had no partner in them. We lived much as before, in reference to our scrambling household arrangements; but I had got used to those, and Dora I was pleased to see was seldom vexed now. She was bright and cheerful in the old childish way, loved me dearly, and was happy with her old trifles.

CHAPTER 48
DOMESTIC

THE old unhappy feeling pervaded my life. It was deepened, if it were changed at all; but it was as undefined as ever, and addressed me like a strain of sorrowful music faintly heard in the night. I loved my wife dearly, and I was happy; but the happiness I had vaguely anticipated, once, was not the happiness I enjoyed, and there was always something wanting.

In fulfilment of the compact I have made with myself, to reflect my mind on this paper, I again examine it, closely, and bring its secrets to the light. What I missed, I still regarded—I always regarded—as something that had been a dream of my youthful fancy; that was incapable of realisation; that I was now discovering to be so, with some natural pain, as all men did. But, that it would have been better for me if my wife could have helped me more, and shared the many thoughts in which I had no partner; and that this might have been; I knew.

Between these two irreconcilable conclusions: the one, that what I felt was general and unavoidable; the other, that it was particular to me, and might have been different: I balanced curiously, with no distinct sense of their opposition to each other. When I thought of the airy dreams of youth that are incapable of realisation, I thought of the better state preceding manhood that I had outgrown; and then the contented days with Agnes, in the dear old house, arose before me, like spectres of the dead, that might have some renewal in another world, but never, never more could be reanimated here.

Sometimes, the speculation came into my thoughts, What might have happened, or what would have happened, if Dora and I had never known each other? But, she was so incorporated with my existence, that it was the idlest of all fancies, and would soon rise out of my reach and sight, like gossamer floating in the air.

I always loved her. What I am describing, slumbered, and half awoke, and slept again, in the innermost recesses of my mind. There was no evidence of it in me; I know of no influence it had in anything I said or did. I bore the weight of all our little cares, and all my projects; Dora held the pens; and we both felt that our shares were adjusted as the case required. She was truly fond of me, and proud of me; and when Agnes wrote a few earnest words in her letters to Dora, of the pride and interest with which my old friends heard of my growing reputation, and read my book as if they heard me speaking its contents, Dora read them out to me with tears of joy in her bright eyes, and said I was a dear old clever, famous boy.

"The first mistaken impulse of an undisciplined heart." Those words of Mrs.

Strong's were constantly recurring to me, at this time;[6] were almost always present to my mind. I awoke with them, often, in the night; I remember to have even read them, in dreams, inscribed upon the walls of houses. For I knew, now, that my own heart was undisciplined when it first loved Dora; and that if it had been disciplined, it never could have felt, when we were married, what it had felt in its secret experience.

"There can be no disparity in marriage, like unsuitability of mind and purpose." Those words I remembered too. I had endeavoured to adapt Dora to myself, and found it impracticable. It remained for me to adapt myself to Dora; to share with her what I could, and be happy; to bear on my own shoulders what I must, and be happy still. This was the discipline to which I tried to bring my heart, when I began to think. It made my second year much happier than my first; and, what was better still, made Dora's life all sunshine.

16 Em'ly's Return

One of the novel's more melodramatic moments comes when Em'ly has returned to England and is confronted by the angry Rosa Dartle, who berates her for the shame she has brought on the Steerforth family. Rosa's ire may be motivated by the fact that it was Em'ly and not she who had so attracted Steerforth. Rosa's is a demented passion; but it is also expressive of her pride of class, claiming falsely that Em'ly's family had 'sold' her to Steerforth. Through this encounter Dickens deepens the characterizations of Rosa as a spurned and jealous woman and of Em'ly as, in Rosa's eyes, the poor girl gone wrong because she desired to be a lady. David, uncharacteristically passive in this instance, makes excuses to himself that Mr Peggotty, whose arrival he awaits, should be the one to intervene and rescue Em'ly. David's anxiety and fascination are evident as he eavesdrops on Rosa's harsh denunciation of Em'ly. The chapter ends with the successful conclusion to Mr Peggotty's long search for Em'ly. But here, as earlier when he had first learned that Em'ly had gone off with Steerforth, David is powerless to act, and as narrator he adds no clarification as to why. Rosa will return to the proud Steerforth house, and Daniel will take both Em'ly and Martha off to a new life in Australia, and thus it is Daniel, and not David, who becomes the hero of this part of David's life. The plight of the fallen woman is well described in Dickens's own 'appeal' in Contemporary Documents (**pp. 22–3**), and commented on by Welsh, Poovey and also by Leavis, who notes Dickens's great success in portraying the psychological and moral nature of Daniel Peggotty, whose persistent efforts to restore Em'ly to her family finally succeed (**pp. 47–9, 59–62** and **66–7**).

---

6   Annie Strong, the young wife of David's Canterbury schoolmaster, has resisted the temptation to love an attractive young man, and her self-judgement of her near error as the mistaken impulse of an undisciplined heart is a lesson David adapts to his own situation with Dora. Some modern critics see this as the self-recognition essential and beneficial to his maturity, but this reading has been challenged by Kincaid (**p. 50**).

CHAPTER 50
MR. PEGGOTTY'S DREAM COMES TRUE

WE proceeded to the top-story of the house. Two or three times, by the way, I thought I observed in the indistinct light the skirts of a female figure going up before us. As we turned to ascend the last flight of stairs between us and the roof, we caught a full view of this figure pausing for a moment, at a door. Then it turned the handle and went in.

"What's this!" said Martha,[1] in a whisper. "She has gone into my room. I don't know her!"

I knew her. I had recognized her with amazement, for Miss Dartle.

I said something to the effect that it was a lady whom I had seen before, in a few words, to my conductress; and had scarcely done so, when we heard her voice in the room, though not, from where we stood, what she was saying. Martha, with an astonished look, repeated her former action, and softly led me up the stairs; and then, by a little back door which seemed to have no lock, and which she pushed open with a touch, into a small empty garret with a low sloping roof: little better than a cupboard. Between this, and the room she had called hers, there was a small door of communication, standing partly open. Here we stopped, breathless with our ascent, and she placed her hand lightly on my lips. I could only see, of the room beyond, that it was pretty large; that there was a bed in it; and that there were some common pictures of ships upon the walls. I could not see Miss Dartle, or the person we had heard her address. Certainly, my companion could not, for my position was the best.

A dead silence prevailed for some moments. Martha kept one hand on my lips, and raised the other in a listening attitude.

"It matters little to me her not being at home," said Rosa Dartle, haughtily, "I know nothing of her. It is you I come to see."

"Me?" replied a soft voice.

At the sound of it, a thrill went through my frame. For it was Emily's!

"Yes," returned Miss Dartle, "I have come to look at you. What? You are not ashamed of the face that has done so much?"

The resolute and unrelenting hatred of her tone, its cold stern sharpness, and its mastered rage, presented her before me, as if I had seen her standing in the light. I saw the flashing black eyes, and the passion-wasted figure; and I saw the scar,[2] with its white track cutting through her lips, quivering and throbbing as she spoke.

"I have come to see," she said, "James Steerforth's fancy; the girl who ran away with him, and is the town-talk of the commonest people of her native place; the bold, flaunting, practised companion of persons like James Steerforth. I want to know what such a thing is like."

There was a rustle, as if the unhappy girl, on whom she heaped these taunts, ran

---

1   Martha Endell, a long-time friend of Emily's and now a prostitute, owes much gratitude to David and Mr Peggotty whose timely intervention prevented her from drowning herself.
2   This scar on her face was from a blow Steerforth had struck her years earlier.

towards the door, and the speaker swiftly interposed herself before it. It was succeeded by a moment's pause.

When Miss Dartle spoke again, it was through her set teeth, and with a stamp upon the ground.

"Stay there!" she said, "or I'll proclaim you to the house, and the whole street! If you try to evade *me*, I'll stop you, if it's by the hair, and raise the very stones against you!"

A frightened murmur was the only reply that reached my ears. A silence succeeded. I did not know what to do. Much as I desired to put an end to the interview, I felt I had no right to present myself; that it was for Mr. Peggotty alone to see her and recover her. Would he never come? I thought impatiently.

[. . .]

"Oh, have some mercy on me!" cried Emily. "Show me some compassion, or I shall die mad!"

"It would be no great penance," said Rosa Dartle, "for your crimes. Do you know what you have done? Do you ever think of the home you have laid waste?"

"Oh, is there ever night or day, when I don't think of it!" cried Emily; and now I could just see her, on her knees, with her head thrown back, her pale face looking upward, her hands wildly clasped and held out, and her hair streaming about her. "Has there ever been a single minute, waking or sleeping, when it hasn't been before me, just as it used to be in the lost days when I turned my back upon it for ever and for ever! Oh, home, home! Oh dear, dear uncle, if you ever could have known the agony your love would cause me when I fell away from the good, you never would have shown it to me so constant, much as you felt it; but would have been angry to me, at least once in my life, that I might have had some comfort! I have none, none, no comfort upon the earth, for all of them were always fond of me!" She dropped on her face, before the imperious figure in the chair, with an imploring effort to clasp the skirt of her dress.

Rosa Dartle sat looking down upon her, as inflexible as a figure of brass. Her lips were tightly compressed, as if she knew that she must keep a strong constraint upon herself—I write what I sincerely believe—or she would be tempted to strike the beautiful form with her foot. I saw her countenance, distinctly, and the whole power of her face and character seemed forced into that expression.—Would he Never come?

"The miserable vanity of these earth-worms!" she said, when she had so far controlled the angry heavings of her breast, that she could trust herself to speak. "*Your* home! Do you imagine that I bestow a thought on it, or suppose you could do any harm to that low place, which money would not pay for, and handsomely? *Your* home! You were a part of the trade of your home, and were bought and sold like any other vendible thing your people dealt in."[3]

[. . .]

_____
3   Rosa is talking about Steerforth's home; Emily's concern is for her former home with the Peggottys.

"I am of a strange nature, perhaps," Rosa Dartle went on; "but I can't breathe freely in the air you breathe. I find it sickly. Therefore, I will have it cleared; I will have it purified of you. If you live here to-morrow, I'll have your story and your character proclaimed on the common stair. [. . .] If, leaving here, you seek any refuge in this town in any character but your true one (which you are welcome to bear, without molestation from me), the same service shall be done you, if I hear of your retreat. [. . .]

Would he never, never come? How long was I to bear this? How long could I bear it?

"Oh me, oh me!" exclaimed the wretched Emily, in a tone that might have touched the hardest heart, I should have thought; but there was no relenting in Rosa Dartle's smile. "What, what, shall I do!"

"Do?" returned the other. "Live happy in your own reflections! Consecrate your existence to the recollection of James Steerforth's tenderness—he would have made you his serving-man's wife, would he not?—or to feeling grateful to the upright and deserving creature who would have taken you as his gift. Or, if those proud remembrances, and the consciousness of your own virtues, and the honourable position to which they have raised you in the eyes of everything that wears the human shape, will not sustain you, marry that good man, and be happy in his condescension. If this will not do either, die! There are doorways and dust-heaps for such deaths, and such despair—find one, and take your flight to Heaven!"

I heard a distant foot upon the stairs. I knew it, I was certain. It was his, thank God!

She moved slowly from before the door when she said this, and passed out of my sight.

"But mark!" she added, slowly and sternly, opening the other door to go away. "I am resolved, for reasons that I have and hatreds that I entertain, to cast you out, unless you withdraw from my reach altogether, or drop your pretty mask. This is what I had to say; and what I say, I mean to do!"

The foot upon the stairs came nearer—nearer—passed her as she went down—rushed into the room!

"Uncle!"

A fearful cry followed the word. I paused a moment, and looking in, saw him supporting her insensible figure in his arms. He gazed at me for a few seconds in the face, then stooped to kiss it—oh, how tenderly!—and drew a handkerchief before it.

"Mas'r Davy," he said, in a low tremulous voice, when it was covered. "I thank my Heav'nly Father as my dream's come true! I thank Him hearty for having guided of me, in His own ways, to my darling!"

With these words he took her up in his arms; and, with the veiled face lying on his bosom, and addressed towards his own, carried her, motionless and unconscious, down the stairs.

17 Heep Unmasked

In Chapter 52, which was part of the seventeenth monthly instalment, the multiple story lines draw towards their conclusions; the previous part dealt with the return of Em'ly and her reunion with her uncle, and in it David learned also of new troubles for the Micawbers. Mrs Micawber, frequently proclaiming that she would never desert her husband, expressed the strength of their ever-expanding love and family. Now working for Uriah Heep, Micawber himself is newly serious, and Mrs Micawber misreads change in demeanour as some vague threat to their marriage. But Micawber soon proves himself the most rhetorical of whistle-blowers. His 'explosion' of Heep's schemes is one of the novel's great comic moments. In terms of plot, Micawber rescues the Wickfields and also Betsey and Mr Dick from Heep's power over their persons and property. As comic characterization, the scene represents the triumph of Micawber's *joie de vivre*. Nowhere in Dickens is ridiculous overstatement so wonderfully employed; Micawber's denunciation of Heep is the triumph of the word. His story logically finishes (although in later chapters less plausibly extends to later great successes as a magistrate in Australia) with the flourish of his finest moment before the company he assembles to expose Heep. Unrepentant, Heep sees himself the victim of the 'precious set of people' above him. Emigration or escape is not a possibility for such villainy, and Heep's last appearance in the novel is as 'model prisoner', confined with Steerforth's former valet, Littimer (Chapter 61, 'I Am Shown Two Interesting Penitents', is not included in these *David Copperfield* extracts). See, for modern critical discussion of this comic climax, Kincaid (**pp. 49–52**), for Micawber as a version of the writer, Welsh (**pp. 65–6**). Poovey (**pp. 61–2**) suggests a rationale, which is scant defence, for Uriah's claims to innocence.

CHAPTER 52
I ASSIST AT AN EXPLOSION

Mr. MICAWBER, with his hand upon the ruler in his breast, stood erect before the door, most unmistakably contemplating one of his fellow-men, and that man his employer.

"What are you waiting for?" said Uriah. "Micawber: did you hear me tell you not to wait?"

"Yes!" replied the immovable Mr. Micawber.

"Then why *do* you wait?" said Uriah.

"Because I—in short choose," replied Mr. Micawber, with a burst.

Uriah's cheeks lost colour, and an unwholesome paleness, still faintly tinged by his pervading red, overspread them. He looked at Mr. Micawber attentively, with his whole face breathing short and quick in every feature.

"You are a dissipated fellow, as all the world knows," he said, with an effort at a smile, "and I am afraid you'll oblige me to get rid of you. Go along! I'll talk to you presently."

"If there is a scoundrel on this earth," said Mr. Micawber, suddenly breaking out again with the utmost vehemence, "with whom I have already talked too much, that scoundrel's name is—HEEP!"

Uriah fell back, as if he had been struck or stung. Looking slowly round upon us with the darkest and wickedest expression that his face could wear, he said, in a lower voice:

"Oho! This is a conspiracy! You have met here, by appointment! You are playing Booty with my clerk, are you, Copperfield? Now, take care. You'll make nothing of this. We understand each other, you and me. There's no love between us. You were always a puppy with a proud stomach, from your first coming here; and you envy me my rise, do you? None of your plots against me; I'll counterplot you! Micawber, you be off. I'll talk to you presently."

"Mr. Micawber," said I, "there is a sudden change in this fellow, in more respects than the extraordinary one of his speaking the truth in one particular, which assures me that he is brought to bay. Deal with him as he deserves!"

"You are a precious set of people, ain't you?" said Uriah, in the same low voice, and breaking out into a clammy heat, which he wiped from his forehead, with his long lean hand, "to buy over my clerk, who is the very scum of society,—as you yourself were, Copperfield, you know it, before any one had charity on you,—to defame me with his lies? [. . .]

[. . .]

"Ury——!" Mrs. Heep began, with an anxious gesture.

"You hold your tongue, mother," he returned; "least said, soonest mended."

"But my Ury——"

"Will you hold your tongue, mother, and leave it to me?"

Though I had long known that his servility was false, and all his pretences knavish and hollow, I had had no adequate conception of the extent of his hypocrisy, until I now saw him with his mask off. The suddenness with which he dropped it, when he perceived that it was useless to him; the malice, insolence, and hatred, he revealed; the leer with which he exulted, even at this moment, in the evil he had done—all this time being desperate too, and at his wits' end for the means of getting the better of us—though perfectly consistent with the experience I had of him, at first took even me by surprise, who had known him so long, and disliked him so heartily.

I say nothing of the look he conferred on me, as he stood eyeing us, one after another; for I had always understood that he hated me, and I remembered the marks of my hand upon his cheek. But when his eyes passed on to Agnes, and I saw the rage with which he felt his power over her slipping away, and the exhibition, in their disappointment, of the odious passions that had led him to aspire to one whose virtues he could never appreciate or care for, I was shocked by the mere thought of her having lived, an hour, within sight of such a man.

After some rubbing of the lower part of his face, and some looking at us with those bad eyes, over his grisly fingers, he made one more address to me, half whining, and half abusive.

"You think it justifiable, do you, Copperfield, you who pride yourself so much on your honour and all the rest of it, to sneak about my place, eavesdropping with my clerk? If it had been *me*, I shouldn't have wondered; for I don't make myself out a gentleman (though I never was in the streets either, as you were, according to Micawber), but being *you*!—And you're not afraid of doing this, either? You don't think at all of what I shall do, in return; or of getting yourself into trouble for conspiracy and so forth? Very well. We shall see! Mr. What's-your-name, you were going to refer some question to Micawber. There's your referee. Why don't you make him speak? He has learned his lesson, I see."

Seeing that what he said had no effect on me or any of us, he sat on the edge of his table with his hands in his pockets, and one of his splay feet twisted round the other leg, waiting doggedly for what might follow.

Mr. Micawber, whose impetuosity I had restrained thus far with the greatest difficulty, and who had repeatedly interposed with the first syllable of SCOUN-drel! without getting to the second, now burst forward, drew the ruler from his breast (apparently as a defensive weapon), and produced from his pocket a fools-cap document, folded in the form of a large letter. Opening this packet, with his old flourish, and glancing at the contents, as if he cherished an artistic admiration of their style of composition, he began to read as follows:

" 'Dear Miss Trotwood and gentlemen——' "

"Bless and save the man!" exclaimed my aunt in a low voice. "He'd write letters by the ream, if it was a capital offence!"

Mr. Micawber, without hearing her, went on.

" 'In appearing before you to denounce probably the most consummate Villain that has ever existed,' " Mr. Micawber, without looking off the letter, pointed the ruler, like a ghostly truncheon, at Uriah Heep, " 'I ask no consideration for myself. The victim, from my cradle, of pecuniary liabilities to which I have been unable to respond, I have ever been the sport and toy of debasing circumstances. Ignominy, Want, Despair, and Madness, have, collectively or separately, been the attendants of my career.' "

The relish with which Mr. Micawber described himself, as a prey to these dismal calamities, was only to be equalled by the emphasis with which he read his letter; and the kind of homage he rendered to it with a roll of his head, when he thought he had hit a sentence very hard indeed.

" 'In an accumulation of Ignominy, Want, Despair, and Madness, I entered the office—or, as our lively neighbour the Gaul would term it, the Bureau—of the Firm, nominally conducted under the appellation of Wickfield and—HEEP, but, in reality, wielded by—HEEP alone. HEEP, and only HEEP, is the mainspring of that machine. HEEP, and only HEEP, is the Forger and the Cheat.' "

Uriah, more blue than white at these words, made a dart at the letter, as if to tear it in pieces. Mr. Micawber, with a perfect miracle of dexterity or luck, caught his advancing knuckles with the ruler, and disabled his right hand. It dropped at the wrist, as if it were broken. The blow sounded as if it had fallen on wood.

"The Devil take you!" said Uriah, writhing in a new way with pain. "I'll be even with you."

"Approach me again, you—you—you Heep of infamy," gasped Mr. Micawber, "and if your head is human, I'll break it. Come on, come on!"

I think I never saw anything more ridiculous—I was sensible of it, even at the time—than Mr. Micawber making broadsword guards with the ruler, and crying, "Come on!" while Traddles and I pushed him back into a corner, from which, as often as we got him into it, he persisted in emerging again.

[. . .]

" 'I have now concluded. It merely remains for me to substantiate these accusations; and then, with my ill-starred family, to disappear from the landscape on which we appear to be an incumbrance. That is soon done. It may be reasonably inferred that our baby will first expire of inanition, as being the frailest member of our circle; and that our twins will follow next in order. So be it! For myself, my Canterbury Pilgrimage[1] has done much; imprisonment on civil process, and want, will soon do more. I trust that the labour and hazard of an investigation—of which the smallest results have been slowly pieced together, in the pressure of arduous avocations, under grinding penurious apprehensions, at rise of morn, at dewy eve, in the shadows of night, under the watchful eye of one whom it were superfluous to call Demon—combined with the struggle of parental Poverty to turn it, when completed, to the right account, may be as the sprinkling of a few drops of sweet water on my funereal pyre. I ask no more. Let it be, in justice, merely said of me, as of a gallant and eminent naval Hero, with whom I have no pretensions to cope, that what I have done, I did, in despite of mercenary and selfish objects,

"For England, home, and beauty."
" 'Remaining always, &c., &c., WILKINS MICAWBER.' "

Much affected, but still intensely enjoying himself, Mr Micawber folded up his letter, and handed it with a bow to my aunt, as something she might like to keep.

18 Death of Dora

Present-tense narration for sustained passages of recollection by David is a distinctive stylistic feature of this novel; Chapter 53 is one of four chapters (with 18, 43 and 64, which is the final chapter) that bring forward past to

---

1 Micawber speaks facetiously of his having gone to Canterbury not as a traditional religious pilgrim to seek spiritual comfort at the Cathedral but rather to have had purely practical motives and outcomes.

present to emphasize both David's process of remembering and the lasting emotional impact of earlier events in his life. By so visualizing David's 'here-and-now' which is the moment of his writing, the present-tense retrospect passages provide readers with an immediacy of voice that harmonizes with the visual immediacy of this accompanying illustration (Figure 5). Here, as in earlier extracts featuring illustrations, we again find an observer built into the picture; this time it is Agnes Wickfield, standing behind David. Beside her and also out of his, but not our, sight is the portrait of Dora. She herself is on her deathbed, but the focus here is on the desolate David, feeling his grief, but with comfort closer than he can yet realize.

Deathbed scenes are frequent and often overwrought in Victorian fiction, particularly in Dickens; but here there is considerable restraint. Readers later learn that Dora had given advisory last words separately to both David and Agnes, but here David is not yet looking towards Agnes, who later moves to the centre of his life (see Figure 6, **p. 162**). We, however, see the background and can read its various consolatory images – the prominence of the cross through the window, the open door, and the patient and prayerful Agnes, and the placid portrait of Dora – as a sequence of eternity, nearer future and remembered young love. Thus the illustration effectively captures the linked relationships of Dora and Agnes, and, more generally, it displays David's failure to yet comprehend his dependency on all the women who love him. For further discussion of these points see Welsh and Poovey (**pp. 66–8** and **59–62**); for commentary on the illustrations, see Lutman (**pp. 68–70**).

CHAPTER 53
ANOTHER RETROSPECT

I MUST pause yet once again. O, my child-wife, there is a figure in the moving crowd before my memory, quiet and still, saying in its innocent love and childish beauty, Stop to think of me—turn to look upon the little blossom, as it flutters to the ground!

I do. All else grows dim, and fades away. I am again with Dora, in our cottage. I do not know how long she has been ill. I am so used to it in feeling, that I cannot count the time. It is not really long, in weeks or months; but, in my usage and experience, it is a weary, weary while.

[. . .]

"Oh, how my poor boy cries! Hush, hush! Now, make me one promise. I want to speak to Agnes. When you go down stairs, tell Agnes so, and send her up to me; and while I speak to her, let no one come—not even aunt. I want to speak to Agnes by herself. I want to speak to Agnes, quite alone."

I promise that she shall, immediately; but I cannot leave her, for my grief.

"I said that it was better as it is!" she whispers, as she holds me in her arms.

Figure 5 My Child-Wife's Old Companion.

"Oh, Doady, after more years, you never could have loved your child-wife better than you do; and, after more years, she would so have tried and disappointed you, that you might not have been able to love her half so well! I know I was too young and foolish. It is much better as it is!"

Agnes is down stairs, when I go into the parlour; and I give her the message. She disappears, leaving me alone with Jip.

His Chinese house is by the fire; and he lies within it, on his bed of flannel, querulously trying to sleep. The bright moon is high and clear. As I look out on the night, my tears fall fast, and my undisciplined heart is chastened heavily—heavily.

I sit down by the fire thinking with a blind remorse of all those secret feelings I have nourished since my marriage. I think of every little trifle between me and Dora, and feel the truth, that trifles make the sum of life. Ever rising from the sea of my remembrance, is the image of the dear child as I knew her first, graced by my young love, and by her own, with every fascination wherein such love is rich. Would it, indeed, have been better if we had loved each other as a boy and girl, and forgotten it? Undisciplined heart, reply!

How the time wears, I know not; until I am recalled by my child-wife's old companion. More restless than he was, he crawls out of his house, and looks at me, and wanders to the door, and whines to go up-stairs.

"Not to-night, Jip! Not to-night!"

He comes very slowly back to me, licks my hand, and lifts his dim eyes to my face.

"Oh, Jip! It may be, never again!"

He lies down at my feet, stretches himself out as if to sleep, and with a plaintive cry, is dead.

"Oh, Agnes! Look, look, here!"

—That face, so full of pity and of grief, that rain of tears, that awful mute appeal to me, that solemn hand upraised towards Heaven![1]

"Agnes?"

It is over. Darkness comes before my eyes; and, for a time, all things are blotted out of my remembrance.

19 The Storm Scene

Through depiction of great storm and turmoil in external nature to illustrate the wrath of gods or to picture it as simply naturalistic and inexplicable, artists often register the turmoil of a troubled human mind in relation to great storms in nature. As two cases in point, there are the literal and figurative storms that

---

1   Clearly he is thinking either of Dora as he last saw her, or now imagines her, or (possibly) as he later comes to regard Agnes. Whatever the frame of reference, it explicitly presents the concept of the 'angel in the house' as a Victorian ideal of womanhood (see pp. 10–11).

Shakespeare's King Lear suffers, and the magnificent sea storms in which the Victorian painter J. M. W. Turner embroils water and sky and drowning people in swirling, kinetic colour.[1] Certainly the tempest in *David Copperfield* can be read in a number of ways. To the story line it is the event ending the story of Steerforth, retribution made tragic by the sacrifice of Ham Peggotty's life in a rescue effort, an act of heroism that David watches from the shore. Less obvious to us, but more evident to contemporary readers, is the fact that shipwrecks were frequent and their economic impact widespread (see **pp. 52–5**). David had prepared his readers for the intensity of this chapter when writing in Chapter 31 (**pp. 127–9**) about the disappearance of Em'ly from Yarmouth; this tempest is the looming dark cloud over his later life. Even in his blissful period with Dora, David had been restless and ill at ease (Chapters 43, 48). But nothing before the storm scene troubles him so greatly, and 'Tempest' (titled, pointedly, without any qualifying 'A' or 'The') is the storm in his mind, driving his pen as he writes this chapter. To the ongoing story of Dickens, this presages the increasing restlessness of his later life, the often-noted 'dark Dickens'. Unsurprisingly, this event was the climax of the dramatic reading Dickens later made of his novel (see **pp. 71–3**).

CHAPTER 55
TEMPEST

I NOW approach an event in my life, so indelible, so awful, so bound by an infinite variety of ties to all that has preceded it, in these pages, that, from the beginning of my narrative, I have seen it growing larger and larger as I advanced, like a great tower in a plain, and throwing its fore-cast shadow even on the incidents of my childish days.

For years after it occurred, I dreamed of it often. I have started up so vividly impressed by it, that its fury has yet seemed raging in my quiet room, in the still night. I dream of it sometimes, though at lengthened and uncertain intervals, to this hour. I have an association between it and a stormy wind, or the lightest mention of a sea-shore, as strong as any of which my mind is conscious. As plainly as I behold what happened, I will try to write it down. I do not recall it, but see it done; for it happens again before me.

[. . .]

"Don't you think that," I asked the coachman, in the first stage out of London, "a very remarkable sky? I don't remember to have seen one like it."

---

1   The storm is in *King Lear*, III, iii; a representative Turner painting is 'Snow-Storm – Steam Boat off a Harbour's Mouth' (1842); it 'demonstrates the puniness of man's creations in the face of the forces of nature', *Turner 1775–1851* (London: Tate Gallery, 1975), p. 126.

"Nor I—not equal to it," he replied. "That's wind, Sir. There'll be mischief done at sea, I expect, before long."

It was a murky confusion—here and there blotted with a colour like the colour of the smoke from damp fuel—of flying clouds tossed up into most remarkable heaps, suggesting greater heights in the clouds than there were depths below them to the bottom of the deepest hollows in the earth, through which the wild moon seemed to plunge headlong, as if, in a dread disturbance of the laws of nature, she had lost her way and were frightened. There had been a wind all day; and it was rising then, with an extraordinary great sound. In another hour it had much increased, and the sky was more overcast, and blew hard.

But as the night advanced, the clouds closing in and densely overspreading the whole sky, then very dark, it came on to blow, harder and harder. It still increased, until our horses could scarcely face the wind. Many times, in the dark part of the night (it was then late in September, when the nights were not short), the leaders turned about, or came to a dead stop; and we were often in serious apprehension that the coach would be blown over. Sweeping gusts of rain came up before this storm, like showers of steel; and, at those times, when there was any shelter of trees or lee walls to be got, we were fain to stop, in a sheer impossibility of continuing the struggle.

When the day broke, it blew harder and harder. I had been in Yarmouth when the seamen said it blew great guns, but I had never known the like of this, or anything approaching to it. [. . .]

[. . .]

The tremendous sea itself, when I could find sufficient pause to look at it, in the agitation of the blinding wind, the flying stones and sand, and the awful noise, confounded me. As the high watery walls came rolling in, and, at their highest, tumbled into surf, they looked as if the least would engulf the town. As the receding wave swept back with a hoarse roar, it seemed to scoop out deep caves in the beach, as if its purpose were to undermine the earth. When some white-headed billows thundered on, and dashed themselves to pieces before they reached the land, every fragment of the late whole seemed possessed by the full might of its wrath, rushing to be gathered to the composition of another monster. Undulating hills were changed to valleys, undulating valleys (with a solitary storm-bird sometimes skimming through them) were lifted up to hills; masses of water shivered and shook the beach with a booming sound; every shape tumultuously rolled on, as soon as made, to change its shape and place, and beat another shape and place away; the ideal shore on the horizon, with its towers and buildings, rose and fell; the clouds flew fast and thick; I seemed to see a rending and upheaving of all nature.

[. . .]

The thunder of the cannon was so loud and incessant, that I could not hear something I much desired to hear, until I made a great exertion and awoke. It was broad day—eight or nine o'clock; the storm raging, in lieu of the batteries; and some one knocking and calling at my door.

"What is the matter?" I cried.

"A wreck! Close by!"

I sprang out of bed, and asked, what wreck?

"A schooner, from Spain or Portugal, laden with fruit and wine. Make haste, Sir, if you want to see her! It's thought, down on the beach, she'll go to pieces every moment."

The excited voice went clamouring along the staircase; and I wrapped myself in my clothes as quickly as I could, and ran into the street.

Numbers of people were there before me, all running in one direction, to the beach. I ran the same way, outstripping a good many, and soon came facing the wild sea.

The wind might by this time have lulled a little, though not more sensibly than if the cannonading I had dreamed of, had been diminished by the silencing of half-a-dozen guns out of hundreds. But, the sea, having upon it the additional agitation of the whole night, was infinitely more terrific than when I had seen it last. Every appearance it had then presented, bore the expression of being *swelled*; and the height to which the breakers rose, and, looking over one another, bore one another down, and rolled in, in interminable hosts, was most appalling.

In the difficulty of hearing anything but wind and waves, and in the crowd, and the unspeakable confusion, and my first breathless efforts to stand against the weather, I was so confused that I looked out to sea for the wreck, and saw nothing but the foaming heads of the great waves. A half-dressed boatman, standing next me, pointed with his bare arm (a tattoo'd arrow on it, pointing in the same direction) to the left. Then, O great Heaven, I saw it, close in upon us!

One mast was broken short off, six or eight feet from the deck, and lay over the side, entangled in a maze of sail and rigging; and all that ruin, as the ship rolled and beat—which she did without a moment's pause, and with a violence quite inconceivable—beat the side as if it would stave it in. Some efforts were even then being made, to cut this portion of the wreck away; for, as the ship, which was broadside on, turned towards us in her rolling, I plainly descried her people at work with axes, especially one active figure with long curling hair, conspicuous among the rest. But, a great cry, which was audible even above the wind and water, rose from the shore at this moment; the sea, sweeping over the rolling wreck, made a clean breach, and carried men, spars, casks, planks, bulwarks, heaps of such toys, into the boiling surge.

The second mast was yet standing, with the rags of a rent sail, and a wild confusion of broken cordage flapping to and fro. The ship had struck once, the same boatman hoarsely said in my ear, and then lifted in and struck again. I understood him to add that she was parting amidships, and I could readily suppose so, for the rolling and beating were too tremendous for any human work to suffer long. As he spoke, there was another great cry of pity from the beach; four men arose with the wreck out of the deep, clinging to the rigging of the remaining mast; uppermost, the active figure with the curling hair.

There was a bell on board; and as the ship rolled and dashed, like a desperate creature driven mad, now showing us the whole sweep of her deck, as she turned on her beam-ends towards the shore, now nothing but her keel, as she sprang wildly over and turned towards the sea, the bell rang; and its sound, the knell of those unhappy men, was borne towards us on the wind. Again we lost her, and again she rose. Two men were gone. The agony on shore increased. Men groaned, and clasped their hands; women shrieked, and turned away their faces. Some ran wildly up and down along the beach, crying for help where no help could be. I found myself one of these, frantically imploring a knot of sailors whom I knew, not to let those two lost creatures perish before our eyes.

They were making out to me, in an agitated way—I don't know how, for the little I could hear I was scarcely composed enough to understand—that the life-boat had been bravely manned an hour ago, and could do nothing; and that as no man would be so desperate as to attempt to wade off with a rope, and establish a communication with the shore, there was nothing left to try; when I noticed that some new sensation moved the people on the beach, and saw them part, and Ham come breaking through them to the front.

I ran to him—as well as I know, to repeat my appeal for help. But, distracted though I was, by a sight so new to me and terrible, the determination in his face, and his look, out to sea—exactly the same look as I remembered in connexion with the morning after Emily's flight—awoke me to a knowledge of his danger. I held him back with both arms; and implored the men with whom I had been speaking, not to listen to him, not to do murder, not to let him stir from off that sand!

Another cry arose on shore; and looking to the wreck, we saw the cruel sail, with blow on blow, beat off the lower of the two men, and fly up in triumph round the active figure left alone upon the mast.

Against such a sight, and against such determination as that of the calmly desperate man who was already accustomed to lead half the people present, I might as hopefully have entreated the wind. "Mas'r Davy," he said, cheerily grasping me by both hands, "if my time is come, 'tis come. If 'tan't, I'll bide it. Lord above bless you, and bless all! Mates, make me ready! I'm a going off!"

I was swept away, but not unkindly, to some distance, where the people around me made me stay; urging, as I confusedly perceived, that he was bent on going, with help or without, and that I should endanger the precautions for his safety by troubling those with whom they rested. I don't know what I answered, or what they rejoined; but, I saw hurry on the beach, and men running with ropes from a capstan that was there, and penetrating into a circle of figures that hid him from me. Then, I saw him standing alone, in a seaman's frock and trowsers: a rope in his hand, or slung to his wrist: another round his body: and several of the best men holding, at a little distance, to the latter, which he laid out himself, slack upon the shore, at his feet.

The wreck, even to my unpractised eye, was breaking up. I saw that she was parting in the middle, and that the life of the solitary man upon the mast hung by a thread. Still, he clung to it. He had a singular red cap on,—not like a sailor's cap, but of a finer colour; and as the few yielding planks between him and destruction rolled and bulged, and his anticipative death-knell rang, he was seen by all of us to wave it. I saw him do it now, and thought I was going distracted, when his action brought an old remembrance to my mind of a once dear friend.

Ham watched the sea, standing alone, with the silence of suspended breath behind him, and the storm before, until there was a great retiring wave, when, with a backward glance at those who held the rope which was made fast round his body, he dashed in after it, and in a moment was buffeting with the water; rising with the hills, falling with the valleys, lost beneath the foam; then drawn again to land. They hauled in hastily.

He was hurt. I saw blood on his face, from where I stood; but he took no thought of that. He seemed hurriedly to give them some directions for leaving him more free—or so I judged from the motion of his arm—and was gone as before.

And now he made for the wreck, rising with the hills, falling with the valleys, lost beneath the rugged foam, borne in towards the shore, borne on towards the ship, striving hard and valiantly. The distance was nothing, but the power of the sea and wind made the strife deadly. At length he neared the wreck. He was so near, that with one more of his vigorous strokes he would be clinging to it,— when, a high, green, vast hill-side of water, moving on shoreward, from beyond the ship, he seemed to leap up into it with a mighty bound, and the ship was gone!

Some eddying fragments I saw in the sea, as if a mere cask had been broken, in running to the spot where they were hauling in. Consternation was in every face. They drew him to my very feet—insensible—dead. He was carried to the nearest house; and, no one preventing me now, I remained near him, busy, while every means of restoration were tried; but he had been beaten to death by the great wave, and his generous heart was stilled for ever.

As I sat beside the bed, when hope was abandoned and all was done, a fisherman, who had known me when Emily and I were children, and ever since, whispered my name at the door.

"Sir," said he, with tears starting to his weather-beaten face, which, with his trembling lips, was ashy pale, "will you come over yonder?"

The old remembrance that had been recalled to me, was in his look. I asked him, terror-stricken, leaning on the arm he held out to support me:

"Has a body come ashore?"

He said, "Yes."

"Do I know it?" I asked then.

He answered nothing.

But, he led me to the shore. And on that part of it where she and I had looked for shells, two children—on that part of it where some lighter fragments of the old boat, blown down last night, had been scattered by the wind—among the ruins of the home he had wronged—I saw him lying with his head upon his arm, as I had often seen him lie at school.

20 David Abroad

Having lost both child-wife and dear friend, a devastated David leaves England to travel aimlessly in Europe. No longer writing, but living on income from his earlier writing, he receives, but at first does not answer, letters from Agnes, which finally give him incentive to resume work and to return home. In Chapter 58, David opens himself to nature's beauty and significance and finds new sympathy and power himself, when 'all at once Great Nature' speaks to him. Such human confidence in nature's power is inherent in three other fictional autobiographies of the time, Charlotte Brontë's *Jane Eyre* (1847), William Wordsworth's *The Prelude* (1850) and Alfred Lord Tennyson's *In Memoriam* (1850) (pp. 27–31).

CHAPTER 58
ABSENCE

[. . .] It is not in my power to retrace, one by one, all the weary phases of distress of mind through which I passed. There are some dreams that can only be imperfectly and vaguely described; and when I oblige myself to look back on this time of my life, I seem to be recalling such a dream. I see myself passing on among the novelties of foreign towns, palaces, cathedrals, temples, pictures, castles, tombs, fantastic streets—the old abiding places of History and Fancy—as a dreamer might; bearing my painful load through all, and hardly conscious of the objects as they fade before me. Listlessness to everything, but brooding sorrow, was the night that fell on my undisciplined heart. Let me look up from it—as at last I did, thank Heaven!—and from its long, sad, wretched dream, to dawn.

[. . .]

I was in Switzerland. I had come out of Italy, over one of the great passes of the Alps, and had since wandered with a guide among the bye-ways of the mountains. If those awful solitudes had spoken to my heart, I did not know it. I had found sublimity and wonder in the dread heights and precipices, in the roaring torrents, and the wastes of ice and snow; but as yet, they had taught me nothing else.

I came, one evening before sunset, down into a valley, where I was to rest. In the course of my descent to it, by the winding track along the mountain-side, from which I saw it shining far below, I think some long-unwonted sense of beauty and tranquillity, some softening influence awakened by its peace, moved faintly in my breast. I remember pausing once, with a kind of sorrow that was not all oppressive, not quite despairing. I remember almost hoping that some better change was possible within me.

[. . .] In the quiet air, there was a sound of distant singing—shepherd voices; but, as one bright evening cloud floated midway along the mountain-side, I could almost believe it came from there, and was not earthly music. All at once, in this serenity, great Nature spoke to me; and soothed me to lay down my weary head upon the grass, and weep as I had not wept yet, since Dora died!

I had found a packet of letters awaiting me but a few minutes before [. . .]. The packet was in my hand. I opened it, and read the writing of Agnes.

[. . .]

She gave me no advice; she urged no duty on me; she only told me, in her own fervent manner, what her trust in me was. She knew (she said) how such a nature as mine would turn affliction to good. She knew how trial and emotion would exalt and strengthen it. [. . .] She, who so gloried in my fame, and so looked forward to its augmentation, well knew that I would labor on. She knew that in me, sorrow could not be weakness, but must be strength. As the endurance of my childish days had done its part to make me what it was, so greater calamities would nerve me on, to be yet better than I was [. . .].

I put the letter in my breast, and thought what I had been an hour ago! When I heard the voices die away, and saw the quiet evening cloud grow dim, and all the colors in the valley fade, and the golden snow upon the mountain tops become a remote part of the pale night sky, yet felt that the night was passing from my mind, and all its shadows clearing, there was no name for the love I bore her, dearer to me, henceforward, than ever until then.

21 The Concluding Chapters

The 'Light' that shines in the title of Chapter 62 is Agnes, and the language sanctifies her as illuminating spirit, good angel, to David, in contrast to Steerforth, whom she recognizes as his bad angel. Epitomizing the moral centre that Victorian literature and culture located in the home which embowered the wife and/or mother, Agnes is an idealized characterization (see **pp. 10–11**). Recent reconsiderations, such as Poovey's and Welsh's (**pp. 59–62** and **65–8**), view her as the construction of David's male imagination. David, in turning to her, either begs or implicitly answers (with what could be either a yes or no) the novel's opening question of whether he or 'anybody else' has become the hero of his life (see **p. 90**). If his concern all along has been self-satisfaction, he here seems satisfied enough. If, as modern critics tend to think, he has had at stake more profound questions of individual autonomy, then his final words about Agnes suggest he has found a heroine instead of a hero. Chapter 64 opens with David's notice of 'the roar of many voices, not indifferent to me as I travel on', obviously a writer's public, but most distinct to him 'in the fleeting crowd' are faces he recalls from his private life. This is as close as David gets in this final instalment to considering the question he raised in the book's first line about whether he or someone else in his life turns out to be the hero. Finally, he speaks of his principal supporters, many of whom are still literally, as well as memorably, present in his life: Clara Peggotty, Betsey Trotwood and Mr Dick, but principally Agnes. She, with the late Dora's full blessing, is his guide and soul mate. So stated in the final paragraph, the implicit point may be that whatever David's conclusion regarding his own heroism, he makes no qualification of her status as his heroine.

The final illustration in Chapter 64 (Figure 6) shares several features of the earlier illustrations reprinted in this Sourcebook. David, facing directly into his drawing room and within his own family circle, is no longer the tentative visitor to other houses or the sad mourner in his own, but is engaged actively with those around him. The bottom of the illustration is filled with children and the clutter of their play, but the rest of the room, unlike the one in his earlier household with Dora, is orderly. Angel figurines stand watch at each end of the mantel at whose centre stands the clock under glass with playful figures circling beneath it. On the wall are pictures of his childhood home and of the beached boat where the Peggottys had lived at Yarmouth. The predominant picture, however, is the portrait of Dora, which was behind David in the cottage at the time of Dora's death (p. 149). But if we look closely, the picture here somewhat alters the position of the arms, and the head and body are more front-facing, with the eyes seeming directed at both David and Agnes. The overall size of the picture is a bit larger this time. Drawn by one of David's young daughters into the frame of the whole illustration, Daniel Peggotty has returned from Australia, and this long-ago first host to the child David receives an appropriate welcome.

CHAPTER 62
A LIGHT SHINES ON MY WAY

The year came round to Christmas-time, and I had been at home above two months. I had seen Agnes frequently. However loud the general voice might be in giving me encouragement, and however fervent the emotions and endeavours to which it roused me, I heard her lightest word of praise as I heard nothing else.

At least once a week, and sometimes oftener, I rode over there, and passed the evening. I usually rode back at night; for the old unhappy sense was always hovering about me now—most sorrowfully when I left her—and I was glad to be up and out, rather than wandering over the past in weary wakefulness or miserable dreams. I wore away the longest part of many wild sad nights, in those rides; reviving, as I went, the thoughts that had occupied me in my long absence.

Or, if I were to say rather that I listened to the echoes of those thoughts, I should better express the truth. They spoke to me from afar off. I had put them at a distance, and accepted my inevitable place. When I read to Agnes what I wrote; when I saw her listening face; moved her to smiles or tears; and heard her cordial voice so earnest on the shadowy events of that imaginative world in which I lived; I thought what a fate mine might have been—but only thought so, as I had thought after I was married to Dora, what I could have wished my wife to be.

My duty to Agnes, who loved me with a love, which, if I disquieted, I wronged most selfishly and poorly, and could never restore; my matured assurance that I, who had worked out my own destiny, and won what I had impetuously set my heart on, had no right to murmur, and must bear; comprised what I felt and what I had learned. But I loved her: and now it even became some consolation to me, vaguely to conceive a distant day when I might blamelessly avow it; when all this should be over; when I could say "Agnes, so it was when I came home; and now I am old, and I never have loved since!"

She did not once show me any change in herself. What she always had been to me, she still was; wholly unaltered.

[. . .]

I found Agnes alone. The little girls[1] had gone to their own homes now, and she was alone by the fire, reading. She put down her book on seeing me come in; and having welcomed me as usual, took her work-basket and sat in one of the old-fashioned windows.

I sat beside her on the window-seat, and we talked of what I was doing, and when it would be done, and of the progress I had made since my last visit. Agnes was very cheerful; and laughingly predicted that I should soon become too famous to be talked to, on such subjects.

"So I make the most of the present time, you see," said Agnes, "and talk to you while I may."

As I looked at her beautiful face, observant of her work, she raised her mild clear eyes, and saw that I was looking at her.

"You are thoughtful to-day, Trotwood!"

"Agnes, shall I tell you what about? I came to tell you."

She put aside her work, as she was used to do when we were seriously discussing anything; and gave me her whole attention.

"My dear Agnes, do you doubt my being true to you?"

"No!" she answered, with a look of astonishment.

"Do you doubt my being what I always have been to you?"

"No!" she answered, as before.

"Do you remember that I tried to tell you, when I came home, what a debt of gratitude I owed you, dearest Agnes, and how fervently I felt towards you?"

"I remember it," she said, gently, "very well."

"You have a secret," said I. "Let me share it, Agnes."

She cast down her eyes, and trembled.

"I could hardly fail to know, even if I had not heard—but from other lips than yours, Agnes, which seems strange—that there is some one upon whom you have bestowed the treasure of your love. Do not shut me out of what concerns your happiness so nearly! If you can trust me, as you say you can, and as I know you may, let me be your friend, your brother, in this matter, of all others!"

With an appealing, almost a reproachful glance, she rose from the window; and

---

1 Her students.

hurrying across the room as if without knowing where, put her hands before her face, and burst into such tears as smote me to the heart.

And yet they awakened something in me, bringing promise to my heart. Without my knowing why, these tears allied themselves with the quietly sad smile which was so fixed in my remembrance, and shook me more with hope than fear or sorrow.

"Agnes! Sister! Dearest! What have I done!"

"Let me go away, Trotwood. I am not well. I am not myself. I will speak to you by-and-by—another time. I will write to you. Don't speak to me now. Don't! don't!"

I sought to recollect what she had said, when I had spoken to her on that former night, of her affection needing no return. It seemed a very world that I must search through in a moment.

"Agnes, I cannot bear to see you so, and think that I have been the cause. My dearest girl, dearer to me than anything in life, if you are unhappy, let me share your unhappiness. If you are in need of help or counsel, let me try to give it to you. If you have indeed a burden on your heart, let me try to lighten it. For whom do I live now, Agnes, if it is not for you!"

"Oh, spare me! I am not myself! Another time!" was all I could distinguish.

Was it a selfish error that was leading me away? Or, having once a clue to hope, was there something opening to me that I had not dared to think of?

"I must say more. I cannot let you leave me so! For Heaven's sake, Agnes, let us not mistake each other after all these years, and all that has come and gone with them! I must speak plainly. If you have any lingering thought that I could envy the happiness you will confer; that I could not resign you to a dearer protector, of your own choosing; that I could not, from my removed place, be a contented witness of your joy; dismiss it, for I don't deserve it! I have not suffered quite in vain. You have not taught me quite in vain. There is no alloy of self in what I feel for you."

She was quiet now. In a little time, she turned her pale face towards me, and said in a low voice, broken here and there, but very clear:

"I owe it to your pure friendship for me, Trotwood—which, indeed, I do not doubt—to tell you, you are mistaken. I can do no more. If I have sometimes, in the course of years, wanted help and counsel, they have come to me. If I have sometimes been unhappy, the feeling has passed away. If I have ever had a burden on my heart, it has been lightened for me. If I have any secret, it is—no new one; and is—not what you suppose. I cannot reveal it, or divide it. It has long been mine, and must remain mine."

"Agnes! Stay! A moment!"

She was going away, but I detained her. I clasped my arm about her waist. "In the course of years!" "It is not a new one!" New thoughts and hopes were whirling through my mind, and all the colours of my life were changing.

"Dearest Agnes! Whom I so respect and honour—whom I so devotedly love! When I came here to-day, I thought that nothing could have wrested this confession from me. I thought I could have kept it in my bosom all our lives, till we were old. But, Agnes, if I have indeed any new-born hope that I may ever call you something more than Sister, widely different from Sister!——"

Her tears fell fast; but they were not like those she had lately shed, and I saw my hope brighten in them.

"Agnes! Ever my guide, and best support! If you had been more mindful of yourself, and less of me, when we grew up here together, I think my heedless fancy never would have wandered from you. But you were so much better than I, so necessary to me in every boyish hope and disappointment, that to have you to confide in, and rely upon in everything, became a second nature, supplanting for the time the first and greater one of loving you as I do!"

Still weeping, but not sadly—joyfully! And clasped in my arms as she had never been, as I had thought she never was to be!

"When I loved Dora—fondly, Agnes, as you know——"

"Yes!" she cried, earnestly. "I am glad to know it!"

"When I loved her—even then, my love would have been incomplete, without your sympathy. I had it, and it was perfected. And when I lost her, Agnes, what should I have been without you, still!"

Closer in my arms, nearer to my heart, her trembling hand upon my shoulder, her sweet eyes shining through her tears, on mine!

"I went away, dear Agnes, loving you. I stayed away, loving you. I returned home, loving you!"

And now, I tried to tell her of the struggle I had had, and the conclusion I had come to. I tried to lay my mind before her, truly, and entirely. I tried to show her, how I had hoped I had come into the better knowledge of myself and of her; how I had resigned myself to what that better knowledge brought; and how I had come there, even that day, in my fidelity to this. If she did so love me (I said) that she could take me for her husband, she could do so, on no deserving of mine, except upon the truth of my love for her, and the trouble in which it had ripened to be what it was; and hence it was that I revealed it. And O, Agnes, even out of thy true eyes, in that same time, the spirit of my child-wife looked upon me, saying it was well; and winning me, through thee, to tenderest recollections of the Blossom that had withered in its bloom!

"I am so blest, Trotwood—my heart is so overcharged—but there is one thing I must say."

"Dearest, what?"

She laid her gentle hands upon my shoulders, and looked calmly in my face.

"Do you know, yet, what it is?"

"I am afraid to speculate on what it is. Tell me, my dear."

"I have loved you all my life!"

CHAPTER 64
A LAST RETROSPECT

AND now my written story ends. I look back, once more—for the last time—before I close these leaves.

Figure 6 **A Stranger Calls to See Me.**

I see myself, with Agnes at my side, journeying along the road of life. I see our children and our friends around us; and I hear the roar of many voices, not indifferent to me as I travel on.

What faces are the most distinct to me in the fleeting crowd? Lo, these; all turning to me as I ask my thoughts the question!

[. . .]

And now, as I close my task, subduing my desire to linger yet, these faces fade away. But, one face, shining on me like a heavenly light by which I see all other objects, is above them and beyond them all. And that remains.

I turn my head, and see it, in its beautiful serenity, beside me. My lamp burns low, and I have written far into the night; but the dear presence, without which I were nothing, bears me company.

O Agnes, O my soul, so may thy face be by me when I close my life indeed; so may I, when realities are melting from me like the shadows which I now dismiss, still find thee near me, pointing upward!

4

Further Reading

University of Virginia Press, 2002), pp. 191–228. By very close reading of sample illustrations, Patten in this recent study points out the close relationship of print and picture text.

Wilson, Edmund. 'Dickens: The Two Scrooges', *The Wound and the Bow: Seven Studies in Literature* (New York: Oxford University Press, 1965), pp. 3–85. Designed for Wilson's University of Chicago lecture in 1939, this essay, building from its emphasis upon the psychological impact of Dickens's early hardships, examines the whole of his career in light of the divided social values and impulses characterized in such figures as the tormented but redeemed Ebeneezer Scrooge of *A Christmas Carol*.

Bibliography

Richard J. Dunn, ed., *David Copperfield: An Annotated Bibliography* (New York: Garland, 1981); supplement with Ann Tandy (New York: AMS, 2000). These volumes provide listings and information about *David Copperfield* editions, adaptations, reviews, criticism, and appreciative and biographical commentary to serve both the Dickens student and the general reader.

Further Reading

Recommended Editions

The following editions are ones likely to remain available, and they contain all the original illustrations, and have helpful introductions and annotations.

Definitive edition

David Copperfield, ed. Nina Burgis, Clarendon Edition (Oxford: Clarendon Press, 1981). Available in many libraries, this is a critical text providing variants that came through Dickens's revisions from manuscript to proof to first serial and subsequent complete editions under his control. Burgis's introduction fully describes the history of the novel from inception through to 1867 Charles Dickens edition (upon which this Sourcebook text is based). It is also the basis for the World's Classics paperback edition (Oxford: Oxford University Press, 1981) edited by Burgis.

Paperback editions

David Copperfield, Penguin Classics (Harmondsworth: Penguin, 1996). Introduction and notes by Jeremy Tambling. This was the first Penguin edition to include all the original illustrations, and is indebted to Burgis's Clarendon edition for some variant readings and for passages in manuscript left out at proof stage. Tambling's excellent introduction focuses on the work as a novel about 'the making (and unmaking) of identity', and examines the functions of memory, the mode of autobiography, gender and sexuality, and the ambiguity of the father-figure.

David Copperfield, ed. Malcolm Andrews, Everyman Edition (London: J. M. Dent, 1993). The 1999 reprint becomes part of the Everyman Dickens, intended to become 'the most comprehensive and coherent edition of Dickens's works to be available in paperback'. Andrews's introduction situates *Copperfield* effectively in a Victorian world of earnestness and purposefulness, and suggests that Dickens's fondness for the work may have been because in writing the novel he may have exorcised what most haunted him from his earlier life. Andrews also appends a good discussion of Dickens and his critics. Fully illustrated and with clear print, this and the Penguin Classics edition rank as the two best available paperback editions.

Recommended Reading

All the books and essays excerpted in Contexts, Interpretations and The Novel in Performance sections are recommended for further reading, and thus full citations appear in the headnotes and footnotes. The works listed below are selected according to pertinence to the respective sections of this Sourcebook.

Biographical studies

Ackroyd, Peter. *Dickens* (London: Sinclair-Stevenson, 1990). Abridged edition (London: Mandarin, 1994). Ackroyd is most helpful for the reader interested in the relationship between Dickens's fragment of autobiography and *David Copperfield* and for the question of both texts' impact on the many subsequent Dickens biographies.

Slater, Michael. *Dickens and Women* (Stanford, Calif.: Stanford University Press, 1983). This is both a biographical and a critical study, biographically covering the numerous women in Dickens's life, critically considering the many women characters in his fiction. For readers of *David Copperfield*, Slater provides insights about likely prototypes for David's mother and various loves as well as a context for more broad attention to the social situation of Victorian women.

Victorian England

Houghton, Walter E. *The Victorian Frame of Mind, 1830–1870* (New Haven, Conn.: Yale University Press, 1957). Houghton draws on a broad range of writers and thinkers and social documents to survey social issues and concerns, and his discussions of love and family, enthusiasm and work can be helpful for readers of *David Copperfield*.

House, Humphry. *The Dickens World* (Oxford: Oxford University Press, 1941). This is a useful, straightforward study of the 'connexion between what Dickens wrote and the times in which he wrote it, between his reformism and some of the things he wanted reformed, between the attitude to life shown in his books and the society in which he lived'.

Critical studies

Butt, John. '*David Copperfield* Month by Month', in John Butt and Tillotson, *Dickens at Work* (London: Methuen, 1957), pp. 114–76. For *perfield* reader interested in Dickens's composition of the novel, Butt pro copies of and helpful commentary about Dickens's working plans monthly part as he developed the characterization, plot and thematic stru

Dawson, Carl. ' "The Lamp of Memory": Wordsworth and Dickens', *Victorian Noon: English Literature in 1850* (Baltimore, Md.: Johns H University Press, 1979), pp. 123–52. Dawson's study well situates Dickens literature and culture of mid-nineteenth-century England ('Victorian noon' shows how memory is similarly illuminating for Wordsworth and Dickens **pp. 27–8**).

Jordan, John O. 'The Social Sub-text of *David Copperfield*', *Dickens Stu Annual*, 14 (1985), pp. 61–92. Jordan's title signals his as one of the mod studies recognizing the novel as more than personal reminiscence; as does Palm (**pp. 52–5**), Jordan finds it a significant document of its time.

Monod, Sylvère, 'At the Top', in his *Dickens the Novelist* (Norman, Okla.: Uni versity of Oklahoma Press, 1968), pp. 275–369. Monod, writing at a period of revived critical and biographical interest in Dickens, devotes much of his critical study to *David Copperfield*, which he finds central to the whole of Dickens's art. Thus, like Leavis (**pp. 46–9**), he values the psychological complexity of characterization and overall artistry of *Copperfield*.

Needham, Gwendolyn B. 'The Undisciplined Heart of David Copperfield', *Nineteenth-Century Fiction*, 9 (1954), pp. 81–107. Needham's was one of the first twentieth-century critical studies to argue thematic coherence, and her focus on the disciplining of the heart opened the characterization of David to closer scrutiny by later critics (see Kincaid, **pp. 49–52**), who, increasingly informed by feminist and gender theory, would regard this as a more troublesome and problematic theme than Needham had realized (see Miller and Poovey, **pp. 44–6** and **59–62**).

Patten, Robert L. 'Autobiography into Autobiography: The Evolution of *David Copperfield*,' in *Approaches to Victorian Autobiography*, ed. George P. Landow (Athens, Ohio: Ohio University Press, 1979), pp. 269–91. Patten provides a useful study of the relationship of Dickens's fictional autobiography (**pp. 20–2**) to the novel, points to the ultimate separation of David's fictional from Dickens's actual life, and makes a case for David becoming the hero of his own life through the writing of it.

Patten, Robert L. 'Serial Illustration and Storytelling in *David Copperfield*', in *The Victorian Illustrated Book*, ed. Richard Maxwell (Charlottesville, Va.:

Index

Further Reading

Recommended Editions

The following editions are ones likely to remain available, and they contain all the original illustrations, and have helpful introductions and annotations.

Definitive edition

David Copperfield, ed. Nina Burgis, Clarendon Edition (Oxford: Clarendon Press, 1981). Available in many libraries, this is a critical text providing variants that came through Dickens's revisions from manuscript to proof to first serial and subsequent complete editions under his control. Burgis's introduction fully describes the history of the novel from inception through to 1867 Charles Dickens edition (upon which this Sourcebook text is based). It is also the basis for the World's Classics paperback edition (Oxford: Oxford University Press, 1981) edited by Burgis.

Paperback editions

David Copperfield, Penguin Classics (Harmondsworth: Penguin, 1996). Introduction and notes by Jeremy Tambling. This was the first Penguin edition to include all the original illustrations, and is indebted to Burgis's Clarendon edition for some variant readings and for passages in manuscript left out at proof stage. Tambling's excellent introduction focuses on the work as a novel about 'the making (and unmaking) of identity', and examines the functions of memory, the mode of autobiography, gender and sexuality, and the ambiguity of the father-figure.

David Copperfield, ed. Malcolm Andrews, Everyman Edition (London: J. M. Dent, 1993). The 1999 reprint becomes part of the Everyman Dickens, intended to become 'the most comprehensive and coherent edition of Dickens's works to be available in paperback'. Andrews's introduction situates *Copperfield* effectively in a Victorian world of earnestness and purposefulness, and suggests that Dickens's fondness for the work may have been because in writing the novel he may have exorcised what most haunted him from his earlier life. Andrews also appends a good discussion of Dickens and his critics. Fully illustrated and with clear print, this and the Penguin Classics edition rank as the two best available paperback editions.

Recommended Reading

All the books and essays excerpted in Contexts, Interpretations and The Novel in Performance sections are recommended for further reading, and thus full citations appear in the headnotes and footnotes. The works listed below are selected according to pertinence to the respective sections of this Sourcebook.

Biographical studies

Ackroyd, Peter. *Dickens* (London: Sinclair-Stevenson, 1990). Abridged edition (London: Mandarin, 1994). Ackroyd is most helpful for the reader interested in the relationship between Dickens's fragment of autobiography and *David Copperfield* and for the question of both texts' impact on the many subsequent Dickens biographies.

Slater, Michael. *Dickens and Women* (Stanford, Calif.: Stanford University Press, 1983). This is both a biographical and a critical study, biographically covering the numerous women in Dickens's life, critically considering the many women characters in his fiction. For readers of *David Copperfield*, Slater provides insights about likely prototypes for David's mother and various loves as well as a context for more broad attention to the social situation of Victorian women.

Victorian England

Houghton, Walter E. *The Victorian Frame of Mind, 1830–1870* (New Haven, Conn.: Yale University Press, 1957). Houghton draws on a broad range of writers and thinkers and social documents to survey social issues and concerns, and his discussions of love and family, enthusiasm and work can be helpful for readers of *David Copperfield*.

House, Humphry. *The Dickens World* (Oxford: Oxford University Press, 1941). This is a useful, straightforward study of the 'connexion between what Dickens wrote and the times in which he wrote it, between his reformism and some of the things he wanted reformed, between the attitude to life shown in his books and the society in which he lived'.

Critical studies

Butt, John. '*David Copperfield* Month by Month', in John Butt and Kathleen Tillotson, *Dickens at Work* (London: Methuen, 1957), pp. 114–76. For the *Copperfield* reader interested in Dickens's composition of the novel, Butt provides full copies of and helpful commentary about Dickens's working plans for each monthly part as he developed the characterization, plot and thematic structure.

Dawson, Carl. ' "The Lamp of Memory": Wordsworth and Dickens', in his *Victorian Noon: English Literature in 1850* (Baltimore, Md.: Johns Hopkins University Press, 1979), pp. 123–52. Dawson's study well situates Dickens in the literature and culture of mid-nineteenth-century England ('Victorian noon'). He shows how memory is similarly illuminating for Wordsworth and Dickens (see **pp. 27–8**).

Jordan, John O. 'The Social Sub-text of *David Copperfield*', *Dickens Studies Annual*, 14 (1985), pp. 61–92. Jordan's title signals his as one of the modern studies recognizing the novel as more than personal reminiscence; as does Palmer (**pp. 52–5**), Jordan finds it a significant document of its time.

Monod, Sylvère, 'At the Top', in his *Dickens the Novelist* (Norman, Okla.: University of Oklahoma Press, 1968), pp. 275–369. Monod, writing at a period of revived critical and biographical interest in Dickens, devotes much of his critical study to *David Copperfield*, which he finds central to the whole of Dickens's art. Thus, like Leavis (**pp. 46–9**), he values the psychological complexity of characterization and overall artistry of *Copperfield*.

Needham, Gwendolyn B. 'The Undisciplined Heart of David Copperfield', *Nineteenth-Century Fiction*, 9 (1954), pp. 81–107. Needham's was one of the first twentieth-century critical studies to argue thematic coherence, and her focus on the disciplining of the heart opened the characterization of David to closer scrutiny by later critics (see Kincaid, **pp. 49–52**), who, increasingly informed by feminist and gender theory, would regard this as a more troublesome and problematic theme than Needham had realized (see Miller and Poovey, **pp. 44–6** and **59–62**).

Patten, Robert L. 'Autobiography into Autobiography: The Evolution of *David Copperfield*,' in *Approaches to Victorian Autobiography*, ed. George P. Landow (Athens, Ohio: Ohio University Press, 1979), pp. 269–91. Patten provides a useful study of the relationship of Dickens's fictional autobiography (**pp. 20–2**) to the novel, points to the ultimate separation of David's fictional from Dickens's actual life, and makes a case for David becoming the hero of his own life through the writing of it.

Patten, Robert L. 'Serial Illustration and Storytelling in *David Copperfield*', in *The Victorian Illustrated Book*, ed. Richard Maxwell (Charlottesville, Va.:

University of Virginia Press, 2002), pp. 191–228. By very close reading of sample illustrations, Patten in this recent study points out the close relationship of print and picture text.

Wilson, Edmund. 'Dickens: The Two Scrooges', *The Wound and the Bow: Seven Studies in Literature* (New York: Oxford University Press, 1965)', pp. 3–85. Designed for Wilson's University of Chicago lecture in 1939, this essay, building from its emphasis upon the psychological impact of Dickens's early hardships, examines the whole of his career in light of the divided social values and impulses characterized in such figures as the tormented but redeemed Ebeneezer Scrooge of *A Christmas Carol*.

Bibliography

Richard J. Dunn, ed., *David Copperfield: An Annotated Bibliography* (New York: Garland, 1981); supplement with Ann Tandy (New York: AMS, 2000). These volumes provide listings and information about *David Copperfield* editions, adaptations, reviews, criticism, and appreciative and biographical commentary to serve both the Dickens student and the general reader.